A Hustler's Wife

APR 2017

SF

A Hustler's Wife

Nikki Turner

www.urbanbooks.net

Urban Books, LLC
97 N18th Street
Wyandanch, NY 11798

Three Legends Press Edition

ISBN 13: 978-1-60162-619-6
ISBN 10: 1-60162-619-3

First Mass Market Printing August 2014
First Paperback Printing January 2013
Printed in the United States of America

10 9 8 7 6 5 4

This is a work of fiction. Any references or similarities to actual events, real people, living or dead, or to real locales are intended to give the novel a sense of reality. Any similarity in other names, characters, places, and incidents is entirely coincidental.

Distributed by Kensington Publishing Corp.
Submit Wholesale Orders to:
Kensington Publishing Corp.
C/O Penguin Group (USA) Inc.
Attention: Order Processing
405 Murray Hill Parkway
East Rutherford, NJ 07073-2316
Phone: 1-800-526-0275
Fax: 1-800-227-9604

A Hustler's Wife

Nikki Turner

Discover more titles by Nikki Turner at:

http://iamnikkiturner.com

Dedication

This book is dedicated to:

The mother beyond all other mothers,
Ms. Denise Turner

No matter how little or much you had to give,
you always gave all of you

Thanks for loving me unconditionally!

My mentor and devoted friend, Ms. Deaudrey
Hunter. Your encouragement means more than
any word could ever express. Thanks for being
my inspiration!

In Loving Memory

A few of you were old and had lived life to the fullest, while some of you were young and hadn't seen what life had to offer. A couple had an awful illness, though most of you fell victim to the streets, and a few of you were just at the wrong place at the wrong time. But each and every one of you added a smile to my world at one time or another. For some, it's only been months since you left, others it's been years, and for a few it's been decades. I think of each of you often, and you may be gone but surely you're not forgotten.

MILTON SCOTT, ESTHER TURNER, NA-THANIEL TOLBERT, BERTHA, RANDOLPH, ALFRED GEE-EL, SAPHONYA WOOLRIDGE, KEVIN WALLACE, THOMAS RANDOLPH, DORIS FOOTMAN, HARROLD "MANNY" WOOLRIDGE, INDIA MORTON, ARTHUR "MAINE" TOWES, KEVIN GRANT, DOMINIQUE BASSETT, CHARLIE CONE (FROM JACKSON WARD), DEBRA "POOKIE" CREWS,

TONETTE "TONI" SNEAD, BUSY BEE (FROM 4TH AVE), NEW YORK CHUCK, BATTLE, MARY PRINCE, CLAYTON BROWN, RODNEY CLANTON, BARRY KEMP, LIL WILLIE (FROM THE WEST END, JULIUS LOGAN, THAERON BASSETT, SNEAK, RAKIE CLOYD, KEVIN-HEAD 44, KEVIN-BLUE ROCKY, LIL MONEY, BLUE JUICE(FROM JACKSON WARD), K.K. (FROM MOSBY)

Acknowledgments

First and foremost, I must give honor to God from whom all blessings flow. It is through faith and believing in Him that I have found a deep, satisfying peace as a writer. I am truly blessed to be able to live out my dream and to have an overflow of favor and especially a large cast of ardent supporters. They have all left footprints on my heart.

To my two biggest fans, Timmond and Kennisha, thanks for your patience while Mommy wrote this book. I love you more than life itself. To my mother, Denise Turner, I am thankful for you always being there whenever I truly needed you, for sacrificing so much for so many years, and for taking on the role as mother and father. Take my love and multiply it by infinity and that's how much I love you. To my grandmother, Margaret Scott, thanks for your wisdom and the support you gave me to live through my own triumphs and tragedies.

To my team who cheered me on and believed in this book as if it was your own, all who have been my foundation long before I ever considered this book. My friend and guardian angel on earth, DeAudrey Hunter, believed in me before I even wrote one sentence, daily pushing me on to the finish line. Angela Yvonne Davis, aka A.D., jumped into character whenever I needed you to, but your most award-winning, outstanding role would be the role of best friend. Abdullah Black, my brother, my friend, I am eternally grateful for your undying concern and support. You go beyond the call of duty. Shauntayne Mccoy, for unconditional friendship and encouragement. Tanisha Washington and Dedria Battle for having my back no matter how far-fetched my dreams were. Deva Plaskette, because you understand. My uncle Andre for believing, inspiring, and following up.

Eternal love to my Triple Crown family: Vickie my sister, friend, for the hype you gave me long before you even read one sentence, the opportunity to excel in this game, and showing me it truly gets greater later, K'wan, my Clyde, and my brother who seen the shine in me from day one, my friend, Shannon, the OG to this hip-hop fiction, thanks for your faith, knowledge, and wisdom. Joy, for your keen eyes, embracing my project as if it was your own and making it airtight. I love you, TCP!

To my technical team, Sandra West, Thomas (Mustafa) Martin, for diligently polishing this novel, Jadi Keambirorio for your input in the first place, and Joylynn Jossel and Angie, for putting the final buff and polish, gotta love y'all! My guys over at Uniquest Designs, for my banging cover design. I've gotta send much love your way! Mr. Tariq, for holding my hand the whole time. Bo, for the concept and design on the knockout cover. Dafina Lovelace, many thanks for your legs and hands on the cover. Keith Witherspoon, playing doctor to "Billie Jean," my computer.

I'd like to express my gratitude to my family for the love of my children and myself over the years. My biological father, Acra, thanks for giving me breath and my name—love ya, Pops. My stepfathers, Balldey and Jeff, thanks. Uncle Gregory Givens, for believing and encouraging, Aunt Bren, for challenging me to get it on bookshelves . . . here it is! Alice Burrell, Margaret Jeffrie, and Iretta King, embracing me as one of your own.

Jhamoul Dean, giving me the ultimate gift . . . Kennisha. Robert, "Bobby" Bullock, for being my Prince Charming when I needed a knight in shining armor. Eric Lundy, for holding. Craig

Acknowledgments

Carthorne Robinson, thanks for inspiration, strength, and unconditional love kept me afloat with moral support when I thought I was drowning. Herbert Halloway, and Claudie Rhodes: Thanks for your open mind, heart, and tons of input and info. To Raquel Byrd, Lisa Dorsey, Stanford "Peter Weet" Dorsey, Butch Lewis, Nicey Butler, "YBC" Yvonne Chesdon, DeWayne Parham, Gloria Williams, Sallie P.Moore, Tammy Taylor offering your faithful friendship, love, and understanding. Ayanna Spurlock-Shackleton, Mary Carter, Seaquanna Smith, Rhoda and Richard Fordham, Isaac Wright, and my ex-coworkers at the MEPS for all the laughs and compassion. Laura Beaton for my journal in seventh grade—look where it got me! Randy Adams, Mr. Lambert, and Gus Nikiforos for seeing the vision in phase one.

Special thanks to my fashion squad: Ebony at DMJ, tightest flat twist in RIC, my seamstresses, Deneen and Avis, Patricia Gray, always fitting me in at the last minute and laying my braids down, Keondra, for laying my hair; Angelina, makeup, photographer, Todd Jagers, CI Photo Studio—thank you, thank you, thank you!

Next, I'd like to send bountiful blessings and thanks to the people in my life who were able to offer me undying support, because they knew firsthand the feeling of having a vision and wanting so badly to bring it into existence. The multitalented Joanne Jefferson "Jo Chansler," blessings come in countless forms and you have been one of mine. Donmashade and Boog for my song, Tyrelle "Big Wig" and Big Khat of Go Hard Productions, and Bay-Bay with your movie, *Girl's in the Game.* Cha of WHY? Ent. and GMAC, thanks for the contacts. To anybody else with goals and aspirations: Dreams do come true; just have faith. To all the single moms, I personally know your struggle. I know it gets rough, but remember: Some of the most remarkable people were raised by the strength and shoulders of single mothers. To all of Richmond's OGs, on lockdown, the streets of RIC will never be the same without you. Anybody else behind prison walls or may have family members who I may or may not know, no storm can last forever!

To every person in my hometown, Richmond, Virginia, thanks for taking a part in the manifestation of this book. It all started here and you blew me up before I even hit the bookshelves and for that I am eternally grateful. To all the businesses who agreed to book signings before I even finished the book. Oodles of thanks to you too. Hermeione, One Force Books, Carla, Readers Choice in Milwaukee, thanks! Much respect to

Donald Goines, Iceberg Slim, Sister Souljah who have definitely paved the way for writers such as myself with a ghetto, urban story to tell.

Then I owe a heartfelt thanks to you, the readers. I love you from the depths of my heart. Without you none of this would be possible. And to anyone whose name is not mentioned here, and you know you made a positive contribution to this book or my life in general. I'd like to thank you too, and I'll get you on the next one.

Last, but not least—no need for names—but to those who never believed, doubted or talked about me when you should have been praying for me, I am going to continue to keep you in my prayers.

BE BLESSED,
Nikki T

A Thought for The Reader

I was questioned about the message that I send out in this novel and the way this story is told. This story is told for the lost, the confused, the weary, the bewildered, and the broken-hearted. I am certain many can relate to this tale. And for those who can't, I hope I've painted the picture vividly enough so that you too can feel the struggle. Through the pages of this story, you will definitely begin to understand the ups and downs, the eternal bliss, as well as the darkest plights, of being *A Hustler's Wife*.

Nikki Turner

1

Mama Didn't Say
There'd Be Days Like This

Yarni sat, stunned, on the cold, mahogany courtroom bench. She couldn't believe the verdict of guilty. The high-profile court case of her notorious, kingpin boyfriend, Des, ended in the worst possible outcome. After seeing the expression of defeat and frustration on Des's face, Yarni broke down in tears as numbness ran through her entire body. Her mind raced frantically as she reflected on what seemed like her life crumbling in front of her eyes.

The trouble began when she returned from Los Angeles. Des paid for her to fly from Richmond, Virginia, to California to shop for her prom dress and accessories. For some reason, she could not get into the shopping spree that led from Saks to Bloomingdale's to boutique shops. Yarni had a bad migraine and a weak stomach the entire time. Des's mother, Joyce, accompanied her as a favor to her son, though it was no secret that she could not stand Yarni. Joyce felt the girl was entirely too young for her son. She did not like the hold Yarni had over Des and she couldn't understand why he loved Yarni so much. She knew if anything ever happened to Des, Yarni would be gone as fast as a speeding bullet.

Joyce had a lot of style and class, which is why Des asked for her help. If anybody could put an elegant ensemble together, she could. Joyce was a big-boned, dark-skinned lady who wore her hair in a flipped-under mushroom style. She had a big and nasty-shaped butt, the kind of butt that one could sit a drink on. She was shortchanged in the breast area with a chest as flat as an ironing board. She drank lots of coffee so her teeth had stains on them. She wore large EK lizard-print frames. With her jewelry, she resembled the female version of Mr. T.

Yarni thought she was feeling pukey because Joyce was up close and personal with her. Joyce made Yarni extremely uncomfortable. She was always in her space. The two of them kept their distance, even on this too-close shopping spree coordinated by the one man who loved them both. Des wanted more than anything for the two of them to get along. Yarni counted the hours until she returned home, away from Joyce's rolling eyes, and back into Des's loving arms.

With the most beautiful prom-wear money could buy, the mission was accomplished! Yarni was back into the comfort of her home and settling into the usual domestic lull after being away for the past four days. Upon entering her home, it was most obvious that Des had not attempted any housework.

Yarni stood at the entrance of the kitchen. Watermelon decor was everywhere, which was a sure sign she was home. Yarni smiled when she glanced at the watermelon calendar hanging on the refrigerator next to the watermelon magnet with her and Des's photo in it. They had taken the picture at the Virginia State Fair.

Yarni was happy to see that Des had circled the appropriate day on the calendar and written, *wifey returns*.

Upon learning that his baby was back in town, Des returned home. With roses in hand, Des greeted Yarni, who he had missed being next to, with a passionate kiss. Later Yarni treated Des to his very own private fashion show of which she modeled her beautiful prom gown. They spent the remainder of the night holding one another, making up for the past few nights they had spent apart.

Yarni fluttered around her watermelon-themed kitchen, putting a load of underclothes in the washer while humming, *"At least we're lucky we got 'em/ Gooood Timmes eeehhh,"* to the end of the theme song. To catch up with the local news, she changed the channel on the thirteen-inch television sitting on top of the refrigerator. The six o'clock news began with the voice of the anchorwoman.

"Covering the news where you live, this is News Six. Lolita Moore joins us from the city's south side with today's latest groundbreaking news."

"This is Lolita Moore reporting live from Midlothian Turnpike. This car wash behind me," she turned with index cards in hand and pointed, "is the crime scene of the city's latest homicide. A man was shot and killed execution-style while getting his car, a 1985 Cadillac sedan DeVille, washed. The suspect fled on a sports motorcycle and was reportedly wearing all black. The victim has been identified as Roy Jasper. Authorities are questioning members of the alleged 233 Mob.

Yarni sprinted over to the television, knocking the watermelon-motif statue off of the wall to turn up the volume. She stood all ears, eyes, and in pure disbelief.

"Yeah, I knew Roy real well," a Jheri curl-wearing bystander spoke at the scene into the camera. "I knew he had a contract out on one of the 233 boys, so they probably did this."

With that powder-keg on-street interview under her belt, Lolita Moore smiled: "This is believed to be drug-and gang-related. Stay tuned. We will be updating you with further information as it becomes available to us. Back to you, Julia"

Yarni ran over to the red and black lip-shaped telephone in their living room and dialed Des's pager number. She gazed at a photo pasted inside the lips of the phone as she waited for the three beeps. She anxiously punched the keys 266-9999 plus 000. This was an emergency.

As the time on the digital clocked changed, Yarni questioned where Des could possibly be. He usually called right back. Yarni paced the floor. She reflected over words her girlfriend, Melanie, had planted in her mind weeks before.

"Girl, I am only telling you this because you are my homegirl and I want you to be aware of the word in the streets. This dude Roy put a contract out on Des because he owed Des sixty thousand dollars that he lost tricking and getting high with some freaks. He figured Des was going to try to kill him, so Roy put out a fifteen-thousand-dollar contract on Des. He didn't have the heart to kill him himself. He knew Des wouldn't have any type of understanding about his money being short. Everybody knows Des don't take partial payments. Roy tried to hire this guy name Smoke, who got his name and reputation from his ashy complexion and doing murder for hires. It just so happened that Smoke had a lot of respect for Des, so he went and told him. And I heard that Des gave Smoke ten thousand dollars for the valuable information."

Tears formed in Yarni's eyes. How could this be? She sat down on the oversized black-leather sectional sofa staring at the phone, wishing it would ring. *We were just together all morning and afternoon. We were in Aunt Sarah's Pancake House eating chicken and pancakes when this occurred, so I know for a fact Des couldn't have anything to do with this. He never left my side for a minute. Why they gotta be messing with him?*

Meanwhile . . . Across Town
On the City's South Side:

Des was kneeling down on the ground, watching the dice like a hawk. Everyone was quiet while waiting to see where the dice would fall.

When all of a sudden the loud *beep! beep! beep!* interrupted the game. Des looked at his pager in panic. *000? In the whole two years we've been together she's never used the emergency code. What the hell is going on?*

"Yo' Slim come on," Des called out to his right-hand man, as he jumped into his gray 1985 turbo diesel 300 Mercedes-Benz, almost forgetting to pick his money up off the ground that he had just bet with. "Something ain't right, man, Yarni just paged me with our emergency code. She's never used that code the whole two years I've been with her." He unzipped the bag that enclosed his cellular phone. Heart pounding as he dialed, he spoke to Slim in a disgruntled tone, "Yo, if something happened to my wife it's going to be a bunch of dead bodies, man, I'm telling you." The phone didn't sound a complete ring.

"Hello," Yarni's sweet voice managed, not trying to muffle the fact that she had been crying ever since she heard the news report.

"Baby girl, what's wrong? Talk to me, baby," Des replied, worried.

"I need you to come home right now. I've got to talk to you; it's extremely important."

"I'm on the way. You all right?" Des said.

"Yeah, I just need you here, that's all," Yarni replied.

"Anybody there with you? Just say yes or no.

"No, baby. It isn't what you think. Now, please just come home!"

"I'll be there in less than fifteen minutes"

"Okay. I love you, baby."

"I love you too, baby girl."

Des pushed the accelerator to the floor, doing 100 mph in a 55 mph zone, weaving in and out of traffic on 95 North. Des almost missed his exit to 64 West, where he just about caused a Volvo to hit a Mustang. The Volvo driver honked the horn at him as he stuck his middle finger up in the rearview mirror. He was listening to the *Paid in Full* cassette in his Alpine tape deck. He sang along with Rakim: *"I ain't no joke/ I used to let the mic smoke. So, I slam it when I'm done and make sure it's broke."* He turned down the music and looked at Slim, who was bopping his head to the beat.

"Yo, man if any of them scandalous hoes done told my wife something, oh I am going to straight pistol-whip one of 'em. That's my word. If any of these local niggas done disrespected my wife, oh, he's going to die," Des raged.

Yarni paced the floor, looking out of the window every few minutes. Des pulled up in front of their Sundance Station apartment, taking up two parking spaces. Almost stripping the gearshift as he quickly put the car in park, he hopped out. His size ten, crisp new blue and white Delta Force Nikes hit the pavement as he sprinted across the wet lawn, avoiding the sprinkler system with Slim trailing behind him. He never acknowledged the mud that splashed on his hundred-dollar sneakers, as his only concern was to get to Yarni. Three steps before he approached the door, he reached under his shirt and pulled out his 9 mm semiautomatic. He then gave Slim the key to open the door.

Yarni ran to the door, put her arms around Des, and laid her head on his chest as she cried. He embraced her tightly as he put the safety back on the 9 mm and laid it on the end table. Slim stood on guard with his .45 Magnum pistol in his hand.

"Baby girl, tell me what's wrong," he said in a comforting tone while holding Yarni in his arms. His whole attitude had changed. Whenever he delt with Yarni, his persona turned into that of a teddy bear. It was like Dr. Jekyll and Mr. Hyde.

"I was watching the news, and the reporter said they were questioning people from the 233 Mob for killing that boy Roy, with you being the leader, I was afraid the cops had you," Yarni sobbed while sniffling and blowing her nose with the tissues she'd gathered while waiting for Des to arrive.

"Baby girl, you don't have anything to worry about. I know the police will probably pick me up for questioning because of my reputation, but they can't hold me. Nothing has changed. I am giving all this up in a couple months once you graduate. You know what we planned, right?" he asked her as he stroked her hair. Yarni shook her head, wiped her tears, and smiled up at him.

The plan was that as soon as she graduated from high school, they were moving to Norfolk. She had been accepted to Old Dominion University. He was going to give up his current lifestyle and open an exotic-car lot near Virginia Beach. He'd had a good run. He'd been flooding keys of powder coke into the streets of Richmond for the past few years. Des had every drug house, corner, strip, block, and neighborhood in the streets of Richmond, and all surrounding counties, on lockdown. He owned and operated every single after-hour, crap, number, and liquor house in the town. The ones he didn't own in the rural areas, got blessing and approval from Des. He was the ringleader of the 233 Mob and ran the most successful and organized crime ring in the state of Virginia. He had found Yarni and wanted to share the rest of his life with her. Amazed that he had gotten away with everything this long, Des was certain it was time to move on. He knew that this life was a trap. He had enough money stashed and decided to quit while he was ahead. The day she graduated the police indicted him on murder charges. He was held with no bond. Yarni wanted to drop dead and die. She was devastated. The funny thing is, everybody thought she was distressed over the money. She was ravaged due to the fact that her husband—her soul mate, her best friend, her confidant, her life, her everything, her all—was gone.

Yarni sat on the mahogany bench, listening to the verdict, knowing he didn't commit this crime. He was dining with her at Aunt Sarah's at the time of the murder and he never left her side. That was Yarni's testimony when she was called to the stand. But the testimony of the others was more damaging. Roy's Mother, Shuckey, a frail, brown-skinned, bald-headed woman, with her front teeth missing or rotten from getting high for so long, testified that she'd seen Des fleeing the scene. She was a junkie. Shuckey had a possession charge pending in another court, which was going to be dismissed after she hung Des. The Commonwealth attorney agreed to the deal. Shuckey was a freebasing, cocaine-addict, lowlife, but they had wanted Des for a long time, so her character was ignored.

Des was sentenced to sixty years. Yarni's vision blurred. She couldn't hear or interpret anything anybody was saying. All she could hear was "guilty" and feel the weight of her own sobs coming like huge waves in her arms. Yarni immediately looked as Des screamed out to Shuckey, "You lying junkie bitch! You reap what you sow. Just because I'm in here don't think it ain't others who can't get to you. You better leave town because this-here town ain't big enough for you to hide in!" Des was taken away chained and shackled. When Des reached the door, he stopped in his tracks. He glared at Yarni and hollered out, "I love you, baby girl, forever and ever! These walls can't stop our love, baby!" Yarni couldn't look at Des. Des's white, bow tie-wearing lawyer explained to her that he would have to do at least fifteen years before he would be eligible for parole, providing good behavior. The lawyer informed her that the longest the state could hold him was thirty-five years. Thirty-five years was a long-ass time. She had to figure something out.

Yarni finally got herself together and left the courtroom to face Joyce, who had been removed earlier from the courtroom for trying to intimidate Shuckey from testifying. Shuckey had a restraining order out on Joyce for threatening her not to go to court to testify against Des. When Yarni delivered the news to Joyce, her first concern was his material possessions.

"How long before you're going to be home because I need to come and get Des's jewelry and also I need to get his cars from over there. You're going to have to sign that Benz in your name over to me too." Joyce was harsh and to the point. She never liked playing second fiddle to Yarni, and now it was time for her to position herself as numero uno, as his mother.

The nerve! How dare she? Yarni thought, speechless. She could not utter a word.

"You can act like you don't hear me, but I'm going to say it one more time," Joyce stressed. "I need to get all my son's belongings from you and I mean that."

Yarni's palms began to sweat and her heart began to pound rapidly as she looked up into Joyce's eyes and said to her in a stern tone, "Did you just comprehend what I said? I said they just gave Des sixty years for a crime he didn't commit, and all you can do is worry about his possessions. I simply can't focus on any car or anything else material right now. Just so you know, I am not giving anybody any of his belongings until I speak to him. As a matter of fact, I can't even talk to you anymore because I feel like you are tempting me to disrespect you, and overall, you are Des's mother." Yarni put her hand on the strap of her MCM pocketbook that Des had rewarded her with for making all A's the next-to-last six weeks of school. She pushed it all the way on her shoulder and turned to walk away.

Joyce followed behind her, making a scene. "Listen to me, you little grown-ass gal. You don't get sassy with me, missy. See, you might have a hold on Des, but I don't care nothing for you, never liked you and never will. You ain't nothing to me. See, Des ain't here to take up for you now." Joyce was so mad, foam gathered in the corner of her mouth.

Yarni couldn't control the tears from rolling down her face as she walked faster and faster to get out of the pathway of Joyce's words. Everybody from the bondsman to the inmate trustee mopping the hall and the lawyer holding a file, talking to his clients, stopped what they were doing to watch the distraction Joyce made as Yarni expeditiously tried to escape. Once she was out of the courthouse she ran to her car, threw her purse onto the passenger seat and just sat in the driver's seat and sobbed. As the tears flowed down her face, then to her neck, she screamed, "*Why me?*"

After Yarni boo-hooed a while, reality sank in. Where was she to go now? She knew she wasn't going to ask her family for any type of assistance. She was too ashamed to after she had moved out from her mother's house and in with Des. She had vowed at that very moment that other than moral support, she would never ask anything else from her family. She would learn to take care of herself, but where would she start?

Somehow she managed to drive herself to the house of her favorite aunt, Andrea. Andrea was a small-featured, cocoa-colored woman with very thin eyebrows and long eyelashes. She wore finger waves gelled neatly across her entire head. Before she could ring the doorbell, she reflected on something Andrea had taught her years ago. The Bible said that if two come together and agree on something, whatever they ask for will come to pass, but Yarni needed confirmation. Yarni asked God to give her the will and the strength to be there for Des and to love him unconditionally. To be with Des always, even through incarceration. She prayed for some of the tension to lessen between her and Joyce. She knew that the only breakthrough and miracle would come from God.

Andrea had already heard the verdict on the evening news. Yarni explained to Andrea in detail the performance Joyce put on as they were leaving the courthouse. To Andrea's surprise, Yarni wasn't really concerned with Joyce's actions. Her focus was on Des and his well-being. Andrea tried to comfort her by sitting beside Yarni on the love seat and placing her arms around her, asking, "Baby, would you rather have twelve people convict him or six people carry him?" That was not comforting to Yarni at all.

"Auntie, no disrespect but somebody dying and someone going to jail is two totally different things. In jail, everything is stripped from you. Your freedom, your self-respect, and your loved ones are all taken away. Yeah, you can still see them and touch them, but at the same time you watch them get conditioned. You watch them get bitter. You watch and hear of your loved ones getting disrespected by some egotistical, control-freak toy cop, who probably doesn't have any authority at home, so they come to work and abuse what little authority they have. I'm sorry, Auntie," Yarni said, shaking her head as she continued. "there is just no comparison."

Andrea said, "Right," as Yarni continued.

"Then we get stripped of our rights as well. We have to be searched when we visit. We can't wear this. We can't wear that. They can search our cars at any given time if it's on their premises. Does prison actually corrupt our people to be more scrupulous? What is the fear now?"

Aunt Andrea couldn't get a word in.

"The way I see it is, one day you're living a regular, everyday life and the next day you're in prison being treated like an animal. Locked in a cell twenty-three hours a day, then they wonder why when you're released you act like an animal," Yarni raged.

Yarni thought about all these things and just began to pray. She had always prayed every night, but now she really pulled out her Bible and started to read it. Her mother had always instilled prayer in her life. Yarni had been through a lot of things and she knew that she would or was to be faced with some unknown obstacles that had yet to be revealed to her, and ultimately, God would be the only one who would carry her through. She knew that God would be with Des no matter what the outcome was. Andrea kneeled in front of the sofa with Yarni. She left her Aunt Andrea's house feeling a lot better.

As Yarni approached the apartment, she could see from the street that the door was cracked open. As she approached the door, she realized it was off the hinges. She automatically thought the police had been there, but for what reason?

Des was already in jail. She walked into the apartment. The living-room furniture was gone. There was only a broken frame on the floor with a painting of Des and Yarni that Des had gotten to hang over the fireplace. She walked to the eat-in kitchen and the table was gone. There was only one bar stool pulled up to the counter with one watermelon placemat. She stepped into the dining room—cleaned out! She proceeded to the bedroom—nothing left! Only Yarni's clothes were hanging up in the closet and her jewelry box. There was a note attached to the jewelry box with duct tape. Written on a brown paper bag with a black magic marker in big bold letters was: *You will not be fucking no other nigger on my son's shit.*

She couldn't believe Joyce was behind all of this. Yarni screamed out, "That dirty bitch!" She broke down crying hysterically.

2

Back In Da Day

Reflect Back, 2 Years:

Yarni was seventeen years old when Des got locked up. She met him when she was only fifteen, a sophomore at Henrico High School. One Friday night, back in the day, her girlfriend Melanie spent the night at her house. Yarni was on punishment because she had gotten a Saturday-morning detention for arriving late to Mrs. Walden's class one too many times, so she and Melanie couldn't go to Skate Land or anywhere else, for that matter. It was a sure gift that she could have company at all, especially company as resourceful as Melanie.

Melanie was bright-skinned with dirty blond hair. She was a little overweight for her five-foot-two height. She had big pop hazel eyes. Being the baby of seven brothers made her quick on her feet. She loved staying the weekends over Yarni's house because there was a loving mother and always a refrigerator full of food. Plus, there was peace and quiet away from the crack-infested, brick bungalow-style projects she lived in. Yarni's house was a mansion filled with all the latest technology. They even had a guest room, although she never slept there. She'd always bunk in Yarni's room.

Melanie loved Yarni's large bedroom. It was the perfect girl's living quarters. The comforter set was a maize, bright orange and hot pink print with a white-wood bedroom suite. The large rug on top of the hardwood floors was a maize print to match the comfort set. She even had a hot-pink telephone. The lighting in the room was hot pink and orange disco lights. The walls were covered with posters out of *Right On!* and *Fresh* magazines. One wall had a bulletin board filled with pictures of her family and all of her friends from school at dances and games. Yarni had her own desk and walk-in closet filled from top to bottom with clothes, belts, boots, and shoes. But most importantly, Yarni's room had her own television, VCR, and all the latest books and tapes on her bookshelf.

Melanie had stolen her older brother's phone book, a book with the numbers for all the big boys who were major players in the drug game. Most were pager numbers, so they couldn't call those numbers since it was after 11:00 p.m. and Yarni's mother, Gloria, had taken her phone line out of her room as part of her punishment. So, they had to sneak and use Gloria's line. No one called Gloria's line after 11:00 p.m. Melanie and Yarni continued to make calls and either got no answer or the big boy was not at home. It was midnight by this time, and they had called all the numbers in the book except one. That number belonged to Des, aka Ghetto Superstar, big-time drug dealer and a treacherous killer.

Melanie had been skeptical about calling the number because she knew Des would not take a phone prank lightly. He had a notorious reputation according to Melanie's older brother, as well as everybody else in the hood. Des was not to be played with in any type of way. Melanie didn't know him personally, but there were stories all over town of his heartless acts. Maybe it was just a rumor that he had killed a boy over a Blow Pop one time. It was also said he'd killed a man for telling his mother to "kiss his ass" because she pulled into a parking space that he had been waiting on. Nobody would dare testify against him because his whole family, including his mother, were gangsters. Nobody messed with anybody who was dear to him. His workers would even steal from their own mother to keep from being short on any of his money.

Des was the worst kind of dope man to deal with. Rumor was—and this rumor was close to the truth—that he was a cold-blooded killer, cunning, and very intelligent. He was charismatic and a master of head games. With his business-oriented mind, he had goals and things he wanted to accomplish in life outside of the drug game. He had book sense—common sense—and street sense. Very rarely would you find a street hustler with all three of these traits. When you did, all hell could and would break loose. Which it did.

Melanie took all these things into consideration and decided, being the thrill-seeker that she was, that they were going to call Des anyway. Hell, it was Friday night and he probably wouldn't be available anyway. She picked up the phone and hung it up, then picked up the phone and dialed. The phone rang twice. She hung up before anyone picked up, and then burst out laughing.

"What are you laughing at?" Yarni asked.

"I am about to call this guy," she said.

"Call him then. Don't keep hanging up," Yarni demanded.

As Melanie followed her orders, a male voice answered. "Hello," the receiving voice said.

"Hello, can I speak to Des?" Melanie said.

"How did you get this number?" the male voice inquired. "Des gave it to me," Melanie responded in a casual tone.

"Well, this is Des and I don't know who this is playing games, and I know you are playing because nobody would or should be calling here for me. Now tell me why you insist on lying?"

Melanie bucked her big pop eyes. She wasn't expecting Des to even be there. She was totally caught off guard. So, she just tensed up. She had to think quickly.

"Des, this is Melanie, Baby Joe's little sister from around the 233."

"Okay." said Des, "is something wrong with Baby Joe?" he asked, sounding sincere.

"No," replied Melanie.

"Then what other reason would you be calling my family's home?"

She immediately came back with: "My friend, who lives in the county, seen you come through 233 and is dying to meet you."

Yarni immediately hit Melanie. Melanie got up off the bed with the telephone in her hand, speaking into the receiver with her hand around the mouthpiece of the phone. Melanie was good on her feet.

"Ever since she saw you, she's been calling me asking who you were. She's very fly. Not to be disrespectful in any kind of way, but she looks better than any of the girls I've ever seen you with. She has real long black hair with copper streaks and ain't got no bumps on her face. She got a real big butt!" Yarni's eyes got big as Melanie continued. "She ain't no yuk-mouth chick either. She got pretty white teeth, and 'bout five-five. I ain't gay or nothing, but she bad, Des."

Yarni was struggling with Melanie to try and hang up the phone. Melanie couldn't believe she still had Des on the phone listening. So she guarded the telephone with her all. She would not dare hang up on Des anyway.

"I told her that you already had a girlfriend and that you wouldn't be interested in her, but would you at least say hi to her, please?"

"Where is she?" Des asked.

"She's right in the other room."

"Put her on the phone," Des demanded, but laughing to himself. *I can't believe these little girls are playing on my phone, but I am gonna go ahead and play along with them.*

Melanie called out, "Yaarrrnnieee", as if she wasn't standing right there. Melanie extended her hand out, handing Yarni the phone. Yarni shook her head no, but Melanie begged and pleaded with her on her knees until Yarni took the phone and softly said, "Hello."

She was sweating from tussling with Melanie to hang up the phone, and tried very hard to catch her breath. She was also a little scared that Gloria might wake up, hear them, and come into her room to hang up the phone. Or even worse, pick up the phone and embarrass her in front of the king of all the big boys.

Des went along, pulling on the jay he was rolling before the phone rung: "Hello, how are you?"

"I'm well, thank you," she said.

"Where in the county do you live?" he asked, just making casual conversation.

"Richmond Hills." He automatically knew that she must come from a good, respectable family. Richmond Hills was an upscale, elite community. There were only a handful of black families living there. She didn't want to tell him that she lived in Richmond Hills because she didn't want him to think that she was the stuck-up type. At the same time, she didn't want to lie. That was something that he could easily find out. They chitchatted for about fifteen minutes. Des couldn't believe how well spoken, confident, and mature Yarni was. He wanted to see who the person was behind the voice.

Des's pager went off. "Give me your number so I can call you right back, because I gotta go take care of something," he said.

I can't give him my number. He cannot call back here this time of night. My mother would flip the hell out. I can't tell him I'm on punishment, and I don't want my mother to tell him either because then he'll really think I am a little girl. Think quick, Yarni, Umm . . . Umm . . . think!

"I need to take a shower and get myself together, so how about I just call you back?" Yarni tried to save her underaged self.

"That's cool So, just ring me back in about thirty minutes." Des was very persistent. He knew he would be in the house for the night because he had been out gambling for three days consecutively. He didn't really have anything else to do and he was in a good mood. Most of the time he had no time to be at home to kick it on the phone with a female. This would be different for him.

From the time that Yarni hung up the phone from Des, Melanie started filling Yarni in about all the good things that were known about him. "Girl, he got money! He is da man, you hear me? He brought every kid in the neighborhood bicycles for Christmas around the 233. He'll never let anybody go hungry. He takes care of everybody around there. Girl, and he fine as I don't know what. He black as midnight, but make you wanna smack yo' mama! He taller than you, 'bout five-eight . . . five-nine. Girl, he got coal-black curly hair like he from some other country or something, but he right from here. He might be Indian. The nigga can dress his ass off, even got a pimp-daddy walk. He got two open-face gold crown teeth in his mouth that are spaced apart. I even heard he got a big dick too."

Melanie boasted on how Des had a different car for each day of the week. Yarni didn't take Melanie seriously about everything she said pertaining to Des. Melanie couldn't believe that Des actually told Yarni to call him back. She secretly thought to herself that Des probably wouldn't even be there when Yarni called back.

Thirty minutes flew by. It was after midnight, but she still waited fifteen extra minutes to call him back because she didn't want to seem pressed to talk to him. It sounded like they were having a party. There was music playing and people talking in the background. She asked, "It's loud, what's going on?"

"My mama and cousin are having a couple of drinks before they go out," Des said.

Yarni and Des talked for over two hours. He asked her mainly about her family life. He felt getting that information out of her would tell him a lot about her character.

"Who do you live with?"

"My mother."

"What does she do?"

"She has her own catering business. She works from home."

"Do you have any brothers or sisters?"

"Yeah, I have a brother by my father, but he doesn't live with us."

"Oh, yo' mother and father divorced?"

"Dang, what are you, *Hawaii Five-o*, asking all these questions?"

"Hell no, I ain't no police," Des laughed. "No, far from the police, baby, just a guy trying to get to know a girl, that's all. Something wrong with that?" He knew it really wasn't.

"No. Now my father is the forbidden story," she joked. "I usually tell people he lives out of town, which is only half the story. He does live out of town, but he's in prison," Yarni said. Des found this interesting, he turned his ears up.

"For how long?" Des asked about the father's jail time.

"Well, for a long time."

"What's a long time?"

"So far, fifteen years plus."

"Yarni, wait a minute, you're fifteen."

"Yeah, you don't have to remind me.

"He's been locked up since I was twelve days old. As a matter of fact, that's how they located him. They went to Richmond Memorial, looked at my mother's records, got her address off of them and there he was with his newborn baby: Me."

"Damn, baby. Sorry to hear that." He paused, then continued prying into her forbidden story. "Damn, ain't that some shit? What, did he murder somebody?"

"Bank robbery."

"And they gave him all that time?"

"Yep."

"What's his name? My mother probably knows him."

"Lloyd Pitman," Yarni said.

"Lloyd 'Slot Machine' Pitman!" Damn, that nigga is a legend in this town. He pulled off one of the most infamous bank robberies in the state of Virginia. They called him Slot Machine because any bank robbery that he pulled off, always paid off like the slots in Atlantic City. This was back in the late seventies and he's still a legend even now in the late eighties.

"Baby, I am sorry you had to grow up without your father. Every little girl needs her father." Des was warming up to her now.

"Yeah, it used to mess me up, but when I evaluated the situation, I couldn't have asked for a better mother. She gets on my nerves at times, but one thing is for sure, and two things for certain: She's always been there when I needed her and even when I don't need her." Yarni threw out a fake laugh when she thought of the reality of the statement she had just made about her overprotective mother.

"Do you write him?" Des asked, getting back to the more celebrated member of the Pitman family.

"My mother makes sure that I write him. For the first few years, my mother would see to it that I visited him. Even though he's in prison, she wanted to make sure he was still a part of my life."

Des thought to himself, *Damn, that alone says a lot about her mother. She is a faithful woman and has a lot of principles and her working from home has given her enough hands-on raising of Yarni. I am almost 100 percent sure that Yarni's mother has instilled those qualities in her daughter. She is only fifteen, but just maybe . . .*

Yarni suddenly realized how late it had gotten. She knew that she had to get up early to go to Saturday-morning detention. She knew she couldn't fall asleep because then she would have to repeat it and would not be able to cheer in the big game next Friday night. Yarni was the

captain of the cheerleader squad. Friday was
the game that Henrico's basketball team played
John Marshall. Everyone who was anybody was
going to be there. So Yarni ended the conversation and told Des it was nice talking to him,
but that she had to go. He told her he definitely
wanted to hear from her again the next day. She
said okay.

Des sat on the couch, looking dumbfounded.
He had never had anyone end any conversation
with him first. Women would always stay around
until he got tired of them and was ready for them
to go. He thought to himself, *The nerve of this
broad to act like she couldn't stay up and talk
to me. Baby Joe must not have informed his li'l
sister of the caliber of the dude she was dealing
with.*

Saturday and Sunday went by, and Des didn't
hear from Yarni. It hurt his ego that after two
whole days she hadn't called. He had even told
his cousin and mother that if she called, to give
her his pager number. By Monday evening he
said to himself, *Whenever she finds out who
exactly I am in this town and decide to catch the
vapors and want to get with me, I am not going
to even accept her calls!* As soon as that thought
crossed his mind, the phone rang. He answered
it, "Yeah," thinking it was going to be for his

cousin. He heard a sweet voice say, "Hello, may I speak with Des, please?"

"Yeah, you finally decided to get around to calling me, huh?" Des said with a nasty tone. "Why even bother calling now?" he said.

She paused. "Excuse me," she asked indignantly. "How about I never call you again, would you like that?" He did not like her tone. She didn't like his either. He was in shock because nobody spoke to him in that tone and expected not to get smacked. But then, he was too far away to hit her and put her in line.

"Wait a minute, baby," he said. "Maybe we should start this conversation over. I don't want you to think this is game I am about to kick to you, but I have been waiting for your call for the last two days. I am a man of my word. My word is bond. When I say something then you can bank on that, and that's what I expect from others. So, when you tell me you are going to do something, that is exactly what you do. So, I don't tolerate anybody lying to me about anything. Nothing big or the least little thing."

"That goes for me as well," said Yarni. "I don't like to be lied to or played with either. There are a few things I need to talk to you about anyway since we're being honest with each other." He braced himself, and to his surprise she didn't back down.

"Melanie lied to you. I have never actually seen you, nor do I know what you look like and I never said that I was attracted to you." Yarni filled Des in on everything. "And even if I had seen you, I wouldn't have ever gotten Melanie or anybody else to approach you. I probably wouldn't have said a thing. And if I'd ever felt like I was at the point where I just had to meet you, I am very much my own person."

She reminded him that she was still in high school and the reason she couldn't call him back was because she had detention, which caused her to be on punishment. Her mother had taken her phone out of her room so she had to sneak to talk to him. She explained that she just didn't feel like sneaking around using the phone. So, she decided to wait to call him when she got her phone privileges back. She also explained that since she was only fifteen, her mother didn't allow her to date or get involved in relationships with guys. Her mother, especially, would not let her even be bothered with Des. He was twenty-one years old, and his street reputation made him older than that. Des could not believe his ears. Yarni was so mature and well spoken. He couldn't believe how honest and to the point she was. She wasn't like the other chicks trying to scheme on his money and wanting to say they were screwing

him for his reputation. As a matter of fact, he
was wondering, *Is she just acting like she don't
know about my checkered past? How I'm living
now, or does she truly not know?* Des had only
dealt with older women, and this young, tender
thing now had his undivided attention. None of
his old heads were even competition for Yarni,
and this was still at the beginning of the game.
Des couldn't understand what was going on with
him. *Why am I entertaining the conversation of
this arbitrary person, and she ain't but fifteen
years old at that?*

He replayed bits and pieces of their conversation in his head over and over again. He wanted
to see her. *Fifteen or not, I must see her.* He
reckoned with himself that beauty and brains
don't come hand in hand. Her conversation was
intriguing. So she probably would look a mess.
Curiosity was killing him. He decided that he was
going to see her and even bet with his main man,
Slim, that she would be busted. After he saw that
she was tore up from the floor up, he would close
out that chapter of curiosity and move on.

For the next three days, he would stop whatever
he was doing to come in the house around seven
p.m. every evening to call Yarni. He wanted to
talk to her on his house phone so there wouldn't

be a bunch of distractions, like people running up to him asking him for this and that, as well as people begging. "Des can I have five dollars? Des, I need help with my light bill . . . Des, Des, Des." He didn't want her to hear none of that. He also wanted her to have his undivided attention. Besides, he didn't want Yarni to have any indications on the extreme status of his lifestyle. He knew what kind of upbringing she had, so he wasn't sure how she'd take to his lifestyle. He expected that Melanie had already given her some ideas, but he wasn't tripping on what Melanie said.

Friday, the big game day, finally came. The game was always a sellout. It was a big deal in this town.

Yarni and her fellow cheerleaders had been rehearsing several cheers to keep the overflow crowd excited. Yarni looked around the gym at all the people who filled the stands. Her girls were really showing off. She could feel that tonight was going to be a good night. Right before they were about to perform in their halftime show, she glanced at the door and an entourage of dudes came in. They all stood out. Pretty much everybody had on all kinds of leather suits or a Dapper Dan jacket.

But these dudes, oh, they took it to another level, and were rocking full-length furs, Gazelle glasses and jewels glistening like the sun on white Bahama sand. Yarni noticed one guy in particular who stood out. She thought he was fine. He had a medium build with a chocolate complexion and black, wavy hair. There was a certain charisma about him. Yarni's cocaptain, Stephanie, was motioning to her, to look over at the dudes, but she didn't want to seem pressed. Right when she looked back over there the music dropped. The song "It Takes Two" by Rob Base played. Yarni just showed off; all the cheerleaders did. She really put her all into it. Her flips, splits, and everything, but never making any eye contact with any of the big hats who had just walked in the door.

Henrico won the game seventy-two to seventy. Afterwards Yarni changed clothes because she wanted to floss her outfit at the after party. Gloria was chaperoning the party. Yarni didn't mind her mother being there because they looked like they could pass for sisters. She and her mother shared the same exact caramel complexion. Most of the time Gloria possessed light brown eyes but they sometimes changed to green or gray. Her mole above the right side of her mouth brought out all the beauty that hid inside of her well-maintained long black ponytail. Gloria, in her forties, not looking a day over twenty-five, still possessed smooth skin and a nice figure. Now, Yarni had more butt and breast than her mother did, but their builds were still the same. One could see that Yarni was more flamboyant and outgoing than her conservative mother.

With Gloria being there at the dance, Yarni pretended like she could really hang. She had on a purple short leather skirt and a purple leather jacket to match. She wore some purple tall riding Nine West boots that tied up at the bottom while everyone else had on black. Gloria had gone on a shopping trip and got them months ago at the King of Prussia Mall in Philly. Yarni hadn't worn them yet because she had been saving them especially for that night. Everybody was telling her how cute she looked, and she knew it. Yarni always stood out in anything she wore. She constantly dressed on a more sophisticated and classier level than her peers. There were girls who wanted to compete with her dressing, but there was just no competition because she had a style of her own.

When she was coming out of the bathroom with Stephanie, one of the guys that was in the entourage came and asked, "Which one of y'all name is Yarni?" Stephanie pointed. He said "oh" and walked away.

The next day, Des called. "You did an excellent job cheering last night. I liked what I saw and I may want you to be my own personal cheerleader."

"You came to the game but didn't make your appearance known to me? You didn't even speak to me!" She was upset and let him know it. He liked Yarni because she had spunk.

"Look, baby, that was yesterday. I can't bring that back. Today is a new day and I want to see you." Yarni was in shock. *Wait a minute, he wants to see me?*

"Can you meet me somewhere around your way?" Des asked.

How can I pull this off? Think Yarni, Okay. I can meet him up the street. Only white people live in that block and none of them know my mom, so I won't have to worry about them trying to snitch on me that I am meeting a grown man.

The date was set. When she saw him roll up in his Cadillac, chills struck through her body and she was mesmerized. *Oh, my God, it's the dude from the entourage at the basketball game last night. This can't be the dude I have been talking to over the phone. Well, shoot me running! Why do I have to be fifteen? Ohhh, I just cannot believe this shit. I know he'll never be my boyfriend, hell, I've never even had a boyfriend my own age, let alone one that's twenty-one years old! Yarni, just keep your cool and lose the thought of him being your boyfriend.*

Once up close she tried not to focus on the anchor pendant on his necklace that was fluttered in diamonds.

"You are even prettier close up," he said as she blushed. "Thank you, you're not too bad yourself," she said calmly as she melted inside.

They talked for a little while longer before she said, "I hate to break this up, but I have to get back home before my mom gets suspicious."

"Okay, I'm glad you snuck out to meet me. I will call you in a little while to make sure you got home safe."

Yarni strolled back down the street, passing all the large houses that sat up on the hill. *Why am I so young? My age stops me from doing everything! He would never take me serious anyway. I'd be his "little girlfriend." Get real, Yarni, he's a grown man having sex, and you are still a virgin.* Taking all those things into consideration, she dismissed the idea of ever being anything to him, and walked on home.

He watched her as she sashayed. The further she got down the street, the more he genuinely wanted her. Not for sex, but just as his own personal teddy bear, so to speak. She was everything he wanted in a female. She had the right build, not too big or too skinny. Her facial features were okay, but she had the cutest dimples. She wasn't any beauty queen, but she was beautiful in her own way. She had long, flowing black hair and a caramel complexion with no acne. Even though she was fifteen, he definitely liked her style.

As Yarni walked in her door, the phone rang.

"Look, I want to take you to the new Jean-Claude Van Damme movie this coming Saturday." She felt like she wanted to just drop the phone. She couldn't believe this twenty-one-year-old man wanted to take her out. All kinds of things started running through her mind. *What am I going to wear? How am I going to wear my hair? Most importantly, how am I going to convince my mother to agree to let me go out with him?*

She thought of every possibility and tried to think of ways to go about this from every angle. *I could say I am going to the movies with Melanie, but then she's going to want to talk to Melanie's mother and insist on dropping us off or picking us up. I could say that it's a school function, but she's involved in every school outing.* She came to the conclusion that her mother may let her go with a seventeen-year-old, but definitely not a twenty-one-year-old. That was a dead issue.

Yarni finally persuaded Gloria to let her go to the movies with her "friend" who she'd been talking to on the phone for months, and she told her mother she'd even been meeting him at Skate Land for the past couple years. She also told her mother that he was sort of like a big brother to her. So, her mother would not look at it as a real date. Now she knew that Gloria would want to meet him, and he would have to come in and meet her before they left.

Yarni knew Gloria was having company on Saturday night and would be more lenient with her guests there. She told Des to pick her up at about 6:30, and he agreed, but he called at seven that evening, saying that time had got away from him. He had gotten caught up gambling, but he was on the way. For a minute she thought he was standing her up. It couldn't be real, that she was going out with this big wheel.

When the doorbell rang Yarni hurried from upstairs to try to get to the door before Gloria could get to it. Yarni had to admit that she looked very cute. She had on tight-fitting black leather pants, a black, red, and white shirt, some red-leather tall riding Nine West boots, and a red-leather jacket.

Gloria rushed into the foyer, looked out of the window to the burgundy-on-burgundy rag-topped Lincoln Continental with the slant back, parked outside with the True Spoke rims along with the Vogue tires on it. She invited Des in. When she saw him with a huge diamond in his ear, Gazelle sunglasses, and exquisite ostrich-skin leather coat with the cowboy-style hat, belt, and shoes to match—and it wasn't that imitation stuff either—her first thought was: *Oh, hell no, my daughter is not going anywhere with this gangsta looking cat. Bottom line.*

But that was before he spoke in that civilized manner that mothers love. He made direct eye contact with Gloria while extending his hand to greet her. "I am so pleased to finally meet Yarni's mother. Yarni has a lot of good qualities, and I can tell that she must have inherited them from you. Would you like to come along with us? We are going to see the new Jean-Claude Van Damme movie. It had a good newspaper review," Des said.

"No, sweetie," responded Gloria in an equally civilized manner. She thought to herself, *That was a nice gesture. He has good manners and he looked me in my eyes while he spoke to me. Hmm . . . I have raised Yarni with certain morals and principles, and I trust her. She knows if he acts a fool that I am only a phone call away. Yarni's mind is set on going on this date. She inspected him from head to toe, and I can understand why. He is definitely a cutie.*

"Sweetie, you all go and have a nice time," Gloria said.

"Is eleven-thirty okay to have her back?" Des wanted to do everything right.

"Yes, sweetie, that'll be fine." That impressed Gloria. Yarni, peeking from around the corner, was bedazzled as well. Des knew it would put Gloria more at ease.

Gloria went in Yarni's maize and hot pink room to get her. She handed her three dollars in change and two twenty-dollar bills. She put her hands on a strand of Yarni's hair that was out of place, fixed the out strand, and grabbed Yarni under her chin. "Rule number one for Dating 101. Never go anywhere without your own money in your possession. Don't let him know that you have money, but keep your own stash in case he acts a fool. And if he does, there's enough change for you to call me. I gave you the change because rule number two states, Never go on a date without change. You may need to use the phone to call somebody. You understand? Now I am going to be here all night, if you need me, baby. You look beautiful." She kissed Yarni on the forehead.

As Yarni was about to turn to walk out of the door, Gloria called out to her and Des, "Wait a minute, smile! I have got to get a picture of my baby's first date." Gloria flashed them with her 110 camera.

Oh, my God I knew she was taking all this too well. She just had to embarrass me by snapping that stupid picture. She is so dramatic and sentimental. I am so glad I did not inherit that trait from her. She always has to overdo it. Like she just could not settle with giving me one dollar of change. She had to give me three dollars of change. The phone is only 20 cents. Now I got all this change weighing my pocketbook down. Don't she know I am smart enough to just call her collect?

Gloria watched from the house as Des opened the car door for Yarni. Tears begin to roll down her face because reality sank in: Her baby, the one she'd given birth to—which seemed like just yesterday—was growing up. As Gloria looked on watching them drive off, a timeline of events in Yarni's life from birth up to this point flashed through her head.

They got to the movie twenty minutes late, which was fine by Yarni. She was fascinated with just being with Des. He was very serious, and to her he seemed a little uptight. The movie was over at about ten p.m. He knew they were working with little time. He stopped by his apartment on the west end. It was something out of a magazine to her. Yarni's mother had a bunch of antique-style furniture, but Des's apartment was very modern. Everything in the apartment was black; black-leather sectional sofa, a large picture of a black panther on the wall in the living room. The tile in the kitchen was black marble. The cabinets and counters were a marble print as well. All the walls throughout the apartment were mirrored. Yarni was intrigued by his style.

He cut the TV on and sat on the arm of the sectional. She sat in front of him. He just sat there. She asked him, "Are you going to give me a hug, or real gangsters don't hug?" He stood up in front of her and put his arm around her, but never responded to the comment. She tried to kiss him, but he turned away, so she kissed him on his cheek, and she could feel his penis getting hard. At that point, he looked at his watch.

"It's almost eleven. I've got to make one stop, and I gave your mom my word that I'd have you back by eleven-thirty." He grabbed her jacket, held it up in front of him so she could slip her arms into it, handed Yarni her barrel-shaped Liz Claiborne purse, and opened the screen door for her so they could exit the apartment. They were off.

The ride back to Yarni's house was silent, besides the radio playing, "Off On Your Own (Girl)" by Al B. Sure! She wondered to herself exactly what his thoughts were. Des was so mysterious. *I wonder, why he didn't try to make a move on me? I can't believe that he was a perfect gentleman. Would he ever see me again? Is he not impressed with what I wore? Is it my hair?* She had her hair in a flat wrap, hanging real straight with the ends bent. *What is it?* He pulled into the 7-Eleven.

"You want something out of here?" He pointed to the store. "No, but thank you anyway." He ran in and left the car running. He was back in a flash. He came back with two bouquets of flowers. He gave her one and placed the other bouquet on the backseat. *I wonder whom the other one is for? The nerve of him to go in the store and buy his other chick some flowers while he's with me! It must be some tramp he's going to go and screw since he can't screw me. It's all too good, though. He probably thinks just because I am young I won't know what's going on. I am not going to say anything, though. I am going to go ahead and play along with his little games, as simple as that.*

They arrived at Yarni's house. He grabbed the other bouquet of flowers. He walked her to the door. Des presented Gloria with the flowers. *Oh, this young boy got his stuff together trying to flatter me, huh?* Gloria thought to herself, loving the attention, but not wanting to display loving it too much.

"Thank you, Mrs. Pitman, for allowing me to spend time with Yarni." As he sat down in the Victorian-style chair in Gloria's living room, he said, "I was wondering if you'd allow me to take Yarni out again to dinner tomorrow night? Because we didn't really get to spend a whole lot of one-on-one time together."

"Oh, and why was that? You picked her up at seven-fifteen, and now it's eleven-twenty." She was anxious to hear his response.

Using his hand to explain, he said, "Well, see, at the last minute my grandmother called, requesting a ride to bingo. I had to stop her at Kmart to get a marker because she left her bingo bag at home, which put me way behind schedule. Yarni and I could not go to dinner as we planned after the movie because we had to pick up my grandmother from bingo and drop her off at home. And initially, I told Yarni we were going to do dinner and a movie. I am a person of my word, and I'd like to keep my word with Yarni, if you'd allow me to."

He seems like he has good characteristics, but at the same time this is my baby, my only daughter, and I got to monitor him closely. Gloria looked into Des's eyes because she wanted to see the expression on his face when she gave him her response. "No, tomorrow night is not going to be good." Des looked at Gloria.

"Okay, Mrs. Pitman, I'd like to thank you for the time you have allowed me to spend with Yarni tonight," Des said in a calm tone. He stood up to shake her hand. "It was a pleasure meeting you."

"Des, you are most welcome to come over tomorrow night. We have cable television. You all can watch a movie and order a pizza, and maybe I'd consider allowing you to take Yarni to dinner next weekend." She had to play it slow.

"That'll be fine. Good night, Mrs. Pitman. And Yarni, I will speak to you tomorrow." Gloria then started feeling like he was a good kid at heart. She decided that she wasn't going to judge the book by its cover.

As Des drove back across town to the crap house to try to win back the twenty-two-thousand dollars that he'd lost earlier that evening, he came to grips with the situation. Yarni was what he'd longed for. She was going to be his. He knew that she was not of age. He was also aware that there was a certain set of rules he'd have to follow concerning her mother. He'd have to cater to Gloria. Kissing ass wasn't something that he was good at. He never had to cater to anybody, man or woman. Not even his own mother, whom he loved very much. As bad as he felt, he wanted and needed to have Yarni as a part of his life. He'd have to play up to Gloria.

Gloria was an excellent mother. She had always taken a part in every activity and function in Yarni's life. Yarni was Gloria's everything. Gloria was an active parent in every organization in Yarni's school, as well as in any other extracurricular activities Yarni participated in. Everyone was envious of the role Yarni's mother played. She was supermom. As a matter of fact, Yarni had been looking for an eligible bachelor to befriend her mom so she could focus a little less on Yarni's life.

Yarni and Des started seeing each other regularly. Every morning he would take her to school. Of course, he was on his way in from gambling and hustling all night long. Des would sleep while Yarni was at school. He stressed school and its importance to her and would never let her skip school to be with him.

One day at Des's house they were watching *Krush Groove* on tape, and she asked, "Des, why do you stress school so much to me? When you don't even go yourself?"

Des was shocked at her question. He turned to look at her and spoke from his heart. "Look, baby, I inherited this life, you haven't—and I won't let you. You think I like this lifestyle?"

"Sure looks that way to me," she said softly and slowly.

"Well, baby, you're wrong."

"Then why do you do it then, if you don't want to?"

Des took a deep breath, then got up and got his brother's picture. "This is my brother, Les, he was a real OG, doing it up. He never let me get involved in the drug part. I only watched while he babysat me while our mother worked three to eleven, second shift. He dropped out of school when he was in the seventh grade because our mother was forced to work her ass off to take care of us. He began providing everything for us. He taught me the game, never, ever allowing me to put my hands on any drugs. When I got to eighth grade, no longer was anything handed to me. I had to work for mines, counting the money and studying anything pertaining to invest-ments." Yarni listened attentively. She had heard Des mention his brother Les, but never had she got any details from Des, only that he and his brother were very close.

"Well, when I was in tenth grade, my brother took a bullet for a little girl who was riding her bike when some dudes came through the 233 projects trying to do a drive-by." Des paused for a moment. Yarni put her arms around him. She could see the hurt and the anger in his eyes. He continued. "So, once he was buried he still had a lot of loyal men on his team, and a lucrative empire, so rather than let it all fall, I was convinced by my homeboy, Slim, to take it over. So I stepped up to the plate, and kept shit rolling."

They both were quiet as she continued to lightly scratch all over his back with her fingernails.

"Did they ever catch the boys who did the drive-by?"

Des looked at Yarni as if she had asked a stupid question. "I was out there that day. When I saw my brother fall to the ground, I just grabbed a pistol and ran out there and started fucking gunning. If you recall, the 233 only got one way in and one way out, right?" Yarni nodded in the positive. Des continued. "Well, when they realized the entrance was blocked off, they couldn't get out, so they hopped out the car and ran across the street to the school, trying to get to those apartments. Baby, we hunted them niggas down and shot them, making them squirm to their last breaths."

Des went into silence for a minute. Yarni, judging by her sheltered life, should have been scared of him, but this only excited her. Des sharing this side of him made her want him more.

"Baby, I apologize. I know I shouldn't be telling you this, but you asked and I had to give it to you real." He was surprised that she wasn't alarmed or in shock.

"So, baby, this is why I want the very best for you. I mean, I graduated from high school and I have even taken some classes after, but due to my lifestyle I couldn't stay focused. You are very dear to me. I want you to have the best education. Because an education can get you a long ways."

Yarni was very intelligent, and he was going to see to it that she didn't lose focus. He started rewarding her for any good work or grades she got in school. He would give her all kinds of expensive gifts: Gucci book bags with a purse to match, every color leather coat and suits, trench coats, as well as short jackets. The jewelry he gave her was on the level of Gloria's jewelry, if not classier. It wasn't long before Yarni had jewelry on every finger stacked; two and three rings on some fingers.

Gloria started questioning all these exquisite gifts. On the one hand, she was relieved that she could finally get to do some things for herself. Gloria always poured all of her money into Yarni. She wanted Yarni to have the best of everything. She secretly felt guilty that Yarni had to grow up without a father, which is why she went overboard and spoiled her daughter. For the first time in years, Gloria started doing things for herself. Yarni even slipped money into Gloria's jewelry box where she kept her money. It was the only way she would ever get Gloria to take money from her. But still, Gloria asked Des to tone down the gifts. He wouldn't, and just kept them coming. Now, it had been six months they had been faithfully together, and Gloria had a certain amount of respect for Des because of his concern for Yarni's education. This is what kept her allowing him to see her daughter: The way he diligently took her to school and picked her up. And before he would take her on any dates, he'd question her about her homework and would get permission from Gloria.

Their six-month anniversary was a few days away. Des and Yarni were in his car on the way to drop her off at school. Des turned down the music from the cassette tape playing, and glanced over at her as he turned into the school parking lot.

"What do you wanna do for our anniversary?"
I thought you'd never ask, she thought.

"Do you have anywhere in particular you want
to go?" Des asked

Yarni smiled. She looked directly into his eyes
as the car stopped at the student drop-off point.
She knew what she wanted and wasn't afraid to
ask.

"Des, the only place I want to go is in your
arms, while we make passionate love." Thrown
off with her answer, Des swerved the car, letting
off the brake by mistake.

"Baby, listen, I want you to be sure you are
ready for that because once you lose your virginity, it's something you can't go back and get."

"Oh, I am ready. I want to consummate our
relationship. Every time I hug you, kiss you, look
into your eyes, I know in my heart that I want you
to be the first person I experience everything with.
I want you to be my first, my everything, my all. I
always think of the presents and gifts you give me.
I think of all the extravagant gifts I'd like to give
you. I'd give you my life if I could, that's how deep
my love for you flows. You've earned my heart;
through all the times you've been there and been
so patient with me. I am not just speaking on the
gifts. I'm talking about your genuine concern for
me, the way you go beyond the call of duty for me

and my circumstances. My virginity is priceless and I'd like to give it to you." The school bell rang and the car behind them honked the horn. She simply said in an energetic tone, "Baby, gotta go. See ya this evening." She kissed him. "I'll call you at lunchtime, okay?" she said as she hopped out of the car.

Des was astonished with the words that came out of Yarni's mouth. He knew that she was a virgin. He'd never pressured her for sex. He figured it would happen in due time. Besides, he got pussy on the regular from the other chicks that he fucked with from time to time. Pussy was no problem. He was leader of the 233 Mob. He had broads throwing pussy his way, coming from the north, the south, the east, and the west. They all wanted him. He was a hot commodity on the streets. His relationship with Yarni wasn't based around sex.

Des had his own selfish reasons. He knew that Gloria was from the old school and she had instilled principles into Yarni, unlike a lot of the last generation of moms. He knew that he had to make love to Yarni mentally before the physical, simply because he was fully aware that the mental love would always last longer than the physical. He knew what type of lifestyle he lived. He knew in his heart that he may have to do some jail time one day. He was totally knowledgeable of the fact that his freedom could be snatched from him at any given time. Des never wanted to lose Yarni, and in order to always make sure she was a part of his world, he couldn't dare base their relationship on sex. He based it on the mental first and foremost. He was always fair and played with principles with anything concerning her. Anything he gave her his word on, no matter what sidetracks and temptation the streets might've had going on, he kept his word with her. He very rarely lied to her. When he had to, he'd simply tell her he couldn't answer her because he didn't want to lie to her. He was a perfect gentleman. He was her best friend. They could communicate about anything from small things to major things. The only level he never communicated with her on was the drug game.

Des never wanted to put Yarni in any situation where she would know anything that could make her an accessory, or that the police could question her on. If she ever was questioned about anything, she couldn't speak on it because she didn't know anything. He did instruct her about some vital rules. Never ever tell the police anything, and never indulge in any drugs, ever. Always keep a close eye on your enemies.

Des naturally spoiled her with material things as well as with small, intangible things. He'd take time out of his busy day to write Yarni letters and to go to Hallmark to read and select the appropriate card for her. Des cooked for Yarni, even though he wasn't a good cook. He practiced chivalry. The things he'd do for her were so astronomical. He'd fly her to New York to go school-clothes shopping. At any given time, he'd take her to Georgetown to go shopping. He'd send her flowers, tulips, for no special reason, or rent a horse and buggy to take her on a ride. Anything he'd see on TV, he'd naturally try to re-create for Yarni. Des sometimes laughed at himself when he looked at some of the things he'd do for her He simply told himself that gangstas need love too! He basically made himself a measuring cup for Yarni to use to measure other dudes she'd encounter, in case he ever got killed or had to go to jail. He hoped that Yarni would be able to do a bid with him, but at the same time, he knew in his heart that the reality was that Yarni was very young and had never been exposed to anything. He was wise to the fact that she'd most likely stray. He was familiar with the reality that there was a limited amount of "sho-nuff real niggas" left. None of the rest of those jokers could offer her half of what he had. She may get with them on the physical side and get into their pockets, but guess what? None would ever have a clue how to get into her heart.

Three days before their six-month anniversary, Des decided that he was going to take full responsibility for Yarni. He wanted to wake up to her every morning, and go to sleep beside her every night. He wanted to marry her. She was still underage. He knew for a fact that Gloria wasn't going for that, and there was no way around that, but he decided to try his hand with Gloria anyway, and went to talk to her. "Gloria, I am not going to talk in circles to you, or play any games. I love Yarni wholeheartedly. I plan to spend the rest of my life with her. I want her to be my wife, to take on my name, and years from now, bear my children, but I need your permission to marry her." Gloria almost fainted. She was outraged, but she managed to keep her composure. She took a deep breath.

"Des, have you lost your damn mind?"

"No, I am serious. I love Yarni with all my heart."

"Des, I truly have a great amount of respect for you and I love you as if you were my own son. At the same time, my first priority is Yarni. She has her whole life ahead of her. She has yet to experience any growing pains. I am fully aware that you and I both want the very best that life has to offer for Yarni. I don't feel it's in her best interest to marry. Christ sake, she's only fifteen, but when she turns eighteen, she will be free to make her own decisions." Gloria raised her voice. "Until then, I am not, and I won't sign anything giving consent for my fifteen-year-old daughter to marry a grown man."

Des decided that even though Gloria wouldn't agree to sign the papers so that they could get married, that still was not going to be a factor. Des decided at that moment that they were going to be married. He bought Yarni a three-karat engagement ring with a two-karat wedding band to match it. He bought himself a phat wedding band. They would wear them. He went to one of those computer places and had a marriage certificate drawn up. Both of them signed it, and that was their commitment on paper. He called his travel agent to take care of the travel arrangements for their honeymoon. He knew if anyone could put this together in short notice, she could. Des assumed complete responsibility for Yarni. He moved her in with him, and took full care of her. He made it clear to Yarni that she was not to go to anyone in her family for any type of favors. He'd provide her with everything she needed. The lovely thing about it was that he meant it from his heart.

Gloria was outraged as well as heartbroken. She felt like everything she ever wanted for Yarni was gone out of the window. She was hearing advice from a lot of people.

Funny how people always can voice their opinion about your child, when they don't even have their own children in check. They said that Yarni was only fifteen, that she didn't have any feelings. She might have been fifteen, but she had her own mind and feelings. *I don't want to forbid her from seeing him,* Gloria thought, *because she would sneak and see him. By no means would I want her to hide anything from me.*

Gloria couldn't sleep. She couldn't think straight. "Lord," she cried, "I don't want to lose my daughter." She realized that this situation was burdening her down. All she knew was to turn it over to the Lord. He'd work this out. Gloria stayed on her knees.

Father up in heaven in the name of Jesus, I come to you tonight in prayer on bended knees, Father, with a broken heart, confused mind, and filled with absolute emptiness. Lord, I have done the best I can to raise my child the best I know how. Lord, I ask you to forgive me for my mistakes while raising my child. Lord, I plead with you, not to allow my daughter's mistake to

*cause her a lifetime of suffering. Lord, I release
control of my child over to you. Lord, I am
leaning on you to show me how to be a blessing
to my child. Grant me wisdom. In the precious
name of Jesus. Amen.*

Gloria concentrated on making her catering
business a big success. She threw herself into
it. She already had a limited, but elite group of
clients who she catered for, and had a waiting
list for clients who desired her to cater their
functions with her gourmet cooking. She pulled
her waiting list out, along with her phone and
address book. She decided that right now, her
business would be her prime focus. However,
when her daughter needed her, she would be
there for her too.

On their anniversary, the travel agent had
arranged for Des and Yarni to go to Sandals
Beach in St. Lucia. St. Lucia was simply beautiful. Sandals Resort was the ultimate place for
couples to go, offering a white-sand beach and
lush, tropical gardens. Yarni could not believe
this place. They thoroughly enjoyed themselves.

Des sat on the terrace in the tropical-color
chair. Yarni came and stood right in front of
him, wearing a red see-through short nightie
with some red high heels. Des looked her up and
down as she posed and turned around. "You see

something here you like?" she said to Des in a seductive tone. He smiled.

"No doubt about it," Des replied.

"Well convince me then," Yarni said, as she bent over and started tongue kissing him. He put his hand on her round, tender butt. She put her hands on his hairy chest and started fondling his nipples, which was a sure turn-on for Des. He took his other hand and put it under her nightie and ran it up her leg. He played around her vagina until he found her clitoris, a spot nobody besides her had ever touched before. He gave her a breathtaking encounter, using only his fingers. She couldn't take it standing up, so she sat on his lap while he reached around and continued to rotate, using his two fingers on her clitoris then inside of her. She sat there, as she knew that she wasn't in control, feeling lost and wondering what to do. He made her feel amazing. She wanted to do something to reciprocate the feeling to her man. She felt his big erection and wanted him inside of her. She moved, trying to position herself so she could sit on it. Des whispered in her ear, "Baby, let's go inside onto the bed. It may hurt more if you try to put it in like that the first time." He picked her up and took her to the bed. She was naked waiting as he laid on top of her kissing and sucking on her breasts. She felt good, but she wanted what she had been waiting on for the past fifteen and a half years of her life. She wanted to know what all the hype about sex was and she wasn't afraid. So she reached between his legs and placed him right where he needed to be. He pushed a little, worked slowly and carefully into her tight, wet vagina. She tensed up. He stopped. "What's wrong?"

"Nothing, I just don't wanna hurt you," Des whispered.

"No, please keep going," she said, but inside it was hurting awfully bad. She wanted to scream, but she didn't want to disappoint him.

"Baby, you gotta relax," Des said softly as he blew in her ear. *Relax shit, this shit fucking hurts . . . damn, and people be acting like this shit feels good, fighting over this and everything.*

Maybe I am missing something. I am trying to thug this shit out, but damn!

Once he was finally inside, the pain immediately turned into pleasure, as she just lay there. She started to moan, "Oh, my God!" He stopped moving.

"You want me stop?" he whispered.

"No, please don't," Yarni replied, not meaning it.

Then she started pumping back, moving around, trying to get with his rhythm. As soon as she started throwing it back to him, he started going fast. So badly wanting to scream, she held on and gripped his back. And then he stopped and collapsed on top of her, as he felt the ocean breeze come through the open balcony door.

"What's wrong?"

He snickered. "I just came, baby."

"For real?" She was sore, tired, and glad at the same. She wasn't sure, being a virgin, if she could even bring her man to an orgasm. Des held her in his arms. *Damn, had I known this shit was going to be like this . . . I would've did this shit a long time ago. She got some bomb-ass pussy. I swear that shit is like wine. It can only get better with time. I hate for another nigga to get a hold of that. Ump, ump, ump, he'll have to die sho 'nuff.*

Now she wanted to learn to put it on him so he wouldn't stray and go anywhere else for sex. From that day on, she perfected her sex game because she knew that it surely played a major part into a man's head, heart, and pocket. She didn't want anyone else to dare get the ultimate prize she had just got from Des. Most definitely, she wanted to be the last person he'd be with on a sexual, mental, and emotional note.

The rest of the vacation they thoroughly enjoyed themselves, making love on the oceanfront terrace while the sun set. They took an invigorating shower in the natural waterfall. They used a hot, bubbling whirlpool under the cool shade of a palm tree. They also went scuba diving, windsurfing, as well as parasailing. Yarni had died and gone to heaven. She just didn't want anybody to revive her.

When Yarni returned home to Richmond, of course the haters were lurking to rain on her parade. It was all over town that Des had married Yarni. Her toxic girlfriends were all jealous. They started bringing up every notorious episode they could possibly dig up on Des.

There was one girl, Weasa, who used to be Des's girlfriend back in high school. She was crazy about Des. She did everything sexually she could possibly think of. He still didn't want her, nor did he pay her any mind. She was outraged that she had degraded herself for all this time and he married this schoolgirl who wasn't even old enough to drive. The nerve! She knew that she couldn't fight Yarni, as bad as she wanted to. Des would probably beat her unmercifully. She knew that much. She would still make Yarni insecure and have second thoughts. She would call the house and wait for Yarni to answer the phone, then she would pick, "Kmart got school paper on sale for twenty-nine cents a pack," Weasa would blurt out, trying to belittle Yarni as much as possible, just to remind Yarni that she was still a little girl.

"I am young but I'm married to the man you desperately want," Yarni would retort.

She would never tell Des any of those small things. She had been warned by her uncle, Stanka, about exactly what type of things Des had been known to do.

Now Yarni's Uncle Stanka was her mother's only brother and he acted as a father, big brother, and uncle to Yarni. He spoiled her. He was a hustler, although he acted as though he worked. He wasn't big-time, but he was no slouch either. Stanka was a well-respected old-timer who pulled off a heist with Lloyd and vowed to watch over Yarni while Lloyd did time. They called him Stanka, because if anybody crossed him, he'd leave them somewhere stinking. Even though it was the late eighties, Stanka lived like he was still in the seventies, wearing a small black Afro, pimp hats, and walking with a cane. Standing six feet-five, brown skin, and weighing 290 pounds, he drove a 1974 black Cadillac Coupe de Ville that was cleaner than any new Caddy. He was shot in his jaw back in the late seventies, so his mouth was twisted. When he spoke, he talked like he had a mouthful of shit, and he always had to spit after every other sentence.

Stanka never sugarcoated anything to Yarni as her mother Gloria and Aunt Andrea would sometimes do. So he told her, "Watch yo'self because Des is a loose cannon. He loves you, but will kill at the wink of an eye. So, just be mindful when you tell him things people say and do. 'Cuse me," he said as he spit. "It's like playing chess. The queen protects the king, you gotta protect him from as much nonsense as you can." He spit again.

Yarni was conscious of the fact that he'd definitely jump the gun and do something crazy to anybody who was disrespectful to her. In Yarni's eyes it wasn't worth him doing anything crazy to jeopardize him getting in trouble and them being separated.

Shortly after the "marriage," Yarni turned sixteen. Des bought her a red Sterling for her birthday with red BBS rims on it. Yarni really had her heart set on a 325 BMW; nevertheless, she was just as happy to have her own wheels. She had never heard of or seen a Sterling before. Des could tell that she was not impressed at all with the Sterling.

"Look, baby girl, I can tell that you don't like it, but I am telling you that these Sterlings are what's happening. People down here just not feeling it just yet, but they will real soon."

"No, boo, I am just glad I got my own car. Thank you, baby," Yarni said with a big kiss.

"Baby girl, I want you to be happy."

"And I am happy to have a car of my own."

"I can see it all over your face. Just keep it for thirty days and if you still don't like it after that, then I'll get you the Beamer you want."

When she realized that he only wanted her to be happy, and wanted her to feel comfortable in whatever she drove, she finally admitted to him that she really wanted the BMW, but she did keep her end of the bargain and drove it for the next thirty days. She put the *For Sale* sign in her window, and everywhere she went, everybody was inquiring about the Sterling. She was the only person in town who had one. A few weeks after she got it, she heard the song by Pete Rock & C.L. Smooth, "They Reminisce Over You" and they spoke on a Sterling. She ended up keeping it.

Even though she was driving long before she ever had a permit, once she got her license, she started strip-hopping—riding through all the projects and drug strips to show off her car. Especially when she was driving any of Des's cars, even though he told her not to take any of his cars through any public housing or drug areas. She still drove it wherever she pleased.

She rode down the streets with the brick two-story buildings on both sides with the dirt-

patched grass. Some of the concrete porches
had people standing on them. The bus stop on
one corner was filled with guys sitting on the
designated bus bench, but when the bus pulled
up, none of them got on because the bus stop
was only a way around the no *loitering and no
trespassing* signs that hung on the bricks of the
end building. Another bunch hovered around
the pay phone, which people telephoned to the
corner to see who was out there, and who had
and was doing what. This all was a cover-up for
the cocaine slanging around the projects. As soon
as a car rolled up, and if it was a car filled with
females, the guys would holler out, "*yo!*" anxious
to know who the girls in the car were. Then there
would be a couple of guys walking over to the cut
or behind a building, with a crackhead following
to make the exchange: money for crack, hand to
hand. There was some of the corner boys who accepted other forms of payment, which consisted
of food stamps, stolen goods, jewelry or a sexual
favor for a little bit of flava (coke).

Then there were the females who got their
hustles on around the projects. Some chicks
got dressed in their Sunday-best coochie-cutter
shorts just to walk up the street to catch the eye
of one of the corner boys' major players. They
didn't want crack, but they wanted these guys

to fund their habits, which could have consisted of shopping, hair done, nails manicured, new sneakers or whatever may have been their fetish. Some wouldn't know anybody over in the projects, but would just hope to ride through and one of the guys would stop the vehicle. Or they would be one of the corner boys' girlfriends just riding through to see her man talking to a girl. Her tires would come to a screeching halt, and she would hop out making a scene, not knowing that the girl he was talking to was a crackhead. Subsequently, there would be other girls coming around the projects with intentions of meeting a friend of her friend's man, another corner boy, so she too could come up.

In the meantime, all kinds of cars were rolling up: new ones, old ones, a car that needed a muffler, and one that had smoke coming out of the tailpipe. Then you had the people approaching the corner on foot, bike or scooter, all in the name of buying crack. This particular corner so happened to be one in Richmond, Virginia, but every town had one.

When Yarni approached the projects, she would make sure all the windows were rolled down, and the music pumping just to draw attention to the car, so people could see precisely that she was pushing Des's whip. She would never make any eye contact with any of the guys out of respect for Des, but she made her presence known and was seen by all the broke-down hoes on the curb that was always hating on her. If she saw a female she was cool with, she'd cut the music down and carry on a conversation with that person, while the whole time exhibiting her newest rock or designer sunglasses, as the haters watched on enviously. Since they despised her anyway, she especially flossed on them. "Hate on that!" was the statement she made.

3

Young But Not Dumb

That had been the sweet beginning, and now Yarni had to pull herself together and gather her thoughts. She wanted to call Gloria so bad. She would come and resolve this whole situation, but Yarni's pride wouldn't let her call. She began to ask herself, "What would my mother do in this situation?" She peeled the duct tape to remove the letter off of the jewelry box and put it in her pocketbook. She picked up the phone and called the police. She reported to the police that there was a break-in at her apartment. She knew none of her neighbors had seen anything because they all were probably at work or they wouldn't say they had seen anything even if they did. The police came and observed the forced entry. They filed a police report. Once they saw the photo of Des on the floor, they drew the conclusion that somebody had robbed him. They honestly were not concerned about who did it or why. The police silently looked at each other, signaling that the case would be closed as soon as they left there. They gave her a copy of the police report and told her they'd keep her posted. All she was really concerned about was the police report anyway.

Yarni sat on the plush carpet and telephoned her Aunt Andrea, informing her of what happened. She also called Des's right-hand man, Slim, and asked him to come over. When he got there, he couldn't believe his eyes. She reached into her pocketbook, unfolded the letter, and handed it to him. Slim had just collected some money that was owed to him. He gave her five-thousand dollars to at least get a hotel room and to look for some more furniture the next day. He also promised that he'd give her five-thousand more in three days. He motioned to a dude waiting in the car to come in so they could try to fix the door until the maintenance people could get there. They also helped her put what clothes they could fit into her Sterling.

Slim picked up Yarni's spirits because he was actually doing hard labor, and he didn't do any manual labor for anybody. Slim was a bright, light-skinned guy who weighed about 270 pounds. Des gave him the name Slim as a joke. He wasn't your average fat kid. Slim was the coolest, smoothest big dude that Yarni had known or ever seen. He might have been overweight, but he was a bona fide fly guy. She never saw him wear the same shoes twice, or anything about his appearance ever out of order. Even his kick-around gear was the average person's top-notch wear. Slim's weight was never a factor to him. He knew that he was a big guy, but he finessed the women and everybody else he interacted with. So to actually see Slim carry her clothes to her car and bust a sweat humored Yarni.

She realized that Joyce had also taken all Des's cars from the complex lot, including the Benz that was in her name.

As Yarni waited while the maintenance man fixed her door, the phone rang. *Rinnnggg. I hope this isn't Joyce. I swear I don't think I can keep from going off on her. Maybe I shouldn't answer it. Rinnggg, I better answer it, it may be Des. Rinnggg.*

"Hello" Yarni said.

"Hey, sweetie, it's Mommy."

"Hey Mommy" *Thank you God, I really needed my mom to call.*

"Listen, baby, I need a big favor of you. I am not feeling well and I don't feel comfortable staying in this house alone tonight. I need you to come over and spend the night. Please, baby, I really need you. I am depending on you."

"No problem, Mommy. I'll be over in a little while. Do you want me to stop at the drugstore to get you something?"

"No sweetie. I'll be fine once you get here."

Yarni hung up the phone and began to think: *Mommy I need you now myself, but I'll be strong for you.*

Nothing was wrong with Gloria. She knew Yarni needed her more than anything now. She'd seen the verdict on TV and Andrea had called and told Gloria the stunt Joyce had pulled. She knew how strong-minded and stubborn Yarni was. She knew Yarni wasn't going to call her.

Gloria had also been keeping up with the trial on the news. She had a bad feeling about the outcome. While the trial was going on, she had a big, oversized bedroom, gigantic walk-in closet, full-sized bathroom, and a den with its own entrance added on to her house. She was hoping that she wouldn't have to put it to use. She prayed that Des wouldn't go to jail. The bottom line was that she had to be prepared for Yarni's sake if he did. She brought a nice canopy bedroom set and a leather sofa for the den along with an entertainment center, a thirty-one-inch

TV, and a mini-sized refrigerator. She felt Yarni could entertain her company as well as come and go as she pleased. She accepted the fact that Yarni wasn't a little girl anymore. She even had Yarni's phone line reconnected so she could have her own phone line back there. Gloria knew that Yarni would need somewhere to stay whenever she came home on the weekends from college. She knew that Yarni would be in school for at least the next seven years. This had been Yarni's dream since she was eight years old and found out her father was in prison and nobody could do anything to get him out. And now since Des had been railroaded, she felt becoming a lawyer was her destiny.

While Gloria waited patiently for Yarni to arrive, all she could think of was Joyce.

I can't believe Joyce's ghetto, no-class-having ass. I should have put her in check a long time ago. She doesn't know whose child she's messing with. I cannot allow this to go. I've got to call this wench and let her know that my child is not to be messed with and she better leave my child alone or else she's going to have serious problems.

Just then, she looked in her beach scene– cover phone book that Yarni had brought her back from St. Lucia, retrieved Joyce's number, picked up the phone and called her. *Rinnnggg, Rinnggg, This hussy better hurry up and answer if she knows what's good for her. She doesn't know who she's playing with. I'll go over her house and sit on her porch and wait for her to arrive. Hum!*

Although Gloria was middle-aged, she possessed a nice figure and up beside any twenty-one-year old, she could hold her own. She was a small-featured lady barely weighing in at 115 pounds, but she was a fighter back in her day. She didn't care. Gloria would fight anybody—man, woman, or child—and couldn't care less about their size. Since she birthed Yarni, she tried to tone down her bad temper. But by no means, she most certainly did not play when it concerned her daughter. Just from looking at her, one would be shocked to learn of her temperament.

"Hello," Joyce finally picked up the phone.

"Joyce, this is Gloria, Yarni's mother."

"Yeah, Gloria, how are you doing?" Just as nonchalant and carefree, as if butter would not melt in her mouth.

"How am I doing?" *The nerve of her to ask me how I am doing. This woman is so fake!* "I didn't call to talk about me. I called to talk about your childish ass."

"I beg your pardon?" Joyce said, and Gloria could tell that she was no longer sitting and no longer trying to play calm. Gloria didn't care, because if she got out of line, Gloria had plans on going over her house anyway.

"No, don't beg my pardon. Beg me not to come over there and personally whip your ass for going out of your way to give my child a hard time. She's been nothing but respectful to you. She's having a hard enough time dealing with the fact that Des is in prison for God knows how long. I am giving you this first and last warning: Leave Yarni alone or you'll have me to deal with me. And honey, let me be the first to inform you that you don't want that. I am so sick of you and I can't believe that shit you pulled today. You take that furniture and shove it up your ass. Have a blessed day." Gloria hung up the phone.

I think I handled that well, considering. I guess she knows where I am coming from now. Just then, Gloria noticed the lights on Yarni's Sterling pulling up in the driveway. Gloria headed toward the door to meet Yarni, then she realized: *I am supposed to be sick. Let me lie on the couch and let her use her key.*

When Yarni arrived, she noticed that her mother had added an addition to the house, as if the house was not big enough already. When Gloria showed it to her and informed her that it was for her, Yarni got real emotional. She couldn't believe that after being away from her mom for two years, how her mom still had her back regardless of what.

As soon as Yarni got her mother comfortable, she wrote Des a letter informing him what his mother did. She enclosed the letter Joyce left on the jewelry box, along with her new phone number and living arrangements. She told him that she would be there on Thursday like she did faithfully every other visiting day. He knew that, though. She also told him that there was no need for him to stress his mom about the stuff she took. She must have needed it more than Yarni anyway.

The next day, Yarni called the renter's insurance company to file a claim in Des's name. The policy was fifty-thousand dollars, she then mailed off the letter that she wrote Des as well as some power of attorney papers.

With the money that Slim had given her, Yarni paid a retainer to Des's lawyer for his appeal. She set up a payment plan. She went shopping with the rest. She brought an appropriate comforter set for her bed with the curtains to match. The one Gloria had on the bed was the typical mother's comforter: pink flowers. She fixed up her room. She bought a cordless phone, VCR, and stereo for her entertainment center, and a nice chaise chair for the corner of her room. She also bought stuff to decorate her bathroom. She bought all new personals, perfumes, Chanel, Chloe, Opium, and the lotions to match. She also bought a few cases of Pepsi and Mountain Dew so she could stock her refrigerator and have cold drinks when guests came. She went to pick up her Uncle Stanka so he could go with her to the apartment to get the rest of her clothes and any belongings that Joyce didn't take. She also got her Uncle Stanka to hook up her stereo and VCR. She bought all kinds of music, mainly rap, but she also purchased R&B to soothe her for the times when things were rocky, and these times were sure to come.

When Yarni and Stanka got to the apartment, she checked her answering machine. Joyce was on there demanding that Yarni bring the title to the Benz to her. She told Yarni to get her mother back in check, because she didn't appreciate Gloria's foul threats. Yarni would never get indignant. She simply told her that she wasn't giving her anything until she spoke to Des. She also told Joyce if she got something to say to her mother, then to address her mother, not her. Pulling no punches, Yarni relayed all of this to Des in a letter.

When Des received the mail from Yarni, he was furious. He could not believe the stunt his mother had pulled. He loved his mother more than anything on earth, but his mother was dead wrong and out of order. He couldn't understand why she even took the furniture, anyway! What did she do with the furniture? Des knew his mother didn't need any furniture. He had just bought her new furniture a couple of months before. He couldn't believe how humble Yarni was concerning the incident with his mother. The way Yarni handled the episode made him love and respect her even more. At the same time, he could not allow his mother to just totally disrespect his wife in such a way. He wouldn't let Yarni disrespect his mother, either.

Down in the city jail, the inmates had a phone list, but Des didn't care about anybody's phone time—he had calls to make. The first one was to his mother. He stressed to her that he was very disappointed with her. He asked her where she got the gall to put her nose in his business. He also stressed to her that until she made the situation right with Yarni, she could not be a part of his life.

He then called Slim to make sure he got the rest of his money from off the street. He instructed Slim to take whatever money he collected to Gloria. Familiar with the old saying, "out of sight, out of mind," he wasn't expecting all his money to be straight. When somebody goes to jail and is not present to get their own money, the money is always short. He also told Castro, his other right-hand man, to give Yarni an allowance of three-hundred dollars a week.

And then the final call was to Gloria. She answered. "Hello?"

"Hello?" She heard an automated operator. "This is C and P with a collect call from Des." The automated voice continued, "If you do not wish to accept this call, please hang up now. To accept this call, press zero now." Gloria hurried and pressed zero. The automated voice responded after she pressed zero. "Your call is being connected, thank you for using C and P."

"Hello, Des. How are you under these crazy circumstances?" she asked with a sincere voice.

"Honestly, Gloria, I am fine. I am just a little worried about Yarni, that's all."

"Yarni will be fine, Des. I promise you that."

"I know you will make sure of that, Gloria, but I have a favor to ask of you."

"Anything, Des."

"I need you to promise me that please, Gloria, by no means will you let Yarni get sidetracked. Even though I am locked up now, she still has to stay focused on pursuing her dream to become a lawyer."

"Oh, I have every intention of doing so," Gloria said without hesitation.

"I am also aware that the seventy-five Gs that I had given you to hold for her college education . . . well, that's not going to be enough. I am going to need you to take out some loans to cover the difference."

"I'd already banked on that anyway since the trial was rigged up. I was prepared to do that."

"My man, Slim, is going to bring you some money later today that he's collected for me."

"Okay."

"Gloria, nothing has changed, I still want Yarni to have the best of everything. At the same time, you've got to be very frugal with that money. She is going to have to tone down her spending." Had he not been in such a solemn position, in prison, he might have chuckled at Yarni's spending habits.

"I know, Des. I will take care of everything."

"I know you will, Gloria, but you know I worry about her. I want to thank you for getting the house addition for her. I really appreciate it.

"Des, say no more. I need you to do me a favor."

"What?"

"Never give up hope and always remember, tough times don't last, but tough people do."

This was a special man, incarcerated or not, and she didn't want him to get lost in the crooked system.

"Man, Gloria, I got mad love for you."

"Yeah, son-in-law, I do for you too."

He and Gloria had their ups and downs, but overall he knew he could definitely trust her.

Slim only collected twenty-six-thousand dollars off the street, which was no surprise to Des. He knew people would put larceny in the game since he was in jail. Slim brought it to Gloria and she put it up. Gloria had already applied for the loans for the full amount of the tuition because she didn't want to bring any kind of heat to herself. Her daughter was going to be a college graduate.

That night when Yarni got home, Gloria approached Yarni's room. She overheard Yarni on the phone talking to Melanie. Yarni was crying.

"I don't know exactly what my plans are now. I don't know exactly how I will go to college now with Des in jail, or exactly how I am going to maneuver going to college, working a part-time job to support myself, study, as well as go see Des. Des is still a priority in my life." Yarni was distant and Melanie had no easy answers for her friend.

When Yarni got off the phone Gloria advanced slowly and told her, "Baby, everything is going to be okay. I don't care what I've got to do to support you. You're going to college. Between the money I've saved for your college education over the years and the money Des has given—Oh, honey, you'll be off to college in a couple of weeks. I've never let you down, and I'm not letting you down now."

The next day they went together shopping for everything Yarni needed for school. They also traded her Sterling in for a brand-new Volkswagen Passat. Des would understand.

A few weeks later, Yarni left for Norfolk, part of the freshman class at ODU.

For the next two years Yarni excelled in school. She was focused on her schoolwork as well as on Des. Not a day went by when she didn't send him some kind of mail. She made sure that his name was blown up at mail call. Every single weekend, she went to visit him. They had him housed at Greenville Correctional Center. She visited him faithfully. She accepted all his collect calls. She would even forward her calls to her cell phone when she wasn't at home. She would never miss any of his calls. Every month, she had at least a five-hundred dollar phone bill. She always managed to pay it and never complained about anything she did for him. It all came from the heart. She also stayed on top of Des's attorney about his appeal. She would look over his transcripts to try finding any type of technicality. She also went to law schools all across Virginia and North Carolina so the law students could look over his case.

Castro faithfully gave Yarni her three-hundred dollars every week, and sometimes he would give her more. He was loyal to Des and his friendship and always kept tabs on Yarni. There was nothing bad to tell, and had it been, he would have never uttered a word to Des. Over the years they became close too, as did her and Slim.

Castro checked in more so than Slim did. Slim only checked on Yarni when there was a problem, whereas Castro called regularly. Castro was handsome. His golden-brown complexion drove the girls crazy. He loved two things: money and the women that came with it. He had slept with most of Yarni's friends, even after she warned them that he was a whore. They didn't care, they only saw his money, and he spent it carefree. He had pretty white teeth with a gold crown on the side, which some girls thought enhanced his appearance. He wore round wire-framed glasses, had a short haircut, and an egg-shaped head. He was about six feet and weighed about 170 pounds. He wasn't the flashy type by day: He wore a brown work suit and some balded up boots everyday all day until nightfall, which was when he transformed into his Don Juan, city slicker type clothes. He sported silk suits, and Stacy Adams shoes were his specialty.

Yarni sat in the tan-colored chair in the visiting room waiting patiently for Des to come out from his building. She had been waiting for forty-five minutes. She walked over to the table set up as a desk in the visiting room and asked the correctional officer if they'd called for Des. "He should be out soon. Maybe he had to take a shower or something. However, I will call again." Just then Des walked in the visiting room and she had to deliver the news to him that his right-hand man, Castro, had just gotten picked up by the jump-out squad.

Yarni smiled as Des walked over to the guard to give the correctional officer his inmate ID. Yarni was so happy to see Des. She laughed with pleasure because he did not look as if he had left the streets. The only thing that gave it up was that prison-blue oxford shirt. He had ordered some blue Levi jeans. He was wearing some Huarache Nikes that Slim wore down there to see him in. Des wore some old sneakers in the visiting room and when the guard wasn't looking they swapped shoes. He also had on some Ray-Ban glasses. He had gotten Castro to pay a doctor to act as if Des had glasses before he left the streets. The optometrist sent the sunglasses to Des so he could have them in the prison. Otherwise he'd have to have state-issued glasses, and no sunglasses are even allowed. Des knew that the state didn't supply any sunglasses. The optometrist talked to the doctor in the medical department at the prison and convinced them that Des had surgery a few years ago and his eyes could not come into direct contact with sunlight. Uncle Stanka, impersonating a clergyman, called the prison's chaplain and convinced the chaplain to accept a religious pendant for Des to wear. That was how Des was able to get and keep his necklace and cross to wear around his neck.

On his way from across the room to greet Yarni, other inmates stopped him and talked with him. The only time he got to see some of the inmates on the other side of the prison was in the visiting room. Yarni shook her head when he finally made it over to the table where she was.

"That doesn't make any sense the way you act like you are still on the streets, people running up to you and you're dressing like you're still in society." Des laughed as he embraced her with a hug and a passionate tongue kiss.

"I am in society, baby. This is a world in itself."

Yarni said, on a more serious note, "Boo, Castro called me, they locked him up."

Des looked off and became distant. He took a deep breath. "Damn."

They both became very silent.

Yarni had already gone to the snack machine while she was waiting for Des to come out.

"Boo, I am going to warm your cheese pizza up. Do you want anything else from the snack machine?" she said.

"No, wait a minute before you go. I am not ready to eat yet."

"Well, what took you so long to get over here? I was waiting at least forty-five minutes. I told you I was coming. You had to take a shower or something?"

"No, baby, I was ready when they called, but I had to stop by building A on my way over here to check on some money that this cat owes me from the game last night."

She shook her head. "It don't make no sense you can take the thug out the streets, but you can't take the streets out the thug. That's a damn shame." Des laughed at her frustration.

"How did your exams go?" He changed the subject.

"Fine," but he noticed that she did not elaborate.

"I tried calling you last night but I didn't get any answer." He stroked her legs as he waited to see how far she would go in creating an alibi. But he hoped she would not go too far.

"My roommate and I went out for college night last night, to celebrate that I had aced the one exam I was actually worried about."

"I tried calling this morning at about seven too," he added, even though he was happy to hear about the A he knew she was capable of getting.

"I heard the phone ringing when I was leaving out the door to come down here. I just assumed that it was somebody for my roommate," she said for comfort.

Des looked into Yarni's eyes, and she saw a look on his face that she didn't recognize: insecurity.

"Baby girl," he chose his words as well as he could. "By no means do I want you to stop living for me. I fully understand that you have needs too. You are not obligated to be my girl anymore, for real." Tears appeared in Yarni's eyes, but Des continued.

"Baby girl, please don't start that. Don't cry. But I've got to be real with you. I am getting too comfortable with you being here for me. I'm going to be here a long time. I know one day you may find someone else to be with, and he's not going to tolerate you coming to see me. Out of sight, out of mind. So, baby, for real, I would rather that you just leave me now verses five years from now." He felt too dependent on her and he didn't like that feeling.

"Des, we made vows to each other. I know there were no legal documents involved, but we took an oath from our hearts, and as far as I am concerned, this is until death do us part. I don't want anybody else. Now stop acting stupid," she said while trying to hold her tears back.

"Baby girl, if you feel the need to be with other cats, then you are free to."

"Yeah, I know that I am free to. You've made yourself clear. Now let me tell you, the only place I choose to be is with you in your heart." Yarni could not believe his insistence.

"Look, we can still be friends. I don't need a woman while I am in here. I need a faithful friend more than anything. That's all any man in prison needs is a devoted friend. Don't get me wrong. Every man locked up wants a woman by his side for his own selfish reasons, but he needs a friend more. Now think about it. What does he need a woman for? He can't have sex with her unless he wants to degrade her and have sex with her in the visiting room, but is that really cool with people's children and other people watching? He can't parade her around town on his arm. He can't lay beside her every night in bed. So, on the real, a man incarcerated doesn't need the headache of wondering if she's laid up with someone else. I know I don't. I don't want to go through that whole shenanigan of why you didn't accept a call or why you didn't write back. Or even me calling to holler at one of my homeboys and he drops some news on me that he seen you with the next dude." Des was just as honest with Yarni five years down the road as he was with her on that first day, when she was just fifteen years old.

"Oh, now I understand. All this is simply because I wasn't in my dorm room when you called last night. So now all you need is a friend? Okay, I got your friend all right," she said sarcastically. Des ignored her sarcasm.

"Yeah, all I need is a friend to talk to, listen to, laugh with, to joke with, and to keep my spirits up. For real, Yarni, you can go your own way. We can end our relationship right now."

He went back into his cell frustrated with the whole ordeal—the legal system mainly, because he did not commit this crime. He was confused.

He knew Yarni was most likely telling the truth, but at the same time, she was young, and if his appeal didn't come through soon, how much time could she really do with him?

He didn't go to dinner that night. Instead he went to a building to check on his money one final time, and when it was short, he asked why. When the dude said the wrong thing, he punched him in the face. He knew that it wasn't that serious, but he had to redirect his frustrations somewhere else. He returned to his pod, went straight to his cell, avoiding any of his homeboys he was cool with, knowing he might lash out on them too. The rest of the night and well into the next morning, Des laid on his bunk wondering what he and Yarni's relationship was coming to.

The following day, he got a letter from Weasa. He thought about how she would definitely be there for him, but at the same time, he knew Yarni would really fly the coop if she ever found out he was corresponding with Weasa. He evaluated the situation.

After taking all those things into consideration, Yarni still knocked the doors down to see him. A few days later, she received a letter from him apologizing for how he acted in the visiting room. She totally understood the mindset of a man incarcerated. People may think, Oh, what more do they want. They have three hots and a cot, but she understood just how hard it was on the inmate mentally to be away from his loved ones. There would be no holidays and no family gatherings, except for the corny ones that the institutions put on once a year.

Joyce finally came around. She realized that Yarni did have good intentions where Des was concerned. Eventually, she also grew to have a lot of respect for Yarni. It had even gotten to the point where they would sometimes ride together to see Des. When Des told Joyce that Yarni had the flu and Gloria was out of town, Joyce showed up on Yarni's doorsteps with orange juice and all kinds of flu medicine. Then a month later, Joyce had to go to the hospital and have surgery on her foot. Yarni was beside her the whole time. She went over to cook for her and checked on her every day.

Joyce and Gloria hadn't spoken in over two years. Joyce even called Gloria, leaving her a message on her answering machine.

"Gloria, this is Joyce, I'd like to apologize for the way I carried on. I've actually grown to really love Yarni and I am so glad that she's a part of Des's life, as well as mine. I never got the opportunity to tell you how much of an outstanding job you did with raising Yarni. You

see, I couldn't understand why Des loved her so
much. I never took the time to try to understand
either. He'd been with so many other girls in
his day, and this young girl came along and just
swept him off of his feet. You know how it is: The
ones we love never love us back. I didn't want her
to hurt my son. See, before Yarni, he'd never—I
repeat, never—loved any of those hoes. The
bottom line is Yarni and Des have made it very
clear that they're going to be together whatever
the weather is. So there is no need for us to hold
ill feelings against each other. I guess what I am
trying to say is, 'I surrender.' I don't want war
with you anymore. Gloria, please call me when
you get this message. 777-9311."

Gloria heard the message. It took a big woman
to surrender, that's for sure, and to 'fess up
to her shortcomings. *Shoot, I realized a long
time ago that Yarni and Des were going to be
together no matter what. I guess I could at least
call her back. I will, but I've got to hype myself
up. I hope she doesn't want to meet for lunch or
anything.*

Everything was going fine until one Saturday
when Yarni was visiting Des and he asked her to
make the ultimate sacrifice. He wanted her to put
her freedom at stake. He asked her to smuggle
heroin into the prison to him so he could sell. He

said she could do it one of two ways. She could put it in her panties or put it in balloons and swallow it and she could throw it up in the bathroom in the visiting room. She felt like the sharpest knife ever had just stabbed her through the heart.

How could he ask me to jeopardize my freedom? Why does he want to break the law still and risk running up his time? He isn't starving for anything in there. His commissary stays stacked. He was a good dude from the street so somebody is always sending him some money. On any given day I could see somebody who knew him from the street and they'd give me a 100 dollars to send him. Shit, why he ain't tell his mother to bring it? What, she too good? Damn, and I am supposed to be the one he loves? Yo, he straight violated.

She didn't have any type of understanding. As she left the penitentiary, she had so many thoughts going through her head. She felt like the one who she loved with all her heart had just crossed her, and she didn't know what to do. She didn't even know how to approach this situation. She didn't want to tell him no and let him down, but at the same time, this one time, she had to think of herself first. She was so confused. For the first time in almost five years, she avoided him. She thought maybe she needed to stay away a little. She started going out, hanging at all the happening places, and meeting other guys.

4

The Joke's On You, Boo

One evening Yarni and her girlfriend, Sophie, were hanging out. Sophie was one of those girls straight from the projects who was just as fly as Yarni was, but her life goals consisted of hooking the biggest drug dealer, being the flyest chic in Richmond, keeping a nice ride, and moving out of the projects to one of the nicer Section 8 communities. Sophie and Yarni met because they both were captains of cheerleader squads back in school. They used to see each other at the games and both saw the material potential in each other. So, even though they were from two different sides of town they always kept in touch, and eventually became good friends.

Sophie was skinny, barely weighing in at 110 pounds. She never wore her real hair, only braided extensions. Displaying long, fat, neatly done box braids neatly in a ponytail on the top of her head, Sophie, without a doubt, set trends with her braided styles. Along with her braids she wore a small diamond earring in her nose and four holes in her ears. There was a permanent scar within her chocolate skin on her temple that she got from a scuffle years ago. Sophie wasn't self-conscience about her cut. Nobody was perfect and everybody had a flaw, and that was hers. She was very confident and couldn't be touched with a ten-foot pole.

Sophie and Yarni were at the summer league basketball tournament over on the west end on Idlewood Avenue. Summer league was packed. All the ballers were there showing off their cars as well as placing bets on which team was going to win. All the young adults knew that in Richmond, back in the early nineties, if you were a female looking for a major player, or if you were a major player looking for a female, summer league was the place to be on Tuesday and Thursday evenings. It was always jam-packed with wall-to-wall people. Girls were in their Daisy Duke shorts riding on bicycles or rolling around with pure white roller skates, and a few guys were sitting or standing near their sport motorbikes. Cars lined up, double-parked, horns honking because they were blocked in. Then there were the set of guys walking around

with the super soaker bazooka water guns, who
were searching for any stuck-up, conceited,
bourgeois-acting female so they could soak her
with their water guns. There were a few dudes
scattered around who had their dogs on a leash,
walking them. They either had Pit bulls or Rott-
weilers. Whenever the dogs would get in a thirty-
foot radius of one another, the owners would
have to pull the chains back to separate the dogs,
as they growled at each other. Throughout the
night during the basketball game, there would
be somebody taking bets on which dog would
win the dog fight, which was scheduled after
the game later that night. The funniest part was
that there was one guy, who always showed up
wearing no shirt, with a super-thick herringbone
necklace on, and an albino, yellow and white boa
constrictor snake around his neck. Now, he knew
nine times out of ten that most the females were
afraid of snakes, so he'd get his entertainment
by walking around watching the reaction of the
ladies when he moved closer to them.

On this particular Thursday, Yarni and Sophie
were standing by the fence, turning heads of the
ballers walking by, acting like they were not paying any attention to all the ooh's and ah's. They
were speaking and mingling with all passersby.
They noticed from across the court on the other

side of the fence, this tall, kind of chubby, bumpy face, dark-skinned dude. He had thick eyebrows and was sporting a bald head and a mouth full of gold teeth. He had just got out of this bright yellow, flip-flop paint job BMW sitting on chrome. Chrome rims are like the shoes on a car. If an outfit doesn't have the right pair of shoes, the whole thing will be thrown off. It's the same thing with an automobile. Rims give it a whole different look as the right shoes would give an outfit a distinct look. They must be eighteen-inch or better. Although, when you take the original rims off a new car, the car depreciates. Some feel it's more important to make the car look good.

As soon as he rolled up, all eyes were on him. Yarni and Sophie immediately acted as if they were not concerned, like they did not even see him. They were like sore thumbs sticking out because they were the only two who were not impressed. He immediately inquired to his homeboys as to who Yarni and Sophie were.

He walked over with his Veryfine fruit punch drink in his hand, held his head back, drank his juice in one big gulp with his lips never touching the bottle, looked at Yarni from head to toe, and reached up to remove his sunglasses. All he could say was, "ummp, ummp, ummp" He quickly glanced at Sophie.

"Didn't you used to go to Fairfield Middle School?" He eyed Sophie in recognition.

"Yeah. How you know?" Sophie said in a snobbish tone.

"I used to go there too for a li'l while."

"Oh, for real? I don't remember you. What's your name?" Sophie squinted.

"Rallo," he said.

"No, I'm talking about your government name."

"Oh, Franklin Black"

"Oh, okay. I remember your name. You look so different." They started reminiscing, going on and on about the good old days at Fairfield Middle School.

"Yo, I am trying to definitely meet your homegirl right there." He turned his attention back to Yarni.

"Yarni, this is Rallo," she said, pointing to Rallo, "Rallo this is my best friend Yarni," and she pointed to Yarni, making the introduction.

Rallo threw up his head, acknowledging her. Yarni extended her hand.

"It's nice to meet you, Rallo," she said in a sweet, innocent voice. Rallo looked and laughed. *Damn, what type of shit she into? This chick gonna extend her hand for me to shake. Do she think she white or what?* He threw his bottle in the trash and reached out and shook Yarni's hand. Yarni thought, *Where in the world did Sophie pick this stray up from with no manners?* She knew she was wrong for introducing him to her.

At that very moment the Southside boys got to fighting with the Church Hill boys. Sophie and Yarni made their way to their car, afraid something more might happen.

The following Sunday Sophie and Yarni drove out to Byrd Park. Byrd Park was off the hook every Sunday. It was the only thing to do on Sundays during the day in Richmond. Luckily, they rolled up when someone was leaving, so they got a good parking space. It was a hassle not having a parking space on a Sunday. Traffic was at a standstill, this one and that one running to and from cars, carrying on conversation, females and guys catching up on gossip. No telling whom a person might run across. One was subject to see anybody and everybody at Byrd Park. You also needed to have a full tank of gas when riding through Byrd Park on a Sunday. People would sit in any one spot for twenty minutes before traffic would inch up even a few feet. Byrd Park was the happening place for all ages, but just like everything else, when there was a whole bunch of blacks folks, the police got scared and overreacted. They started blocking certain sides of the park down. Then they put signs up: *No Parking, on Sundays 2:00 p.m.–8:00 p.m.*

Nevertheless, Sunday life at Byrd Park went on. The crowd just moved the party over to the other side of Byrd Park. The police posted *No Stopping or Standing* signs all over the park enforcing hundred-dollar fines.

They saw Rallo again, and he tried to get Yarni's number, but she wasn't pressed.

"Yarni, how come you don't like Rallo?" Sophie almost knew the answer, but she had to ask.

"I don't think I want to talk to no man who drives a canary-yellow BMW." They both laughed. "Besides, that car looks like it could be a female car. To me, only a female would drive that bright yellow car."

"Yarni, you know a brother is getting some money and want to shine."

"The only place shining gets you is in the penitentiary or in the diary of a stick-up kid."

"Yarni, you right."

"But the crazy thing is, these brothers know this. They see so many of their boys right in their immediate circle fall victim. You would think they would learn. Right?" Yarni, in her own way, tried to make sense of the high rate of black men in prison, more than at ODU and all the colleges in Virginia.

"You would think, but I guess their motto is, Ball 'til you fall." Sophie fell out laughing at her own poetics.

"Guess so, but you can't tell them nothing. When they sitting in da clinker, they be wishing they had listened," Yarni said.

Later that night, Sophie wanted to go to Tropicana *baddd!* Yarni didn't really have any money to be jerking off at the club. She had just gotten her car out of the shop so her funds were very limited. To her the club wasn't where she wanted to spend her last money.

"Yarni, I'll pay your way in, and once we get in, some clown will buy our drinks and pay for our pictures." They still were not old enough to drink.

"I don't even like rolling like that. I like having my owns. Just the thought of some wack-jack nigga, giving me the impression that because he buys me a little five-dollar drink that I have to entertain him and act interested in his conversation for the rest of the night. No, I am not feeling that." Gloria had trained her daughter well.

"Yarni, don't you got the money for your polo lessons?"

"Yep"

"Well, use that for your pictures and drinks and I'll give it back to you when I get paid tomorrow."

Yarni saw that Sophie was determined to go, so she went. When they arrived at Tropp the line was all the way up to the next corner. As soon as they walked by they saw Rallo and his crew at the very front of the line. He called out to Yarni.

"I got y'all, come on." He paid for them to get in, bought their drinks all night long, as well as paid for about six or seven pictures. He pulled Sophie to the side, peeled off five twenties and told her he was paying her a hundred dollars for Yarni's number. Sophie told him she'd get back to him before the end of the night.

"Look, Rallo is giving me a hundred dollars for your phone number. I'm going to give it to him. If he'll give up a hundred for your number you could probably get some shit out of him." At the end of the night, when they were walking to their car, he rolled up beside them in his canary-yellow car with neon yellow lights under the bottom. Yarni was not feeling that yellow car. *I hope when he calls he doesn't ask to take me out anywhere. I am not riding in that car looking like it came straight from the Universal Soul Circus*, she thought to herself. He called Sophie over to the car.

"You got that for me?" Sophie reached in her back pocket and handed over the number to Rallo. Rallo passed Sophie the hundred for the number. He then produced another hundred.

"Put in a good word for me," Rallo said, handing Sophie the second hundred-dollar bill.

Yarni thought to herself, *This clown is really trying to shine, huh? I should've told Sophie to write* 1-800-Joke *on the paper.* Once they got in the car, Sophie handed Yarni a hundred dollars.

Rallo's first impression of Yarni was she was a "missy prissy" type of chic. After conversing with her over the phone for two weeks, he felt her personality was down-to-earth. Judging by the way she spoke, it would make one think that she was slow to the street life. She was very thorough.

Their first date was to Kings Dominion amusement park. They played and rode all the games and rides. Rallo won Yarni a teddy bear, and she won him an even bigger teddy bear playing skeeball. He was shocked when he found out she was actually a lot of fun to be around. They laughed and joked. She was pretty too. He was attracted to her and she didn't have a ghetto demeanor, which he wasn't used to. She was the best chick that he had ever dated.

They started hanging out a lot. Yarni was on her summer vacation from school so she was in Richmond for the next three months. They went to see Jamie Foxx's comedy show together and went out to eat just about every day. They went bowling, played pool in the pool hall in Shockoe Bottom, and saw every single movie together.

He even took her shopping. Everything they did, she'd make sure none of their dates ran into the wee hours of the morning. She never put herself in the situation to have to feel pressured for sex. He actually was so intrigued with Yarni he forgot what his initial intentions were.

That got old soon. Rallo had paid for all these extravagant clothes and hairdos to make her look drop-dead gorgeous and for what? He couldn't even take them off her. He wasn't able to mess up the hair after he paid top dollar for it. Half of the time, he really didn't go out to any clubs. She'd come through the spot to get money to go out and he'd see exactly how good she looked. She wouldn't even come back around there to be with him after she left the club. She'd go straight home and kick it over the phone for the rest of the night. He decided they needed to have a heart-to-heart talk and now was the time.

"I need to see you," Rallo telephoned. "I've got something important to talk to you about."

Yarni and Rallo went to Red Lobster. Understand that back in the day, Red Lobster was a big deal. If you were a female and a guy took you to Red Lobster—oh, he was really doing something. Yarni was curious to know what exactly he wanted to talk to her about. Once their appetizers—mozzarella sticks—arrived, he dipped them into the tomato sauce and looked at Yarni with a serious look. *Here comes the game*, Yarni thought.

Rallo pulled no punches. "We have really been hanging tight and I want you to be a permanent part of my life. I want you to be my girl. I want us to be on some one-on-one– type shit. *I want us to carry it to the next level.* Now I've showed you how I get down for mines and I haven't even had sex with you. Now imagine how lovely it can be if we step this up a notch." This was the game Rallo kicked to Yarni.

"Honestly, I don't need a boyfriend right now. It wouldn't be fair to you because I already have a man! I love him very much and I am not leaving him for anybody. So me sitting here pretending that I can carry it to the next level with you, is a dead issue. I appreciate everything you've done for me and I value your friendship, but at the same time, I told you this in the beginning and I still feel the same way. I hope we are still cool." She bit into her mozzarella stick.

Oh, it's cool for you to accept my money and eat up all my damn food, but you don't want to be my girl. Now all of a sudden, you want to remember that you got a man. This no good, ho!

Yarni's response cut him down. He wanted to smack the cowboy shit out of her, but he kept his composure.

"I respect you for being real about it." He shook his head and drank some of his Heineken.

The realness was that he wanted to fuck her and just had to go at her from another angle. He continued to talk to her on the phone as nothing had changed. He called her six nights later.

"I want to ask you something. I don't want you to take any offense by it, though. It's very important." Rallo put on his sincere, serious voice.

"Go ahead and ask," Yarni responded.

"I am so attracted to you, mentally and physically—you know this, and I feel like you got a wall up against me to shield yourself from my feelings. I've tried to come at you from various different ways, but you keep turning me away. You turn me on and off like a light switch. Now, don't cuss me out when I ask you this, but if I give you a G, could we have sex?"

I can't believe he is propositioning me. I am broke as a broke-dick dog. At the same time, I don't want to seem like a trick. I was planning on doing it to him in the next couple of days anyway. I think I have been jerking his chain long enough. What the hell? I would have to do it to him doggie style. He's so ugly, I can't stand the thought of looking at him in his face.

"It's really not about the money, Rallo, but I am broke as I don't know what. You can come over. That's no problem," she said, holding her breath.

He went right over her house with the G in his pocket. His plan was to fuck the shit out of her and not ever speak to her gold-digging-ass again.

When he arrived, she had candles burning all through her den, bedroom, and bathroom. She ran him a candlelit bubble bath, washed him up from head to toe. When he got out of the tub she wrapped him in a big, oversized towel, and wiped him off. She pulled her Dr. Scholl's foot massager out and gave him a pedicure. She put lotion on him, and gave him a full-body massage with sensual massage oils. She then fed him some fruit, grapes off the vine, cherries, as well as chocolate-covered strawberries. Then hopped on his little, itsy-bitty dick and rode him backwards. He came in approximately forty-five seconds and he had on a rubber. "If that wasn't a damn waste, I don't know what was." Nevertheless, she got up to wash up and brought a washcloth back to the bed to wash him up. Rallo was asleep, knocked out, snoring. When he felt the warmness of the washcloth on him, he opened his eyes and went right back to sleep.

The next morning he woke up to her voice.

"Rise and shine, big daddy," Yarni said. His eyes opened when she placed a tray on his lap. Turkey bacon, fried potatoes with onions, scrambled eggs, two almond croissants, some Smucker's grape jelly, and a glass of Sunny Delight orange juice occupied the tray. *Nobody* had ever cooked for him except his mother. The thought of somebody bringing him breakfast in bed was almost too much. He questioned her because he didn't know what a croissant was. He cleaned his plate empty, gave her the thousand dollars and an extra two hundred dollar tip. It was worth every penny, the best 1,200 he'd ever spent.

How could he possibly leave her alone? It wasn't as easy as he thought. Romancing him, she took fucking to another level. He'd gotten plenty of pussy in the hood, but that was all it was: sex, no romance, no feelings behind it. None of the things that Yarni had done had ever even crossed his mind.

For the next two weeks, they saw each other every day, just like before. They had sexual encounters two more times. He paid her each time. The third time when he went to give her the money, she wouldn't take it. She told him that it wasn't that type of party anymore. She informed him that they were better than that. When she came in, she looked at the mail. There was a letter there from Des. She tore it open.

My Dearest Yarni,
Just exactly how long do you plan to stay mad at me? I miss you and I love you very much. I want to apologize for asking you to jeopardize your freedom for my own selfish reasons. I also apologize for taking you for granted. You have every right not to speak to me ever again. I hope you won't take that avenue, though.

Anyway, I need to put you down with something. I heard that you were hollering at that nigga, Rallo, out there. He made sure it got back to me. He and Roy were boys. He hates me.

He and I were beefing before I left the streets. He is telling niggas how he is fucking my wife and how he really don't want you, and some other things I rather not say. What I will say is there's no need for you to get upset. Because the word is the dude is gone behind you. His plan to fuck you over blew up in his face. Now, what you've got to do is to take this dude for everything he got.

And when you feel you tired of that nigga
YOU just bounce on his ass. That's how you
get revenge on him. And never ever let this
dude know you know what his intentions
were. The joke is on him, Boo!
   Come and check me soon!!!!
   Forever and Ever,
   Des

Yarni was furious. Was Des just trying to
throw salt in the game for his own selfish reasons? Nah, Des wasn't that petty. But when you
love somebody, love will make you genuinely do
crazy stuff.

Right after she finished Des's letter, Stanka
came by. He basically gave her the same info. So
it was about to be on now, for real.

After Yarni turned down that last money Rallo
had offered her, his mind was blown. In his
mind, that confirmed that she wasn't just out
for his money. She knew that he'd never had a
woman in her league and she used that to her
advantage. She'd make sure that when she was
with him, she'd always have some new type of
thing going on. She'd always wear the sexy, but
not sleazy, lingerie. She'd walk around him buck
naked with nothing but some "come fuck me
boots" on. Sometimes he'd never know who she

was going to be until he arrived. She might come to the door with a blonde wig on, asking him, "Is it true that blondes have more fun?" She'd cook for him and bring him back presents from the mall when he'd give her money to go shopping for herself. He wasn't used to any of this. All he ever dealt with was sleazebags. So, everything Yarni was doing was just getting him wide open.

Rallo fell in love with Yarni. All he thought about all day was Yarni. He catered to her in his own little way. He gave her money freely. Anything new that came out for females, he got it for her. He took care of her upcoming school expenses. He gave her a brand new candy-apple Saab convertible with license plates that said *NO NOTE* because it was paid for. He said that he wanted them to have his and hers BMW's. She convinced him to get her a Saab because people were not really into the Saab convertibles back then.

After all this, Yarni still continued to go see Des faithfully. The only difference was, she was riding in the Saab that Rallo bought her. She'd drive any of Rallo's array of cars as well. Every Saturday morning, she'd get out of the bed with Rallo to go see Des. At the same time, Rallo believed if he did everything for Yarni and just was patient, she would eventually drop Des. That wasn't the issue, though, because Des was in her heart. Rallo wasn't aware that Yarni knew what his initial intentions were.

Every Sunday morning, she'd go to church. After all, it was God who made all these things possible. She'd invite Rallo to go. She'd preach to him.

"You throw bricks at the penitentiary all day, every day. God watches over you even though you are doing wrong. The least you could do is devote Sunday to Him and go to church to say thanks and give God the praises," Yarni preached.

Rallo didn't hustle on Sundays, but he would never go with her. However, he'd always send his tithes and offerings.

"Don't you think God want to see you in church every once in a while?"

"No, I need to get myself together first." He hugged her and rolled back under the cover.

"Well, you start with hearing and studying the word. You doggone for sure ain't going to hear it on the strip."

Richmond was a small town where everybody knew everybody. So, news traveled around the town. It got back to Tina, the mother of Rallo's baby girl Ralleshia, he'd gone out and bought Yarni a brand-new car while she drove around in a raggedy Chevy Chevette. She flipped. Oh, it was about to be on.

Tina wasn't as unruly as she pretended to be, but the crew she rolled with went for bad. However, her deep voice made her bark louder than her bite. She was light-skinned with short hair on the top and long weave sewn in. She had green eyes, a big nose, and buck teeth. She stood five-feet-seven, weighing 195 pounds; the two-size-too-small clothes she squeezed into really added a good twenty extra pounds to her visual. No one could ever figure out why she continued to wear the gold earrings with *Tina* and *Rallo* inside of them. Was it because she couldn't afford to go and get some more? Or was it because she still loved Rallo? Or was it that she wanted everybody else to think she was still with Rallo? Whatever it was, she wore the earrings faithfully.

Rallo always took care of his daughter. Yarni would even buy Ralleshia the cutest stuff when she went to the mall. He never told Tina that she bought it because with her ignorant self, she never would have accepted it. *Come on, what difference does it make who bought it? It wasn't for you anyway. It was for Ralleshia,* he would most likely argue with Tina in his mind. Little-dick Rallo was at least a peaceful man when it concerned his daughter.

Tina, on the other hand, was hot. Anytime she would see Yarni's car anywhere she would flatten the tires. Rallo would only give Yarni one of his cars to drive and he'd take care of getting new tires. Tina would throw eggs at Yarni's car, but never approached her when she saw her.

One night, Doug E. Fresh made a guest appearance at the grand opening of Polo Bay Lounge. Richmond was live this night. Everybody was out. Yarni drove Sophie, Jerri, and Monica, but something was wrong. She didn't feel right for some reason.

"If I was to get to fighting, would y'all help me?" she asked out of the blue.

"No doubt," the three replied in harmony.

"Girl, you know I got your back. I don't know 'bout anyone else, but I got you." Sophie made her position known.

"Girl, don't ask no crazy questions, you know we got you," Jerri said.

"Girl, please, I wish somebody would try to roll up on you while you with me," Sophie said.

Yarni had on sky-blue suede coochie-cutter shorts, with the suede shirt tank top to match. She was definitely turning heads in the club. She made eye contact with this dude. She asked the three girlfriends if any of them knew who he was. None of them did.

She pushed her way through the hot, smoke-infested, congested crowd. She stopped to chat with folks she knew on the way over to the bar. When she approached the bar somebody she knew from high school came up to her, and gave her a hug. They gave each other a brief catch-up. She didn't notice who was behind her. She inched her way up to the bar, and squeezed in to place her drink orders.

"Umm, one pina colada, Absolut and cranberry juice, Baltimore Zoo, and a Heineken," Yarni told the bartender.

"Wait a minute, sweetness. You just walked right up and cut in front of me. I am trying to order a glass of Alizé," the man sitting on the bar stool said while using his hand to clarify what he was saying over the loud music.

The waitress looked at them both.

"Go ahead, ladies first," he said, with a toothpick in his mouth. In the meantime, he started talking to one of his homeboys.

"May I have a tray to carry all my drinks?" Yarni asked the waitress. She put the drinks on the tray except for the glass of Alizé, tipped the waitress and tapped the dude on the shoulder that she had made eye contact with earlier when she first arrived to the club.

"Good things come to those who wait. Thanks for allowing me to go in front of you." She slid the drink over to him and picked up her tray of drinks. She walked away from the bar leaving him speechless!

Not ten minutes later, he was walking over to her table carrying a tray with drinks on it for her and her girlfriends. He kept the drinks coming all night. He sat over at Yarni's table and talked to her. He looked good to her. He was a russet-brown complexion with the sexiest full eyes and long eyelashes. He rocked a perfect rounded fade haircut with a little, short beard on his face. His face possessed a few razor bumps, which didn't matter because Yarni was definitely attracted to him. He was a medium build, tight abs, not too muscular, but she could tell he worked out. He wore money-green suede shorts with a short-sleeve shirt with gold buttons to match. His footwear made the ensemble; some green and gold dress shoes with no socks and a diamond ankle bracelet. They laughed and giggled together. He bopped a cool dance for her, and moved just the right way. She took a dollar bill from her pocketbook and was shaking it while he danced. They were having a ball. Yarni put on her sunglasses and was dancing in front of the mirror around him. They were all into each other—and boy, did they put on a show.

The females in the club were *upset* that Yarni had the attention of this man. No one really knew who he was. They knew he had plenty of dough. He had come home from jail about two years ago. He was a dude who played the background. He was rarely out at a club. And when he did come to the club, it was through the back door, and he left through the back entrance where his car would be waiting. They couldn't believe that he was over there in her face and dancing for her too. What the hell was going on?

Yarni saw Tina and her hood-rat friends from a distance. She thought to herself, *How did they even get in here with sneakers on, them no-class-having bitches*. She whispered in her girl Sophie's ear.

"Girl, Tina and her girls are over there."

Sophie alerted Monica and Jerri. Yarni never let Tina know that she'd acknowledged them. They tried to make it known that they'd seen her. They were watching her like a hawk. She kept acting like she was having a ball with the mystery man. When she saw them out of the corner of her eye looking at her—oh, she showed off more. A couple minutes later, Sophie told her that she was going to the restroom. Jerri said she was going to get a drink. Mystery man said he'd be right back because he had to go to the restroom.

Monica was talking to some dude. Monica asked Yarni if she had a pen in her pocketbook. She started fumbling around in her bag for a pen. When she finally looked up, she saw Tina and her two other girlfriends walking up. They were less than fifteen feet away from her. While her hand was still in her pocketbook, she felt around for her knife. She knew it was about to go down!

She saw Sophie come out of the bathroom and walk back over there in that direction. They finally got in front of her. Not Tina, but Tonya, one of Tina's girlfriends who was about thirty pounds bigger and three inches taller than Yarni, black as tar, a gap between her front teeth and broad shoulders, approached her.

"Why you be talking about me?" she asked Yarni while Tina and the girl stood behind her.

"I don't even know you to talk about you," Yarni told her. "Why you rolled your eyes at me then?" Tonya asked, fishing for an argument. Yarni looked straight in Tonya's eyes.

"Look, I don't know you, nor have I ever seen your bamma ass before, but straight up, get the fuck out of my face."

Tonya turned and started to walk away. Tina, wearing the gold earrings with *Rallo* and *Tina* inside of them, with the *Rallo* popping out a little, said something to Tonya. Tonya turned back to Yarni and smacked her. Then Tonya proceeded to turn and walk away. *Wait a minute, does she actually think she's going to smack me and just walk away? Oh, I think not!* Yarni was dressed to impress. She was very prissy, but at the same time, she wasn't a punk! Yarni jumped up, grabbed that guttersnipe from the back, and started slicing and dicing her. Yarni caught her by surprise, had her on the ground and was on top of her, whipping her. Tonya was not even fighting back. At this point, Tina jumped on Yarni's back and started pulling Yarni's micro braids. Yarni started fighting Tina, trying to get her off of her to stop pulling her hair. Yarni reached her hand behind her head, put her fingers in Tina's eyes, and Tina released her hair immediately. At that moment, security grabbed Yarni. They picked her up off of her feet and carried her to the back of the club. She was still kicking when she went past Tina.

The big bald-headed, dark-skinned security guard with a deep voice tried to be patient with Yarni.

"Look, I don't know how much damage you did to the girl laying on the floor. Normally under these circumstances, we'd lock somebody up and press charges, but since you are a personal friend of the owner's best friend, we're not," he continued as he made it clear to Yarni. He instructed her as he pointed, after he heard another security guard over the walkie-talkie.

"*Smokey the Bear has just arrived. Get li'l mama wolf outta here.*"

"Go into the bathroom and clean yourself up. The police just arrived. In order to protect you from them, we're going to have to hurry and take you through the back entrance."

Yarni had never been in an official fight. She was in shock over her reaction to the whole situation. She had no idea that she could ever get violent if the situation presented itself. *I can't believe I actually got into a fight. Oh, my God! Where did I get all that strength and rage from out of nowhere? I could feel my heart beating fast, but I had no idea that I would go off like that. I know am going to look a wreck. I am going to be messed up.* To her surprise, she only had three scratches on her back, but her braids were all over her head. All the bobby pins from the way she had it styled were gone. Most of all, she was mad that her suede outfit was ruined. She looked in the mirror, focusing in on the blood on her new outfit. *Shit*, she thought, *this was the last one like this. I can't even replace this outfit. I know blood ain't going to come out, and especially since this is suede too. Shoot, I really like this outfit. I wonder where my girls at? I hope they don't get locked up behind this foolishness. I hope they just left on their own, but I am driving. Man, I hope they are okay.* As she tried to pull it together, some girl walked up to her and looked at Yarni through the mirror.

"It's so foul that your girls didn't even help you, but you was still rumbling by yourself. Girl, I give you your props."

Yarni couldn't believe her ears. "What?" She balled up her face and looked at the girl.

"Yeah, your friends, left you," the girl said, and right then and there, Sophie walked in.

"Girl, you all right?" Sophie asked.

"Sophie, where were you?" Yarni fairly bawled.

"I knew they were coming over there to start something, so I went to get security!" Yarni saw red.

"What? You went to get security?" Yarni punched Sophie in the face. She commenced to beat her down as if she had stolen something. Security rushed in the bathroom and the guard couldn't believe it: Yarni had Sophie in the stall of the bathroom beating her head up against the wall.

"Need backup in the ladies' room. L'il mama wolf is at it again," the security guard screamed over the walkie-talkie. As soon as the security grabbed Yarni, Sophie tried to escape by crawling under the stalls. Yarni was walking in front of the security guard and caught a glimpse of Sophie in the last stall closest to the door. She moved so expeditiously that security was caught off guard. Yarni ran into the stall. Once she got into the stall security grabbed her, but not before she kicked Sophie in the face with her clog-style, sling-back suede shoes. The security guard was amazed with Yarni's energy.

"Do you want to go to jail?" he had to ask.

"No." Yarni replied.

"Didn't I tell you to be cool?" Security escorted her to the back door and the mystery man was waiting in the alley for her.

"Did you drive?" he asked.

"Yes, my car is right in the front of the club."

"I'll give you a ride home. I'll get my homeboy to get your car and meet up with him in an hour."

"Thank you, but no thanks. I don't go anywhere with strange men."

"Yeah, under normal circumstances, I wouldn't recommend it, but these aren't normal circumstances."

"Do you have a cell phone? I lost mine somehow in the club." She suddenly thought to call home.

He pulled out his Motorola cell phone attached to a black bag. She called Gloria to tell her
what was going on. She gave her his license-plate
number in case he turned out to be a psycho.
Yarni let Gloria know that she would be there in
a half hour. Gloria insisted that she stayed put
until she got there. Yarni knew for a fact that if
Gloria came to pick her up, she would add fire to
the situation, as Gloria used to be a real pistol in
her day.

While she still had access to the Motorola,
Yarni called Rallo and filled him in on what just
happened. She instructed Rallo to find out the
outcome of her battle with Tonya. She also told
him to make sure they don't press any charges
out on her. He'd already heard what happened.
Tina had already called. He said that Tonya had
to get a lot of stitches. She also let him know
that dude was all in Yarni's face, and how Yarni
looked like she was enjoying mystery man's
company.

On the ride to her house, the mystery man revealed that his name was Benjamin. His mother
named him Benjamin because when she looked
at him, she knew that he'd make plenty of them.
However, he was called Bengee for short. He was
the silent partner in four different restaurants
in town. He owned and operated a landscaping

business also. She thought to herself just how typical it was for every dude who claimed he was out—or getting out—of the drug game, always got one of two businesses: A detail shop or a lawn-care business. Bengee explained that he lived alone and had done six years in the pen. He was now the most eligible bachelor on the street. By the time they got to her house, she basically knew his whole life story. But she didn't focus on a word he was saying.

5

Enough Is Enough

All Yarni could think about was that she'd had enough of the whole situation with Rallo. She was sick of his little dick and fed up with his baby-mama drama. She especially didn't like his attitude when she called him to inform him of the fight. It was time to move on.

After Bengee dropped Yarni off, Rallo came over to make sure everything was cool with Yarni and, more importantly, to give her the third degree about who the nigga was she was talking to all night at the club. She denied everything and did a flip mode on him.

"How can you believe anything that Tina says? Why would you even approach me with anything that skank had to say? You should know yourself that Tina is only going to bring lies." She knew that after this whole ordeal, she wasn't messing with Rallo anymore. He never meant her any good anyway. All the money wasn't worth all the drama. She just needed a way to get some money from him as her severance pay as well as to throw salt one last time for his trying to be disrespectful toward her husband, Des. She knew just the plan.

Yarni knew that Rallo felt awful about the fight, and he should have. She knew he was in the street life. She also suspected that he messed around on her. She felt like if you're going to cheat, at least keep your women in check. Inform them of their place and make them play their position. Taking all this into consideration, she decided to use this to her benefit. He knew that the fight was because of him. He felt guilty because he was still sleeping with Tina every now and then. He'd explained to Tina that it could be "no more them," that he was with Yarni now. He shouldn't have slept with Tina. He knew that she was going to get out of hand. Tina just gave the bomb head. This week, especially—oh, he spoiled Yarni. He bought her a seven-karat tennis bracelet and her allowance was tripled. He agreed to go on a seven-day cruise with her. He gave her the money to go pay for it. She didn't because she wasn't going on any cruise with him. She just kept the money.

After all this, she decided she had gotten enough from him. They went to Tysons Corner Mall. They just put out their new fall line. She knew she was going to be going back to school soon. She shopped early for her school clothes. She figured she'd better get it now. She knew when she left him alone she wasn't going to able to afford shopping sprees in the exquisite boutiques. They actually had a nice day together. All good things must come to an end, huh?

When he dropped her off at her house, she gathered all her bags and told him that she was going in the house to lie down because the Thai food they'd eaten was making her feel nauseated.

The next morning, she changed her phone number to an, unpublished number. She pulled her car into the closed garage, so it appeared that she wasn't home. When she did leave the house, she drove her mother's spare car, a Toyota Cressida. When he called on her mother's line, her mother would just say Yarni wasn't available. He wouldn't dare ask Gloria any questions.

After about four days, he realized she really didn't want to mess with him. *I can't believe how she just booked up and left me like that. After all the good times*, he thought, *she let one incident come between us, and I went all out to make it right, not hustling, just straight catering to her that whole week. That cruddy bitch!* Then, to put the icing on the cake, his cousin's girlfriend told Rallo she'd seen Yarni down at the prison, visiting Des. She described what Yarni had on from head to toe. It was one of the outfits he had bought her. The gall of her. She had him looking like the laughingstock of Richmond. What was he to do now?

Rallo decided to tell all the hood rats from around the projects that if any of them saw that bitch, Yarni, anywhere at all—he didn't care if it was at church on Easter Sunday—he wanted her beat down. He'd pay anybody $250 dollars to beat her every time they saw her.

It didn't take long for Yarni to get a whiff of the rumor. One day she was in the beauty parlor, some girls were talking about her and didn't even realize that she was right there. She got her beautician to go over there and ask who and what they were talking about. They let the cat out of the bag.

When she got home, she was so furious with the whole thing. She paced the floor, trying to make sense of this matter. She looked at Rallo's picture that she had on her dresser.

"Now, enough is enough! I let you get off easy when I just stepped off. Now, you don't appreciate it when a sister walks away! No, you gotta have drama. Well, let the games begin, Mr. Rallo. We'll see who gets the last laugh: He who laughs last, laughs the longest. You just *haaadddd* to take it to another level. Now it's on!"

She pulled herself together and paged Rallo. She put four-thousand in after her number to make it look like it was somebody trying to spend four-thousand dollars. Just as she thought, he called right back.

Yarni made her voice sound real weak. "Hey, it's me. Sorry I haven't called you. I've been feeling so bad ever since we came back from Tysons. I've been feeling so weak that I didn't call and give you the new number. I changed it because somehow, Tina got my number and was playing on my phone. I really need you right now. My doctor's office gave me a sick-patient appointment, and I can't drive myself. I need you to come and take me." Of course, Rallo agreed and rushed right over.

Yarni threw on some sweatpants and sneakers and she kept her hair wrapped up in a doobie. She planned out every single detail. She let him go back in the room with her to see the doctor. They asked her for her urine sample so Yarni peed in the cup. When they did a pregnancy test, it came back positive. She had gone by her cousin's house, who was pregnant, and got her to pee in a cup with a top. She had the cup in her pocket all along and used her cousin's pee instead of her own. They asked her when her last period was. She told them a date two months before. She reminded them about how irregular her periods were. They told her she was six weeks pregnant, and the doctor prescribed prenatal vitamins.

Rallo was happy, although he had ulterior motives when he first met her and messed around on her, but now he truly loved her. He wanted to marry her. He even told her to set up some marriage counseling with her pastor, but Yarni wasn't thinking about marrying him. Rallo was a snake. *How could he even think I would dare to even entertain the thought of marrying him after, just earlier today, he had the dogs out looking for me? Am I just supposed to forget about that?*

Yarni knew that Rallo, more than anything, wanted a child with her. He thought that was his way of trapping her and the ultimate revenge on Des. But really it was her way of imprisoning his mind. He'd never find out the truth. The fact that he truly loved her, just the thought of him knowing that they'd conceived a child together, and she aborted it, would damage him for sure. Not like a gunshot wound that would eventually heal if nursed right. She wanted real damage. Injury to the heart was the worst kind of bodily harm. Now, if he didn't love her, it wouldn't have had any effect on him, but that wasn't the case.

On the way from the doctor's office she explained to him that having a child right now wouldn't be a good move for her. Yarni could be very persuasive. She'd always been able to debate and argue her point. So she explained to Rallo while he drove.

"Rallo, I am still trying to complete my schooling and we're not ready for a child. I'm not even legally divorced from Des, and Des isn't going to take no divorce papers lightly." She said, even though she knew that she and Des weren't legally married, but Rallo didn't know that. She continued to assure him.

"We have plenty of time to get married and have a baby. I'm not going anywhere anytime soon. Do you plan on messing with somebody else?"

As soon as she said that he consented to the abortion.

"I'm not real good with these type of things, but if you absolutely need me to, I'll go with you."

Yarni paused for full effect.

"Rallo, for real, it's going to be hard enough to do it. I don't need you there making the situation worse. As a matter of fact, I need some time to myself to get my mind right."

Rallo respected her wishes. When he dropped her off he told her he was going to bring the money back. He left and came right back and gave her three-thousand dollars. He said it was some extra money in case she might've wanted to go shopping afterwards. He thought it would help her feel better.

She went straight to Cloverleaf Mall, aka, "the ghetto mall of Richmond," and every city had one. Whenever you went to Cloverleaf Mall you were subject to see anybody and run into some of everybody. She ran into this big-mouth girl Amy. Now Amy was a gossip box who grew up in the suburbs near Yarni, but as soon as she got a job, she moved to the city just so she could be closer to the action.

Every town was equipped with three or four Amys. Amy was the person who knew everything about everybody. She knew who drove what, who had a baby by whom. You didn't even have to request a blood test because Amy knew. She knew where everybody worked, who was getting money, as well as who was bankrupt. If you needed to locate or get a message to someone, she could take care of that too. The only thing she didn't know was how to take her gossiping ass up to Channel 12 and get a job so she could get paid to report the news instead of being a broke bootleg gossip columnist.

Amy was pretty as a little girl, but now she had so many scrapes and scars from being in scuffles about he-said, she-said– type messes. All of her bruises had given her a hard look, which added about seven years on to her actual age. Thirty years old, standing five-feet-five, birthing three children, she still maintained her brick-house-type shape, and was up on all the trends to hit the fashion scene. Amy's complexion was a walnut shade of brown and she had nice round, full lips. Most of the time when she was out during the day, her hair was wrapped around in a doobie under a scarf to match her outfit. Although she could maintain the upkeep of her hair herself, she was faithfully in the beauty shop every Friday and Saturday to get her hair and nails done. But while she was getting pampered, she was gathering and passing on gossip.

Amy informed Yarni, "Girl, that dude Bengee has been looking all around town for you. He's been trying to locate you. He said he didn't want to show up at your mother's house unannounced." She remembered telling Bengee that was her mother's house and she was never there, because she had just met Bengee and didn't want him to know exactly where she lived. She thanked Amy for the info and kept it moving.

She also ran into Tina, Ralleshia, and Rallo, looking like a big happy family. *Oh, I'm glad to see them out doing a family outing. This is all I need. This is surely a valid excuse to be rid of him.* He stopped to talk to her.

"Come here, Yarni. Let me holler at you for a minute." Yarni giggled a little with one of those fake laughs. *Ohh, he got big balls, don't he? He got the nerve to stop and want to carry on a conversation with me when he is with that guttersnipe. I ain't even going to act stupid. Oh, but I'm going to stop and talk to him just to make Ms. Tina mad. Watch and see.*

She didn't get upset; she just stopped and chitchatted with him. Ralleshia stood by Rallo, holding his leg, smiling.

"Hey Ralleshia, you're so cute," Yarni said in a goo-goo ga-ga way.

"Hi, what's yo' name?" Ralleshia asked, but Rallo cut in.

"This is my good friend, Yarni." *Oh, I'm his good friend now, huh?*

"Daddy, that's your girlfriend?" Ralleshia asked her father, knowing the score.

"Yeah, baby, that's my girlfriend."

Tina was furious. She looked like a time bomb about to explode. She stared at her watch and sucked her teeth.

"*Rahhlow*, come on. Time's up. I thought you just said we was going home to lay up?" Tina said in her most ghetto-fabulous voice while twitching her neck and placing her hand on her hip.

Yarni acted as if she didn't hear Tina. Yarni simply turned to Rallo and asked for some money. He went in his pocket and pulled out a bankroll. He peeled off four hundreds. She grabbed the bankroll and left him with the four hundreds.

"Big daddy," she whined in her most seductive voice, pissing Tina off. "Call me when you drop them off, all right," and she kept on going, laughing to herself how funny she was.

Before she got in her door good the phone was ringing. It was Rallo and she told him that it was over. There was nothing he could say. Yarni hung up on him after telling him to never call her again, but those words didn't mean anything. He kept calling, so she simply got her number changed again.

Yarni called Information and asked for the number and address to Right Choice Landscaping. The operator gave her the information she needed. Her next phone call was to Vogue Florist. She ordered a dozen sunflowers. The card attached read, *Thanks a bunch for being my Superman when I was truly a damsel in distress.*

She was sure that some of his homeboys would be hanging out up at his shop. That's usually how it went. A brother who was trying to go legit still kept company with dudes from his past. Yarni's guess was that he might be trying to lay the foundation for the other brothers so they could know that they could do it too. Yarni knew as soon as the flowers arrived, the other guys would be hyping it up. She gave them until about five p.m. for the flowers to arrive. Just then, her next-door neighbor, Ms. Jackson, called her to inform her that somebody was over by her car. She slipped on her shoes and ran outside. Her first thought was that it was Tina or Rallo. She was wrong. It was Bengee, leaving a note on her car.

He smiled when he made sight of Yarni and was clearly happy to see her. "I didn't have any way of getting in contact with you. I knew your mother lived here. I was hoping to catch her outside watering her flowers or doing some type of yard work." He stared into her eyes and said, "Today must be my lucky day! I have been looking for you ever since I dropped you off. I didn't want to come back here all unannounced at your people's house. Then today, I surprisingly get these sunflowers from you. Nobody has ever sent me flowers." Yarni already figured that anyway. She just smiled back at Bengee and was pleased with herself.

"The guys at the shop couldn't believe it," he continued. Then they exchanged numbers and agreed to see each other the next day. He bent down, kissed her on the cheek, and got into his truck. She looked at his work truck and just shook her head as he pulled off.

She immediately ran in the house and called him on his cell phone. "I have to ask," she said, laughing, "why do brothers who are most likely using a business for a front, go get a work truck and have it sitting on eighteen-inch rims or better. They have their work trucks chromed out." Yarni mentioned how she'd seen a work truck the other day with TV's in it. "Come on brothers, then you wonder how the police know what you're doing?" she went on. He just started laughing. He knew she was sharp.

They went out for brunch the next day at the Jefferson Hotel.

For the next sixteen days, he sent her some type of flowers. It had been sixteen days since they first met at the club. He explained, "These are for every day I wanted to bring you flowers and couldn't." Bengee wanted to make up for it now. They met at the movies the next day. When she came out of the movies, somebody had spray painted *Bitch* on her car. Another time they met at TGI Fridays for happy hour, to have a cocktail

after Bengee got off work. When they came out,
somebody had stolen her tags and colored her
inspection sticker and her county sticker black
with a marker. He then told her that from now
on, he'd drive his car. Yarni knew that she really
had to get a new car. With her car being paid for,
she could surely trade it. The value had depreci-
ated so much from all the times it had to be
painted from the many times of being vandalized
by the playa haters, plus her insurance premium
was escalating as high as gas. She felt helpless.
She couldn't help but to think.

*Shoot! It doesn't make any sense. Why do
people who have a problem with a person,
always mess with their car? What did the car
do to you? Why are you taking it out on the
car? Take it out on the person. The car can't
fight back. Sabotaging somebody's car is a real
cowardly move. What people fail to realize is
that when you vandalize somebody's car, nine
times out of ten, the person has insurance. And
if their car is paid for, then you are probably
putting a few extra dollars in their pocket.*

After all this drama with Yarni's car, Bengee
decided he needed to get her away from all
this madness. He decided to take her to the
Poconos. They stayed at Caesar's Resorts with
a champagne-glass Jacuzzi, swimming pool and

fireplace in the room. It was truly the getaway she needed.

When she returned from their four-day weekend getaway, she heard that Rallo had raised the stakes up to five-hundred dollars, and if somebody broke a bone or made her have a fracture or anything of that nature, it was $750. She couldn't believe what was happening all because his heart was broken. *Who does he think he is, that he could put a price on my safety?*

Throughout the years, Slim, and Yarni had become very good friends. He was a brother to her. He never got into anything concerning her and Des. He wanted no parts of it because he knew that they may go through things, but ultimately Des and Yarni would always be together. She tried not to involve him in any of her negative situations because she knew that he was a certified tickbird and would overreact.

Slim already had his differences with Rallo before Des left the street. He found out Yarni was messing with Rallo; Rallo became a part of Yarni's life and was her sole provider, and for the most part she seemed happy with him. So, he spared Rallo for the sake of his sister, Yarni. But he had carried it to another level now. He didn't like what he was hearing on the streets.

Two days after Yarni came back from the Poconos she met Slim for lunch and she was driving Bengee's Porsche. He could tell that she was a little shaken up. She told him that she really didn't want to drive it because it was too flashy, but she had no choice. She told him how Rallo was so petty to get Tina or some female to call the insurance company and cancel the insurance on her car. While the car was parked outside the front of her house, he came and set it on fire. She couldn't get any money for it. It was burned to a crisp. She explained the whole story to Slim.

"I am not going to worry about it. I'm just going to get me a little hooptie to kick around in, get me from point a to b." She joked, "After all, it's not the car, it's the star driving it." She continued to make jokes. "Now, had I spent one penny of my money in that car besides putting gas in it, oh, I'd be pitching one. He's the stupid one. He should've just taken the car up top to the chop shop. He's the one that lost out because his money gone down the drain. What did I lose? Shoot, I rode all summer at this cat's expense."

Slim wasn't having that. He told her that he was going to help her get a car. Slim tried to keep his cool, but he knew what had to happen. This dude Rallo's life had been spared time after time, like a cat who only has nine lives, he thought to himself.

This cat Rallo was on his last one. One way or the other, Rallo was going to be just like Christopher Columbus: history.

A couple of weeks later, the feds did a sweep in the 643 Killa Villa where Rallo hung at. They picked up twelve people, including all of Rallo's homeboys. All of them got indictments except for Rallo. Now these were the guys who Rallo was with every day, day in and day out. They all hustled and gambled right there around the 643 together. The boys wondered, How come Rallo didn't get picked up? It looked suspect to his boys in jail as well as to everybody on the streets.

On their warrants it stated that a "confidential informant" was snitching on them. Rallo's drug supplier cut him clean off. He couldn't find anybody to buy any dope from or anyone who would buy any from him. He was slowly going broke. He lived off his stash money, but he pinched off of that because he didn't know exactly when the police were going to come and pick him up. Nobody wanted to be around him. Everyone kept his or her distance.

Rallo started driving to Baltimore to buy dope. They were beating him in the head with those high prices because he was an out-of-towner. He was going to Dinwiddie County in the boondocks to hustle, but them country dudes wasn't having it. They kept robbing him. He didn't know what to do. Hustling was all he knew.

He couldn't sleep. He was too paranoid, not knowing when the police was going to come or when niggas was going to kick up in his house and kill him. He was wearing a hard label. The label of a snitch was the worst kind of label. In all actuality, he was locked up, just minus the bars. And for Slim, that was the best get-back. With the label of a snitch, he might as well be dead. He was invisible to all the people he once cared about. So he was just deadweight walking around. A label of a snitch is like a tattoo, a mark that one will have for the rest of his life. Once that label is placed on somebody, it is damn near impossible to take it back and fix it.

6

Throwing Bricks

Des called Yarni. "Am I going to see you, Saturday?" he said.

"Boo, I don't have a rïde. Andrea's motor went out in her car. She's driving my mother's Cressida, and you know how my mother is, since she got this new boyfriend. If she's not at work, she's out with her man."

"What, Gloria got a man?"

"Yep."

"Where she get him from?" Des was happy for Gloria.

"She met him at a singles conference through the church."

"Is he a square?"

"I don't know because I haven't met him. She always goes out to meet him for coffee and doughnuts. She's still scoping him out. She says once she gets to know him, then she'll introduce me. All I know is his name is Sam."

"I am happy for Gloria."

"Me too." Yarni was quite serious.

"Baby girl, I am going to call Castro or Slim, to tell him to get you the rental car. He's going to call you later." Des changed the subject.

Castro got the rental car for Yarni to go visit Des. Yarni woke up bright and early Saturday morning to get on the road. On the way, she got a flat tire on 95 South. She pulled over, opened up the trunk, only to find that there was no spare tire. *Now ain't this some shit?* She slammed the trunk and went to sit in the car. She called roadside assistance. They told her it would be at least three hours before they could get there. She tried to call her mother, Slim, Castro, and Joyce; not one of them were available. She called Bengee, who asked, "Why didn't you call me earlier?" He arrived the same exact time the roadside-assistance people showed up. They towed the car. Bengee took her to the nearest rental-car place where she got another car. After she had gotten everything straight with the rental car, it was too late to get on the road to go see Des. This was the first time in almost three years that she didn't go see Des when she said she was. Awful was the feeling she felt, and she really had her heart set on seeing him.

What a day, she thought as she walked into the door. She kicked off her shoes. She looked at the caller ID. She saw some out-of-areas on the caller ID, and some numbers she didn't recognize. She checked her answering machine.

Beep. "Baby girl, it's twelve-thirty and you're not here yet. I spoke to Castro and he told me he got the rental. I guess you should be showing up any minute now."

Beep."Yeah, Yarni," *Des never calls me Yarni.* "If you needed a rental car for something other than coming to see me, you should've just said so, and it wouldn't been no thing. No love lost. No need to rush to get up here. Guess I see you whenever."

The next morning Yarni was up bright and early to get on the highway to go visit Des. She arrived at the prison at 8:46. She knew they had to call for Des before 9:15 because of the count. The correctional officer sitting at the front registration desk looked Yarni up and down from head to toe when she approached the desk. The masculine-looking guard sat there on the telephone carrying on a personal conversation, not even acknowledging Yarni other than the stank look she gave her when she walked in the door. Yarni was patiently looking at her watch, knowing that time was not on her side right now.

"Excuse me, miss, are you working or am I waiting on someone else to come and check me in? If so, would you call them, please?"

"Would I have on this uniform if I wasn't working? I am going to check you in when I get off the phone." *What do I do? Should I ask to see her supervisor or should I just chill, since I am trying to get in there? I really don't need any holdups.* Right then and there, the bell rang for count. Yarni knew she had to wait now.

"Oopps, look at there. You've got to come back after ten-thirty when the count clears."

I can't believe this jheri curl–wearing heifer. I'm not even going to comment on all that Jheri–curl activation on the collar of her shirt.

Yarni left and came back around 10:35 when the lobby was packed with tons of people. When Yarni reached the front of the line the same guard informed her, "Oh, your jeans are too tight. You can't go in. Let me make a suggestion to you. There's a Dollar General store down the street, maybe you can go and purchase some jeans."

The nerve of this big dyke-looking wench, she could have told me that before, when I was here the first time. I feel like smacking the hell out of her, but then I know that I really won't be able to get in there to see Des. Be cool, Yarni. And if

*you want to, you can show your ass, but wait
until you come out from seeing Des.*

Yarni left the prison and returned with some
jeans that were on the clearance rack for six
dollars at the Dollar General store, the only store
in the town. She left her shirt and shoes on. She
was then processed in. She went into the room
with this other guard that looked like she was an
amazon.

"Face the wall, hold your hands straight-like,
level with your shoulders." She began to pat
Yarni down. *You are too into this. Is this the
highlight of your job?* "Take off your shoes. Lift
up your feet." *The things a girl's gotta do to be
supportive of her man while he's in prison. I
realize, though, that this is the way the system is
set up, to discourage us from coming in here to
see our loved ones. These people want us to just
say, "Oh, I'm not going through all this to get
into a prison to see him. I'll see him when he's
released." So me giving into these people would
be allowing them to win this political war.*

Yarni walked in the visiting room, and handed
her visitor's pass to the correctional officer sitting at the entrance door. "Ma'am, he's at table
thirty-three. He's already visiting with another
visitor so you can just join them. Table thirty-
three is outside. Walk through those double
doors and you should see him."

"Thank you," Yarni said. *He's about the only person who works at this place who has some sense. I think it must be a thing with the female guards. Most of the women are mad because you coming in here dressed all fly, with the hairdo to match. You got your head all up in the air. They know you know that you looking good, so the only way they know they can mess with you is by trying to use the little toy badge and imitation police uniform to try to make your day rough, when all they gotta simply do is ask, "Where did you get those shoes, or who did your hair?" I'd surely tell them, alls they gotta do is ask. No, that's just too easy, they've gotta reveal that nasty disposition instead, and guess what? They still don't know where I got the shoes from, either. Wonder who's in here seeing Des? It's probably Joyce. Wonder why she didn't call to see if I wanted to ride with her? She knows my car was just torched.* Yarni looked around the visiting room to see who was visiting whom. *I can't believe there are chicks in here with jeans way tighter than mines. Ooh, look at that plump chick over there with some stretch pants on, and they got the nerve to make a big issue about me coming in here with my jeans on.* Just then, Yarni had the table in sight. *The nerve! No, he don't have some chick up here visiting him!*

The girl sitting at the table with Des was a bright, light-pale complexion, with sandy brown hair. Her hair was gelled back into a neat ponytail with a scarf wrapped around it. She had a single red pimple on her face that stood out from afar due to her light skin tone. She was tall and slinky, possessing no shape at all. Her eyes were dark brown with black eyeliner around them, along with the same liner for her lips, which possessed candy-apple red lipstick. She had on some bell-bottom jeans with some Bass denim bobo sneakers, a blue and white Guess shirt, with her neck, fingers, and ears possessing an assortment of gold jewelry.

Yarni was trying to keep her composure. *After all I been through yesterday and today to get here, and I'm greeted with my man sitting at the table with somebody else. And on top of everything else I got on these cheap-ass six-dollar jeans. Oh, hell NO!*

"Oh, isn't this just cute!" Des and Madame X both were in shock when Yarni snuck up from behind. Des always sat with his back to the police when he was in the visiting room. It was his way of being disrespectful to the correctional officers. "Surprise! Surprise! Surprise!" Yarni pounced upon them.

"Hey, baby." Des got up to embrace her with a hug and a kiss. Yarni turned her face away from Des and he ended up kissing her on the cheek. She sat down.

"Oh, Flo, this is my wife, Yarni. Yarni, this is a friend of mine, Flo." *Your friend, huh?*

"Nice to meet you, Yarni," Flo said.

"Can't say the feeling is mutual, honey." Yarni looked Flo up and down. *This bitch gonna try to extend her hands out to me, flashing her big, cheap, ninety-nine-dollar rings that she got from Broad Street, all in my face like she doing something!*

"On that note, Des, I am about to go," Flo said as she stood up.

"Look, sweetie, you ain't going anywhere until I get an explanation about what the hell is going on here," Yarni said in a firm tone.

"Baby girl, calm down. Don't make a scene. I'll explain everything." Des tried to get the situation under control.

"Yeah, I want it right now while your ho—excuse me, I meant while Flo is here."

"Baby, calm down, this is not what you think."

"How did I know you were going to say that?"

"Sit down, Flo, because you ain't going nowhere," Yarni said as she pointed to the chair.

"Baby girl, I know I went against the grain when I asked you to bring narcotics in here. I know the severity of me asking you to jeopardize your freedom. My man hooked me up with Flo. She's a mule. She goes to different prisons visiting dudes to take them the pack. That's her hustle. All those money orders I been sending you, I get them from doing my thing in here, not just from cigarettes."

"I am still trying to understand why, Des? Your commissary stays stacked. You don't want for anything. I just don't understand why you'd resort to this?" Yarni was truly at a loss.

"Well, Baby girl, opportunity was there. There is a lot of money to be made in here."

"Every time opportunity knocks you can't open the door for it. Des, what you have failed to realize is that you were a major player on the scene. Simply because you walk in the spotlight, believe me, there's a rat or a snake in the shadow, because all a nigga needs is to get a whiff of what you doing and they'll drop a note or a kite on you. Then here comes the heat. They put you under investigation, then they control your destiny." Yarni could feel her blood pressure increase knots.

"Baby girl, calm down"

"Calm down? Let me enlighten you to this, Des. I am out here ripping and running up and down the damn road to every place that I think will listen to me to help out with your appeal. Wouldn't it just be ironic if I get a break on your case and you mess around and get a drug charge in here? That's a street charge. All it takes is for them to do a shakedown on the late night-early morning shift. Even if you got somebody else holding it, who do you think is going to take the charge? Not even a flunky junkie is that stupid. No, baby! Brothers are doing anything to get outta here. People are snitching like crazy. You should know just from reading your subscription to *Don Diva* magazine? That's the proof in the pudding right there."

Just then, Flo stood up. "My work is done here. I am about to go."

"Flo, I am not finished with you, either, and it's to your best interest that you sit your bony butt down. Don't worry, I am going to get to you in a minute."

Des couldn't say a word because he knew if Yarni had never been right about anything else, she was right this time.

"Just think about this. Now, suppose somebody got a whiff of this whole conspiracy going on, and set the whole thing up." She pointed to Flo as she continued. "Flo, they wait for you to come in here with the pack, and catch you in the process. Oh, I don't know if you can hold your own, but say they put the pressure on you. They want you to tell on the person who gave it to you." Flo interrupted, "Oh, I can do mines if I catch a case. I'm not going to tell on nobody. It was my choice to do it, so I can handle the consequences."

"Flo, they all say that, that's until you're presented with all that time." Yarni rolled her eyes in disgust. "Now, back to what I was saying. Then they connect the mule, you, Des, and then everybody's locked up with a rack of time, all because you say opportunity knocked. How much money could you make in here? A few hundred dollars, Des? You were never a hundred-dollar dude when you were on the streets, so why come to jail and become a hundred-dollar man? You're in the penitentiary throwing bricks at the exit door. You must really like it here, huh? Are you trying to come home or what?

"And you, Flo, for the love of money, right? Is this all really worth it? Let me tell you this, if I ever catch you in here bringing my man some damn drugs, I will beat you down unmercifully, you hear me? You can sit there and pick your fingernails as if you don't hear me, but this is from the heart, baby. Now, you are dismissed. You are free to go now."

"Yarni, listen to me, baby. Please don't be hard on me, I understand your feelings about this, but try to recognize my plight. I know that you like nice things. I know that things are tight due to the fact you are trying to further your education. I don't want you to have to go through the bullshit with those clown-ass niggas just to be able to keep your head above water. I feel that the main reason you're so caught up in that lifestyle is because I introduced you to it. By all means, I want you to have the best of everything, and I will do whatever's in my power to make sure that you're okay."

Yarni touched Des's cheek and gazed into his eyes. "Des, don't try to turn this around on me. Let me tell you: It doesn't matter what I drive, what I wear, or how much money I got if I don't have you with me to share it with. It's meaningless. If I won a million dollars tomorrow and had to pay nine hundred and ninety-nine thousand dollars to get you outta here, it would be done in a blink of an eye."

Yarni maintained her serious disposition. "Des, I love you with all my heart, but sometimes a girl's gotta do what a girl's gotta do. I need you to choose. Now, is it going to be me or your little prison drug ring? That's my bottom line."

Des tried to respond but Yarni cut him off. "Don't answer right away. Think long and hard over this whole ordeal." Yarni got up as if she was leaving. Des jumped up, followed Yarni over to the exit door, and grabbed her hand.

"No, baby, where you going, baby girl? I've made my decision. Yarni, I quit," Des said, motioning his hands as if he was the umpire at a baseball game. Of all times, he knew she was serious by the look in her eyes.

"Yarni, you're all I have, all I need, and all I want. If it takes me to give up hustling, it's out the window."

"If you truly love me and are willing to sacrifice and prove it to me, then give me what Flo just brought you." Des did not hesitate. He quickly reached into the pocket of his jean jumpsuit and handed it to Yarni. She took it out of his hand, balled it up in a paper towel, proceeded to the bathroom, and flushed it down the toilet.

They went back to sit at the table. She developed tears in her eyes, as she absorbed the idea of Des throwing the towel in on selling drugs. The streets had practically raised him, and him excluding drugs from his life for her was one of the ultimate tests of their love. It wasn't Rallo or Bengee who'd passed the test. It was Des. Time and time again, it was always Des.

7

Da Clinker

All kinds of blessings were coming to Yarni all at one time. Joyce returned the Benz that she had taken over three years ago from the apartment as she wanted to start with a clean slate. She realized that Yarni had Des's best intentions at heart. With the 300 Benz, part of the money from the savings bond her grandmother had left for her, and the help of Bengee and Slim, Yarni was able to get her a black M3 BMW.

Things were going well between her and Bengee. They actually clicked as well as complemented each other. They liked a lot of the same things. They both liked to travel. They went everywhere together. Any time she had a break from school or long weekends, they would always be off out of town exploring or relaxing.

They went on a Carnival Cruise. He would take her to Las Vegas to go to any of the fights that were there. She absolutely loved Vegas. He'd send her flowers for no reason. He'd take the initiative to plan scavenger hunts for her. The way he treated her reminded her a lot of Des. She never had to tell him what to do because he just did it. He had a way of looking at her. It could be a roomful of beautiful, exotic women and he would only see Yarni.

This was the first man besides Des that she'd ever genuinely cared about. They were tight as jeans. They communicated well. Communication was the key to any relationship. The sex was good. Now that they were in a deep relationship Yarni had no desire to go out to the clubs anymore. Bengee didn't tell her to stop going. He wasn't the going-out type, just more of a homebody. They found things for them to do at home, or outside of the club scene, which were worthwhile.

Though Bengee and Rallo were slightly similar in the method of operation, there was a difference between them. Bengee was eight years older than she was and more attentive with anything concerning her. Bengee definitely wore the pants in their relationship. Yarni could not just come with some lame excuse and expect Bengee to accept it. He was sterner with her than Rallo ever was. She respected him as well as his wishes. He made it clear that she was not to go see Des in prison. She would not disobey, but she still stayed in contact with Des via letters.

Des had been transferred to a prison nine hours away from Richmond. Norfolk, where Yarni attended ODU, was two hours outside of Richmond. Des was considerate enough to tell Yarni that eleven hours was too far to drive to see him. He was more worried about her safety when driving the distance and through the winding country roads to the facility. Just corresponding on a regular basis until he was moved from up there, would suffice in his eyes. In all actuality, Bengee's demands never affected the relationship with Des and Yarni.

During the weekdays when she was attending classes in Norfolk, Bengee would be there at least two of the four class days. She would stay with him when she was in Richmond on the weekends. She had keys to his house. He was becoming a permanent part of her life. After attending three years in Norfolk at ODU, she transferred to the University of Richmond. When she moved back to Richmond, she moved in with Bengee. This was the first time in her adult life that she had actually lived with a man.

One summer night, right before Yarni's senior year at the University of Richmond was to begin, she and Bengee were riding down Azalea Avenue. The cops pulled Bengee over for no apparent reason. In reality, the reason was they were DWB—Driving While Black. The typical situation: The police spot an 850 BMW with rims on it and see a young black man driving and automatically think, drug dealer! The cop put the blue lights on them. Bengee pulled his BMW into the Brookhill Azalea shopping center. The officer approached the back of the car and broke the tail light. He went around to the driver's side of the car. He looked down with his round, shiny, mirrored reflected sunglasses and big brim hat while chewing tobacco.

"License and registration please?" The officer said with a deep down-south accent. Bengee cooperated. The officer studied Bengee's license hard. "Mr. Whales, do you have any drugs or weapons in here?" the officer asked while pointing his flashlight around the car.

"No," Bengee politely responded.

"Then you shouldn't mind if I search your vehicle, right?"

"Sir, I apologize, but you can't search anything of mine," Bengee said in a firm tone. He knew his rights.

"We'll see about that, Mr. Whales. We'll just see, won't we?" the officer said as he spit his tobacco. The officer walked back to his squad car, sat in his car for twenty minutes, and returned to Bengee's car when another police cruiser rolled up. The other cop proceeded to Yarni's side of the car.

"Mr. Whales, please step out of the car," the younger cop demanded.

"For what?" Bengee asked. He ignored Bengee. The officer opened Bengee's car door while spitting his chewing tobacco.

"Mr. Whales, I said step out of the vehicle."

As soon as Bengee proceeded to put one foot on the pavement the officer grabbed him, literally pulling him out of the car, and slapped handcuffs on him. Yarni could see something out of the corner of her eye on her side of the car. She called out to the police, "What's going on?" When she looked to her right, there was another police officer standing there with a loaded shotgun pointed at her. "Ma'am, step out of the car." Yarni slowly got out of the car.

"Mr. Whales, your license is suspended," the first officer said to Bengee. Bengee knew for a fact he had a valid driver's license. Taking his lifestyle into consideration, he'd never let his license get suspended. At this point, two more police cars rolled up. The second police immediately removed Yarni out of Bengee's sight. She was placed in a minivan while they searched the car.

"What's your name?" the police asked in a calm voice. Yarni ignored him. "Is that your boyfriend?" Yarni only moved around the backseat to try to get out of the van. They had her locked in. A lady cop entered the van wearing some black jeans with a white polo-style T-shirt and some combat-looking black military-style boots. "Hi, are these guys giving you a hard time?" Yarni only looked at her as if she was crazy. *Oh, they trying to play good cop-bad cop, huh?*

"You mean to tell me y'all don't have anything else to do, but harass me? Why don't y'all go try to find some child molesters to catch? Listen lady, I haven't done anything," Yarni complained to all who would listen.

"I know you haven't, but it's just standard procedure," the lady interrupted. "What's your name, honey? Whose car is that?" Yarni never responded to any of her questions.

"That's some nice jewelry. Did your boyfriend give them to you?" Yarni ignored the lady cop as she moved around the van, trying to see out of the windows that were taped up. The male policeman said, "Yeah, her boyfriend gave it to her because you know he's a drug dealer." He opened up the door to get out of the van, leaned back in, and shook his head at Yarni, "But sweetie, you can kiss that big, nice rock on your finger good-bye because my wife's going to be wearing that soon and very soon," pointing directly at the cluster ring that Bengee had given Yarni just a few weeks before.

"I kinda figured your boyfriend sold drugs just by your jewelry. How else would you be able to afford such extravagant pieces? I wish I had somebody to buy me some nice presents," the lady cop said in a sarcastic tone, but trying to make Yarni comfortable so she could loosen up.

I betcha you do. Don't try to act as if we're really friends and I don't know what's going on here. Shit, you ain't no friend of mine and can best believe I'm not muttering a word.

"Look, you need to talk to me. I can help you." Yarni rolled her eyes and laughed. Everything else the woman cop said Yarni continued to laugh at in a cynical manner, even when the male cop entered the van with a 9 mm in his hand.

"Laugh now, but cry later," the officer said. "Yarnise Pitman, you are under arrest for possession of an illegal firearm. Now, I bet you want to talk to us, huh?"

Yarni continued with her sarcastic giggle. "Do you really think a ride downtown is going to scare me? Oh, I'm shaking in my boots!" Yarni said as she continued laughing on the outside, but crying on the inside. She'd never been inside a police car before or been to a jail, other than to visit. She was fully aware of the notion that they were only taking her to jail out of spite. The police knew that gun wasn't hers, but since she didn't utter a word, they gave her the gun charge too.

Before they took her in front the magistrate to get a bond, they made her sit in a cold, empty room for about three hours before anybody came in. She couldn't fall asleep because the room temperature was so uncomfortable. Her nipples were hard, and chill bumps were all over her body. When the interrogation officer entered the room, the first thing he asked was, "Are you cold? Would you like me to adjust the temperature to make you more comfortable?" He banged on the door: "You guys ought to be ashamed of yourself. It's freezing. Cut the air down, and get me some hot cocoa or coffee in here right now!" Yarni didn't budge; neither was she impressed.

"Ms. Pitman, this is how it works. One hand washes the other around here. See how I got you instant results with the heat, coffee, hot chocolate, and all? That's how I work. Instant gratification. You give me some instant info and I will give you on-the-spot results. This little fiasco that you had earlier can all be erased." Yarni just stared at him with a timid expression on her face. He pulled up a chair beside her. "Do any of these people look familiar to you?" He started spreading pictures all across the table of the city's neighborhood drug boys from all over Richmond. Some she knew, or had seen around, and some she didn't. She studied the photos and what she found interesting was the fact that the photos were not mug shots. Most were taken at clubs, some at car lots, the mall, summer league, shows, the block—just anywhere the ballers were subject to be found. Yarni didn't allow her astonishment to show as she stared at the photos of the players and pimps from all over the communities of Richmond, from the 358, the 233, the 643, and the 321. Still she maintained her silence. The interrogator observed her looking, so that's when he started laying more photos on the table, "Whose car is this?","What about this car?" *Damn these people ain't joking. They taking pictures of cars and everything.*

"Yarnise, if you can give me some info about any of these people, I can make your little charge disappear as if I was David Copperfield. Poof, be gone. Just like that."

"Just like that, huh? That easy?" She finally broke her silence. The detective got happy as he grinned. "Just like that!"

Yarni looked as serious as she could. The detective moved the photos around on the wood table. "See, I know that gun wasn't yours. I can persuade the right people of it. What do you say, Yarnise?" He asked as if he knew he was just about to hit the jackpot. He was certain she was about to spill her guts on everything she knew or heard of on every nickel-and-dime hustler to the big-time dealers. Oh, Ms. Yarnise Pitman was going to be his Christmas bonus, his raise, and that promotion he'd been looking for.

Yarni looked in his face and made direct eye contact with him, and fell into laughter. "Poof, be gone? Disappear like David Copperfield, right?" she asked as she held her stomach with rays of laughter roaring out. He shook his head and started laughing too. "Just like David Copperfield."

Yarni seized her giggles and got serious as she paused and looked into his eyes. "David Copperfield works with illusions, and that bullshit you talking is nothing but a mirage, a fallacy, a hallucination! You understand? Now, get me a lawyer, and while you're doing that, realize that I walk with two legs. I don't lay on my belly and slither around on the ground. I'm no snake, rat, snitch, informant, mole, spy, understand that. Oh, and one last thing, never ever compare yourself to David Copperfield. One thing is fo'sho, and two things for certain: You're not Houdini or David, so you can't make jack disappear."

Both Yarni and Bengee posted bail that same night.

A lot of sleepless nights followed. She had a lot on her plate. Every time she closed her eyes to sleep she thought about the pictures that lay on that table. What was her responsibility here? Did she warn the hustlers of the fact the police were asking questions and they better prepare themselves for what was about to come? She was fully aware of the fact that it didn't take much to convince a weak individual of treason, especially when they were under the gun. *The rules to the game changed in their eyes. Was it fair to let innocent people fall victim? Granted, they were all breaking "the law" even though the law wasn't set up for my people to come in first place? And certain people possess these get-out-of-jail-free cards. I mean, these people in the photos, they shouldn't be sacrificed to save somebody else, who simply got caught up. Okay, I wanna approach each and every face I remember in those pictures and just put them down with the conspiracy, but at the same time, where does that leave me? People will get suspect, think I got ulterior motives, and I'm the one trying to play fair.*

Yarni knew that Bengee already had twenty-two years suspended time over his head. Plus, he'd be violating his parole if he got that new conviction. After constant persuasion from Bengee, she ended up taking the charge. Bengee hired her a lawyer, Mr. Plucktime. The lawyer assured her that the state would dismiss the accusations or only knoll process the case, and the worst that could happen is that she'd get probation, and after six months of good behavior, they'd bring the case up and dismiss it.

Bengee asked her not to tell anybody. She didn't tell a soul, especially her mother or Des. She knew it would break Gloria's heart. She also felt ashamed that she had let Bengee talk her into this. This was really putting her career on the line, her schooling, her life—her everything. She loved him and knew that he'd never steer her wrong. So, she just believed in him.

While all this was going on, she still went back and forth to school maintaining a high grade-point average. When she went to talk to the pre-sentence officer, she said that she'd recommend to the courts no jail time, and assured her that everything would be fine.

The court date came around fast. When she woke up, Bengee said that he was sick and he couldn't go to court with her because he thought he had a stomach virus. She ended up driving herself to court. As soon as she pulled in the court parking deck she called Gloria. She told her she had to go to court and she didn't want to go by herself. Gloria had arrived right before they called Yarni's name. She knew that Yarni was in serious trouble due to the fact that she was not in general district court, but circuit court. Gloria was furious because she knew Bengee was the masked man behind all of this madness and now he was nowhere in sight.

Yarni was sentenced in Henpeck circuit court. Henpeck County was very strict. The judge who presided over the case was a real redneck. The irony of it was, his name was Judge Redneck. He was old and should have retired fifteen years ago, when he was seventy or so. He made an example out of Yarni. He looked dead in Yarni's face and asked her, "Do you expect me to have some sympathy for you? You're in college. You should know better." He looked at the paper-work, page after page, with his pen in hand and asked the Commonwealth attorney, "Did she cooperate with you in questioning and turning state's evidence?"

The Commonwealth attorney laughed as he said, "Judge, she didn't utter a word and simply turned her back to me the whole time I was trying to question her."

The judge shook his head in disgust and interrogated her. "I've looked over your letters from your professors, your grades, as well as your pre-sentence report, and how could you possibly have all this book sense and not an ounce of common sense to speak up and save your own butt? I'm looking around the courtroom, and the male whose gun it really was, isn't even here to show his support. You young girls better wake up and smell the coffee because it is definitely perking. I've never wanted to send someone to jail, until now. I really don't feel you deserve to be sentenced to jail time. However, I feel obligated to sentence you to one year in jail, simply for being a fool for love."

In Virginia, one year was equal to ten months. Yarni would have to serve ten months in the Henpeck County Jail. With good behavior she'd be released in nine months and fifteen days. Yarni was devastated and was outdone with the outcome. Gloria jumped up in court and yelled, "You prejudiced *motherfucker*!"

The bailiff marched over to Gloria to lock her up for the profane outburst, but the judge simply said, "I am going to let you get that one for free. After all, I am having a good day and I've been called worse behind my back, but never in my face." He added, "Remove this woman from my courtroom!"

Yarni walked slowly out of the courtroom in disbelief. Her attorney approached her, smiling at her. "I think the outcome went very well, considering the guidelines for this type of case." Yarni exploded, "You never mentioned anything about any guidelines to me. You promised me no time, you sellout motherfucker!!!" She walked up to him, got face-to-face with him, and spit. "You're fired and I am reporting you to the bar association."

She called Bengee at the house since he was supposed to have been so sick. She didn't get an answer. She called his cell phone. He answered.

"Oh, you've recovered, huh?" Yarni said in a sharp tone.

"No, I just had to go meet somebody real quick. I am on my way back to the house now," Bengee explained quickly.

"You sold me out, Bengee. You got me that bullshit-ass lawyer who you claimed was top-of-the-line. He really was the bottom of the barrel. You better go get your money back. You knew that those white folks were going to give me some time, didn't you? That's why your stomach was hurting this morning, huh?" Bengee hung up in her ear.

The judge did give her work release. She'd lied to him, telling him that she did bookkeeping at a day-care center. She neglected to mention that it was her Aunt Andrea's day-care center. He gave her until the following Monday to turn herself in. She hired another lawyer to work on an appeal, sentence reduction, and home incarceration.

Yarni told Melanie what had happened and expressed to her friend that she was going to need to call her collect as a backup in case she couldn't reach Bengee or her mother. Melanie said that her phone was about to get cut off from dudes calling her house from the penitentiary. Yarni paid Melanie's phone bill—$536 dollars— so she'd be able to call her collect. She also told Melanie that she would get Bengee to give her the money to pay her phone bill for the months to come.

Monday rolled around and Yarni turned herself in. She kept telling herself it wasn't going to be that bad because she got to leave during the day. All she had to do was sleep there. When she left for work during the day at Aunt Andrea's day care, she'd go check in, then leave and go to her classes at U of R. There was no way she was going to let any of this stand in the way of her graduation. She had promised Des and her grandmother she was going to graduate and she meant it. She would go back to the day care for the rest of the day when her classes were done.

Two months into the work release it was running smoothly and one day, the work-release sheriff showed up at the day-care center looking for Yarni. They tried to cover for her and said that she was gone to the bank. Andrea ran to the back office and tried to call her on her cell phone, only she had left her cell phone at the day-care center. She was up the creek with no paddle. When she returned to the jail that night they removed her from work release. She had to do the remainder of her six months straight jail time. This was the greatest difficulty she had faced yet.

When they first put her in population, she cried every day. Not because she was scared of being in jail, but simply because she wasn't used to jail life or the mentality. Having to eat what was chosen for her to consume was hard enough and the food was disgusting, so she wouldn't eat. She lost about twenty pounds in a four-month time frame.

When she went into the jail population some of the girls knew her from the streets. Or, if they didn't know her personally, they had heard of her by tying her to Des, Rallo or Bengee. Some gave her the utmost respect on the strength of Des or Bengee, but some of her fellow inmates were jealous of her. They were especially envious of the way she lived out of jail as well as in confinement.

Sometimes when a person went to jail, they were forgotten about. People on the outside world thought, out of sight, out of mind. So, they forgot all about the inmate. What they didn't realize is unless a person was sentenced to death or had consecutive life sentences—and even so—convictions were overturned everyday, which means they were not going to be confined forever. And one day, they would meet again.

This wasn't the total case for Yarni. First of all, she only told a selective few that she was in jail. The people she did inform showed her love. She got mail on a regular basis, and even though she didn't want any visits, Gloria visited every week. Whenever she made a phone call, the charges were always accepted. She could call as much and talk as long as she wanted. Her inmate account was always stacked. She continued to get yellow money-receipt slips even though she already had hundreds of dollars in her inmate account.

She also ran a store in her dayroom. In jail, inmates only get to go to the canteen once a week. At the end of the week, some of them may run out of certain products. So, an inmate would allow that person to get an item from them, providing when they go to the store, they give them two items back. It is called two-for-one.

Yarni only provided one-for-one: Whatever was gotten from her was just reversed with that item.

Most of the girls in jail were there because of some crime they committed for drugs. The majority of them were conniving on the streets and shiesty in jail. They may have done so much low-down dirty stuff that when they got to jail, nobody thought enough of them to send money or any expressions of love. So, naturally, when they saw somebody like Yarni, one of two reactions happened: They either tried to befriend her to get whatever they could from her, or they just envied and hated her, and tried to give her a hard time. They'd send trouble her way anyway they could.

Yarni had never thought about breaking the law before in her life. The lifestyles of the men she dated caused her to know the hustles of the world, such as buying clothes hot from a booster, buying food stamps for half price, dudes getting robbed, people selling drugs, or whatever crime that had been committed. She was aware of all these offenses and personally knew people who did all of the above plus some, but she never thought of ever committing a crime.

Overall, Yarni was a good person. She would help anybody. Girls would come in going through withdrawals from heroin. That was a sad sight.

They would shake, sweat, and vomit, just be sick desiring chocolate to ease their urge. She would give them a couple of chocolate candy bars and some Ivory soap to help clean up the vomit, not looking for anything in return. Her heart was compassionate. She looked out for anybody in need, but don't get it twisted, Yarni was no fool or no lame for anybody.

The first two months were the hardest for Yarni to adjust to. She stayed in some type of trouble. She got into two fights back-to-back with girls wanting to try her. She knew if she didn't straighten the situation out, things would go from bad to worse.

Yarni had picked up a lot of her jail-survival skills from Des and unknowingly, her father. For instance, she told the deputy who processed her in, that she'd just gotten her ears pierced and was afraid if she'd removed her diamond-studded earrings her ear may close or worse, get infected. The deputy allowed Yarni to keep her earrings, because the jail was awful when dealing with medical incidents. They hated the hassle and were shorthanded on medical staff.

Yarni also removed the underwire out of her bras so she wouldn't have to wear the county-issued underwear. She was allowed to have eight T-shirts, soft bras, socks, and panties.

She instructed Gloria to bring her all colors of T-shirts with socks to match, not any white, because she could buy white T-shirts and socks from the jail canteen. Her mother also brought her a Guess watch. These things were nothing to Yarni. She was only trying to make the best out of a horrible situation. Having these belongings made Yarni stand out, so there was a lot of jealousy surrounding her.

Although Yarni had a good heart, she wasn't going to let anybody take advantage of her by any means. This dirty, junkie girl, Key-Key, who she knew from the street, was locked up too. She was light-skinned, with shoulder-length curly hair and had a petite frame. Pretty she wasn't, but her complexion, clothing, and cute shape attracted the men.

One day Key-Key walked over to Yarni when Yarni was leaving out of her cell to go play spades.

"Can I get a honey bun and a Baby Ruth from you? I'll pay you when we go to canteen on Tuesday. I'm supposed to get a money slip on Monday," Key-Key asked.

"Hold up, Key-Key," Yarni said as she went back into her cell. She returned with a honey bun and a Milky Way. "Here, you can have this. Don't worry about giving it back to me when your money slip comes. Just get stocked up on your personals. Okay?"

"Thank you, Yarni." Key-Key was more grateful than her stoic face would show.

Yarni went to the card table with three bags of potato chips in her hand. She had to use the chips to put up to bet in the spade game. She played spades for the next two hours. When the game was over, she ran up to her cell to get her a Baby Ruth. She looked in her box where all her snacks were, but there were no chocolate bars left. She knew she should have had at least seven or eight left because she never gave them away, as they were her favorite. Yarni flipped out. She ran out of the cell.

"Who been in my cell?" Nobody said anything. "Well, if anybody saw anything, oh, I got a ten-dollar reward out to know who been in my cell." Yarni knew money talked, even in "da clinker." She went back in her cell and took off her gym shorts and her tank top she'd been walking around in. She replaced it with her sweat suit and her tennis shoes, and went back to play cards.

A girl approached Yarni. The girl didn't want to get caught up in the hype, so she just passed Yarni a note. Yarni put the note in her pocket. Later that night, she read it. *Look in Key-Key's cell.*

Yarni waited until Key-Key went to take a shower. Yarni snuck into her cell, and there it was. Seven Baby Ruths, dry ramen noodles, two Secret deodorant sticks, and the Victoria's Secret underwear that Yarni had on the day before, which she had washed out by hand and had hanging up in her cell to dry. *A dirty bitch. She had the nerve to steal my drawers! How trifling can you be? I gave to this broke-down ho and she gonna steal from me. I can't believe this!*

Yarni walked fast with her hands swinging by her side. She had a one-track mind and was in a trance trying to get over to the shower. She opened up that shower door and pulled Key-Key out, buck naked. "Oh, you wanna steal from me?" Big, bad, bully Key-Key who had so much mouth, didn't try to fight back while slipping and sliding all around the dayroom. It only made Yarni madder, because she had to chase her around the dayroom. The deputies came in and broke up the fight, but they only locked the both of them in their cells for the rest of the night.

After the fight, Yarni didn't have anybody else trying her. Thirty-eight days of her jail term was spent in the hole, in solitary confinement. Most people would have gone crazy having to be locked away twenty-four hours, seven days a week, but Yarni handled solitary well, better than the average inmate.

In the dungeon, the lights were very dim, and the female isolation was located over one of the male pods. Yarni kept hearing vague voices carrying on conversations. At first, she thought the solitary confinement was getting to her, but then she realized that wasn't the case. She wasn't losing it after all. While she lay on her cot, writing a letter to her father, she heard a voice that sounded like it was somewhere near.

"Hello, hello, hello. I'm talking to you down there in cell block two or three."

Yarni jumped up and ran to the door to respond through the slot in the door that the guards used to hand her mail or meal trays through. "Hello, back. Where are you? And who are you?" Yarni replied

"This is Zurri and I am down here in cell six. What's yo' name?"

"Yarni," She was as happy as a kid in a candy shop to finally hear a friendly voice.

"What you doing in here? And didn't they just let you out a few days ago?"

"Yep. How you know?"

"Because I was back here then too."

"For real, well why you didn't say nothing then?" she asked suspiciously.

"I don't be fuckin' wit these broke-down chicks in here. I don't be trying to make friends wit none of them. They all fake as hell. These bitches in here is just like the hoes on the street: backstabbing, throat-cutting, larceny-jealous-hearted, snitching bitches, who don't mean themselves no good, so how could they possibly mean me some good?"

"I feel you, gurll! You ain't never lied!" Yarni felt a little comfort to finally be talking to someone who could actually feel her struggle.

"Too bad it caused me to come in here to figure that shit out," Zurri said.

"What are you in here for?"

"In jail period or back here in the dungeon?"

"Both? If you don't mind telling me, I know it's kind of personal." Yarni didn't mean to pry. She knew how she felt when people tried to inquire about her situation.

"I don't usually tell anybody, but for some reason, you seem cool. I am in for worthless checks. And back here in the dungeon for a variety of things, except for dyking, you name it. Cussing out a few deputies, arguing with these broke-down chicks, not following direct orders, blah, blah, blah, and the list goes on."

"Oh, okay." Yarni smiled to herself because she could tell that Zurri was a bit ghetto, but cool. "You got kids?" Zurri asked.

"Nope, thank God for that. You?"

"I got three."

"Oh, my God, who got them while you're in here?"

"My family."

"Well, that's good."

Zurri and Yarni talked all day and night. Zurri was impressed with Yarni, as Yarni was intrigued with Zurri. She learned all about Zurri's struggle as a single mother. When Zurri started thinking about her children, she got depressed and Yarni comforted her. She felt it was God who put them together because time really flew by. When she was released from isolation to go back into jail population, she was sad because she realized she wouldn't be able to talk to Zurri anymore. Zurri had to be in the dungeon for the rest of her time in the jail. She promised Zurri she would write her through the mail and they would always keep in touch, no matter what the storm in each other's life was.

Another issue that annoyed Yarni was the women guards. They were so disrespectful. They thought that all females in jail either got high or were tricking when they were on the streets. They tried their best to humiliate the women inmates as much as they could.

There was one female correctional officer who processed her the first day she'd turned herself in. Her name was Officer Rita Plenty. She recognized that Yarni was different from the other girls who'd came through the jail. She was certain that Yarni had been "caught up." Yarni's mannerisms, the clothes she wore in, and the way she spoke, were confirmation. Once Yarni was removed from work release, Deputy Plenty would observe her actions. One day she accompanied Yarni to the nurse and they spoke briefly.

"Why were you removed from work release?" She interrogated Yarni.

"Before I was arrested, I was in the process of finishing my last year in college. I wanted to finish, so when I left the jail in the mornings I'd attend my classes." Yarni shrugged her shoulders and said in a nonchalant manner, "Somehow they found out."

"I am not mad at you. I would've done the same thing," Deputy Plenty said in a sincere tone.

Later that day, Deputy Plenty was escorting a male inmate, who was Castro's homeboy, to the nurse.

"Could you give a kite"—a note folded up real small; inmates usually throw them to the recipient—"to Yarnise Pitman for me?"

"How you know Ms. Pitman?" She reached out her hand to get the kite from him.

"Yo, she's good peoples. She goes all out for the people she loves, that's why she's in here now." He explained the lifestyle Yarni lived on the street and that Yarni was "real." He had only good things to say about Yarni. Deputy Plenty felt compassion for her plight and they became friends. She made Yarni's stay at the Henpeck County Jail a little more comfortable. She was concerned that Yarni had lost too much weight. She'd bring in food from home to her. She'd pass messages between Yarni and Castro. Yarni never asked Deputy Plenty to do any favors for her. She respected the fact that, this was her job and her livelihood. Although the circumstances they met under were odd, they turned out to be genuine friends. Deputy Plenty would tell Yarni of problems she was dealing with in her own life. Yarni was a good listener, and she offered the officer some good advice.

When Castro heard that she was being housed on the other side of the jail, from where he was, he got one of the trustees to pass her some food, toiletries, and some cigarettes. Yarni didn't smoke, but she could sell them. The facility she was being housed at was smoke-free. Cigarettes were sold for four dollars per cigarette. Everybody wanted cigarettes. They were hard to come by. Whenever a female acquired cigarettes, the smokes were treated if it was dope on the streets.

She hung as tough as she could, but jail eventually corrupted Yarni. Her attitude was so bitter. She wasn't afraid of anything. There was no fear in her heart. She developed a jailhouse mentality and learned to master the ins and outs of jail. She realized if she socialized with one of the guys who worked in the kitchen she could get extra helpings of the food she liked. She also flirted with some of the male deputies. Yarni learned to manipulate while she was in jail. She once stopped up her commode, so the deputy on duty had no choice but to call the plumber, who was a trustee. When the trustee came into her cell, he passed her a package full of cigarettes and marijuana, which she, of course, sold. She would have never touched marijuana, tried to sell it, or experiment with it on the streets.

Jail introduced Yarni to a world she'd never known and if she had never experienced confinement, she would never be able to relate to anyone else who'd been there and done that, to the extent as her being locked up had. Maybe her incarceration made it just that much harder to walk out and turn her back on Des. Her imprisonment may have been a factor as to why she never stopped fighting for Des's release upon her discharge. Or maybe her own incarceration was the reason that she always dropped a card in the mail to other inmates she knew, and never seem to forget anybody dear to her in prison, as the average person may have.

"*M-a-a-ill c-a-l-l,*" yelled the high-pitched voiced deputy. She called out Yarni's name.

My Dearest Yarni,
What have you let that nigga get you into? Why didn't you let me know what was going on with you? I am crazy worried about you. Please don't shut me out. I know you need me right now. I am here for you, baby. I love you unconditionally. That will never change. This wasn't in my plan for you. I know that you are definitely a warrior. You'll be O.K. and no storm lasts forever.

You have got to cool down. You can't allow them broke-down hoes to run up your time. You only have to be there for a few more months. Don't put yourself in a situation that could get you a street charge and add more time to your sentence. I know you ain't accustomed to this jail shit, so focus on what you going to do when you get out of there. Them hoes going to be there when you leave.

One thing to think on, if somebody controls your emotions, they can control your attitude. If they can control your attitude, then they control your actions. If someone can control your actions, then they control your destiny. You do the time, baby, don't let the time do you.

Let me know what the hell is going on with your case!

Much love,
Des

It took her two weeks to get up the nerve to write Des. Let the truth be told, she knew Des was the only one, besides God, who could carry her through this whole ordeal.

Once Yarni got Des's letter, she turned her focus elsewhere. She started doing the time, not allowing the time to do her. She signed up for every recreational activity the jail offered. Every opportunity to get out of the dayroom she participated in. She wrote the sheriff, the judge, as well as the governor, one letter a week, asking for a sentence reduction or to be placed on home incarceration. They wouldn't respond, but she diligently wrote them.

Whenever Bengee knew that Yarni was going to call, he would be at Gloria's house to talk to her. He'd send cards, letters, and money, even though he knew that she had money already. He never visited her. He claimed "visitors made prisoners." That was just an excuse.

Yarni had mixed feelings about Bengee. She never totally grasped the concept of exactly why *she* was sitting in jail. Was it because of the fact that she was loyal to Bengee and the principles she'd been taught about the people she loved? Was it that she knew her mother was very submissive to the man she loved? Or, was it because she loved Bengee?

She sat Indian-style on her three-inch thick mattress trying to make sense of the trial.

Yarni sobbed. This was the first time in her life she'd regretted not consulting her mother. *My mother would have never let me get myself into this mess.*

Even though Yarni felt like she was at her lowest point in her life, she never thought for one minute that God had left her or forsaken her. She never knew why going to jail had to be her destiny. She never asked God, "Why me, Lord." She only asked God to make her stronger and asked what was it that He wanted her to learn from this experience? Every night before Yarni would go to sleep she would pull out her Bible and read Psalm 23, or Matthew 11:25–30. She'd also pray that God remove her from that situation. Yarni thanked God in advance for removing her from jail. She didn't know how exactly God was going to pull it off, but she knew and believed, with all her heart, that she wasn't going to do the full ten months.

One day, a girl named Cyn came in the day-room. She knew Cyn from the street.

"Girl, not trying to piss in your Cheerios, but Bengee has gotten *bucckkk* wild since you left the streets. He is always in the clubs balling out of control, buying three and four buckets of Moët at a time. And to top it off, my man told me that Bengee be having strip parties on a regular. Yarni, Bengee is out of control."

"Oh, for real," Yarni said in a calm tone, showing no emotion. Then Yarni continued to carry on the conversation. "How's your daughter, Cyn? I bet she's gotten big, huh?" Anything to dilute a conversation about Bengee.

"Girl, she has! She weighs one hundred and four pounds, and is only nine years old." Cyn answered Yarni while searching her face for some kind of sentiment. Cyn couldn't believe Yarni wasn't upset about the news she'd just given about her man. She just had to let her know that her man was out of control. Cyn knew it was bothering Yarni. She thought Yarni would go to her cell and cry, or at the very least call Bengee and cuss him out.

Yarni's feelings were hurt. She didn't know if she should take what Cyn said into consideration or not. Chicks were always trying to kick a sister when she was down, this she did know. And Cyn wanted to see her break. She was yearning for her to crumble, but Yarni continued the conversation like the news that Cyn had just given didn't mean anything. They sat and talked for the next hour, and Yarni didn't return to her cell until the bell rung at 11:00 p.m. for lockdown.

The next day, she tried calling Melanie's house collect, for the first time since she'd been locked up. She heard Melanie's voice when she picked up the phone and said "Hello." Melanie didn't take the call. She thought that maybe Melanie hit the wrong button or something. She knew that there had to have been some mistake. She tried two more times and Melanie still rejected the call. She couldn't believe it. Melanie had been her ace since sixth grade and now she wouldn't even take a dollar phone call. That just intensified the whole situation.

The nerve *of Melanie, I never knew just how petty she was. She doesn't know if it's* an emergency or what. *Dag, I thought we were better than that!* The sound of the dial tone in her ear from Melanie hurt Yarni's feelings. Was she concerned that Yarni was going to run up her bill? That couldn't have been the circumstances because Bengee or Gloria would've taken care of the bill. Why would the bill even been an issue?

Yarni remembered something Gloria once told her a few years ago. "You'll always find out who your true friends are when you're down and out." The whole time Melanie and Yarni had been friends, this was the one time she ever needed Melanie for anything at all. Melanie had forfeited her friendship with Yarni at that very moment. To comfort herself, she simply looked at it as it only cost out 536 dollars to find that her so-called friend wasn't worthy of her friendship.

She didn't want to call Gloria to involve her in what was going on. Gloria couldn't find out any of these things about Bengee because she knew if she let Gloria know anything bad about Bengee, Gloria would always harbor ill feelings toward him. When mothers and family members got involved in a couple's relationship, they still held a grudge, even if the couple got back together. She knew that she couldn't let Gloria know anything until she was sure it was completely over between them.

After a lengthy deliberation, Yarni decided that she wouldn't mention to Bengee any of the rumors she'd heard. She'd keep them to herself for now, but prepare herself in case the rumors were true.

After being in jail for exactly five months—a total of seven months, counting the two that she was on work release—Yarni's lawyer came to visit her. He told her that she had a court date scheduled for the next day. The judge agreed to hear arguments for her alternative sentencing. He told her not to get her hopes up too high because he was going to take into consideration that she had gotten removed from the work-release program. Not one ounce of doubt set in, for she was certain that she was being released. This was only God working on her behalf. She knew the judge didn't have any jurisdiction over God. That night was the first night that she had actually slept for the entire seven months.

When they called Yarni, she only had fifteen minutes to get ready for court. While she waited in the holding cell she wasn't a bit nervous. She had a sense of peace and security that she was about to be released.

She overheard the judge having very little sympathy for the defendants before her, but when she was called to go in front of the judge, she could feel that she was walking on still waters. The judge had a sense of compassion for her, she could sense. It was almost as if he wasn't the same person who had sentenced all the people in front of her to harsh sentences.

He reviewed her letters of character from her minister, a U of R professor, and her mother. He allowed her to explain why she was taken off of work release. Yarni explained to the judge that she simply wanted to get the degree that she had worked so hard for. She made it clear that what she did was wrong, but that she felt it was what she had to do, as she knew now, she was a convicted felon. She may never be allowed to make her dream come true, so she thought at least she could finish out her classes. But she was unable to because she was removed from work release.

Yarni went on to tell the judge that no matter how much jail time she had to end up doing, no time could ever outweigh the punishment of her not being able to complete her studies. The judge took all these things into consideration. He suspended the rest of her time providing she volunteer one hundred hours of her time mentoring teenagers, report to a probation officer for the next year, and not write the judge any more letters.

Yarni was released from jail that same day. Before she left, she asked the deputy to take her to isolation to see her friend, Zurri. She hugged Zurri, gave her all the canteen she had left over, colored T-shirts and socks along with Gloria's address, and phone number. Zurri was happy to see Yarni leaving and told her she would be going home in a couple of months.

Yarni had written over twenty letters to the judge and now that chapter of her life was closed.

8

The Wake-Up Call

While they waited on the paperwork to come over from the courts to the jail so Yarni could be released, the deputy sheriff informed Gloria that it would be approximately three hours before Yarni's discharge.

Gloria left and went to Regency Square. She bought Yarni a Guess jean outfit along with some Air Max Nike sneakers. She wasn't sure if Yarni would be able to even wear the jeans because she had lost so much weight. Yarni was wearing a size 8 before she went away to jail, so Gloria got one size smaller. When Yarni went to court, the outfit she wore was falling off of her.

It would have been easier for Gloria to go to Yarni and Bengee's house to get some sweatpants or something from there. When Yarni called the night before informing Gloria on her court date, she specifically told Gloria not to tell anyone, not even Bengee. Gloria immediately called Ukrop's and ordered a "welcome home" cake, as well as balloons. She wanted to do more, but she was trying to get back to the jail on time so she could get the deputy to pass the new clothes to Yarni.

Yarni was in shock, riding in the car. She rolled down the window, something she never did because she always rode under air-conditioning. Today she wanted to smell fresh air and admire the trees.

The little things we take for granted and never appreciate, she thought to herself. Her mother took her to Hooters. Yarni loved Hooters chicken wings. Gloria wanted to spend the rest of the day out with her, but Yarni only wanted to go home and take a long, hot bubble bath. Gloria understood, and she took Yarni to Crestar Bank to let her cash the check the jail had given her for the balance of her inmate's account. She then dropped Yarni off at home.

"Mommy, make sure I get in before you pull off. I don't know how Bengee is carrying it since I've been locked up. I hope he hasn't changed the locks. You know how men are. They'll switch up on you in a heartbeat." She said to her mother as if it was a joke, but her mother knew she was serious.

Gloria tried to be very selective of her response because she didn't want to ignite an argument with her daughter who had already been through enough. "Sweetie, you know you don't have to put up with no man's shit. I've always got a place for you. You're never too old to come home."

"I know, Mommy—I love you, and thanks for everything. I am sorry for all the heartache and embarrassment I've caused you."

Gloria could see the tears forming in Yarni's eyes. "Baby, don't feel bad. Don't start dwelling on the past. You've already paid your debt to society and the bottom line is, it doesn't matter if you'd murdered sixty people. I am still your mother and will always be here for you. You hear me?"

"Yeah, Mommy, I know. I just hate the fact that you can't live your life due to the fact you always have to come and rescue me from my constant drama."

"Honey, please. I've got a life and have been living it out to the fullest. Even got a man who loves me and wants to marry me," Gloria boasted as Yarni cut her off in surprise and astonishment.

"Back up, Mommy. What do you mean, You got a man, who loves you and wants to marry you?" Yarni put her hand on her hip and waited for Gloria's answer.

"Yeah, Sam and I are dating exclusively and he wants to marry me. I told him I am not sure because I don't know how you'd feel about me divorcing your father after all these years. And I—" Yarni interrupted.

"My father? Mommy, I don't care about you divorcing my father. As far as I'm concerned, you guys were divorced a long time ago. Mommy, I just want more than anything for you to be happy. I would like to meet this Sam person, though. You've got to give me the lowdown on him." Yarni was curious about this mystery man who had her mother glowing.

"Yarni, he's a good man! Oh, my goodness, he's a God-fearing man." Yarni could see the exhilaration all over her mother's face "He's wanted to meet you from day one. He's been so supportive to me throughout your whole detention term. I felt accountable because my husband and my daughter were both in jail. I blamed myself."

"Mommy, how dare you point the finger at yourself? You had nothing to do with any of our decisions."

"I know, baby, but I can't help but wonder where I went wrong?"

"Mommy, where did you go wrong? I could never ask for a better mother. You were the

perfect mother, and don't you dare blame yourself for my poor judgments and mistakes. As a
matter of fact, I don't think I'm ever having kids
because I could never fill your shoes."

"Oh, Yarni, that's so sweet." Gloria blushed as
she wiped the tears out of her eye.

"Did you tell Sam that I was in the clinker?"

"Yeah, I shared it with him. Sam has been by
my side. Every single time I came to visit you,
he waited patiently in the waiting area with
his cell phone and agenda book taking care of
his business until I was finished visiting you. I
always knew that he had more important things
he had to do, but he felt being with me right then
and there was far more significant than any business proposal. I knew you'd be uncomfortable
meeting him under those circumstances, and I
promised him that I'd introduce you two when
you came home."

"Mommy, I am so happy for you, and I can't
wait to meet him. You deserve this. I am going
to call you later to get details because I can't
believe you were holding out on me. Right now, I
gotta go. Love ya much!" Yarni shut the door and
walked up the sidewalk to her house.

When Yarni reached the door and put her key
in, it opened the lock. She walked into the house.
The first thing she spotted were her pictures

still in place. *That's a good sign,* she thought to herself. She thought again. *Pictures of me don't mean shit. That has no bearing on them shiesty hoes. Most of them are just trying to get theirs and cutting throat any way they can. So my picture still being up, what the hell does that mean?*

She walked over to the telephone. The caller ID held eighty numbers. She got a piece of paper out and wrote down every single number. Any number on there two to three times, she put a star by the number. Any number showing up more than three times, she put a question mark beside it. She also put down the names of each person showing on the caller ID, and took the paper and tucked it in the back of her wallet behind a picture of her godson just in case she might need to recall the numbers at a later date.

The trash was running over. It was smelling so she took it out. Half-empty Heineken and Corona bottles were all over the house.

When she looked in the refrigerator there were only beers and sodas. Then she looked in the freezer. It contained frozen, microwavable foods, pizza, Eggo waffles, and Hot Pockets; no meat, no veggies. Next, she went into the bedroom and found price tags from new clothes Bengee had bought, empty hangers and plastic from the dry cleaner's all over the place. The hamper was running over with dirty boxers, socks, and wife-beaters.

In the closet, there were a lot of club gear: gator boots, python-skin boots, gangsta hats. From the looks of things she could tell he had been going all out on the club tip. He always dressed real classy anyway. Her clothes were exactly how she'd left them. She noticed an Alan Furs coat bag hanging up and opened it. There was a full-length black-sable mink coat dangling there. She took the coat out and tried it on. While she was admiring it in the mirror she noticed that it had been engraved in the inside: *To My Yarni, All My Love, Bengee. How sweet,* she thought to herself. On the closet floor there was a hatbox with a mink hat inside and behind that box, was another one containing a mink collar and the gloves to match. Then she noticed a few Versace suits with the tags still on them. Yarni hugged herself, all wrapped up in fur, as she admired the coat in the mirror. *Bengee had been thinking of me while I was away.*

Yarni stripped the sheets off of the bed and replaced them with clean ones. She dusted and vacuumed because she could tell it had only been done once or twice since she'd been gone. She cleaned the house thoroughly. She wondered if she'd run across any bobby pins or anything that would indicate a female presence. She went through that house with a fine-toothed comb. She washed his clothes and got the house back in order to her liking. There was not one indication that any female had been there. She even looked under the bed to see if there was any underwear there. She remembered the first time she stayed over Rallo's house. Just to be spiteful, she left her underwear under his bed. She knew how women think. They're scandalous. It was their way of saying, "Oh yeah, you aren't the only one fucking your man. Here are my panties for the evidence, bitch!" What better proof?

After the house was spotless she lit Glade rainshower-scented candles throughout the house and took a hot bubble bath. She sat there for a while to try and gather her thoughts. As soon as she got out she wrapped herself in her pale-pink terry-cloth Victoria's Secret robe. Just then, she heard Bengee coming through the door. He knew immediately that Yarni was home. *But how did she pull this off?* he wondered to himself. He didn't care. He was just glad she was home.

"Yarni!" There she stood with her robe hanging open with nothing on under it. He dropped his keys, the bags he had in his hand, and his mouth fell open from the sight he had not seen in so long. He picked her up and spun her around. He could smell the scent of the "exotic bouquet" Victoria's Secret fragrance as he hugged her tight.

"I missed you so much." He grinned and brought her closer to engage in a passionate French kiss.

As his arms were around her, he lowered them and felt her naked, soft, round, tender, smooth "ummp, ummp, ummp" behind. When she placed her arms around his waist, he realized just how much he'd missed her. He started fondling her breast. He slowly moved from the breast down to her navel. Bengee dropped her robe on the floor, then laid her in front of the wood-burning fireplace. She started to quiver as he kissed her inner thighs. Both could feel the temperature rise and started to feel dizzy. She was trembling, about to burst into her climax when Bengee looked into her eyes with burning desire.

"Please don't stop," she moaned.

"Hold it baby, please don't cum now. I'm not ready for you to cum yet." He immediately moved from her upper body and proceeded to kiss her knees. He then slowly ran his tongue up and down her calves as he reached his hand to grab her right foot. He eased her Victoria's Secret bootie off and then slid off the left slipper. He slowly and methodically kissed and massaged her feet. The room began to spin as she was blazing with desire. She was yearning for him to insert his large penis. As he entered the tight, wet threshold, she tensed up. "Be gentle with me, baby, you know it hasn't been tampered with in a while," she whispered in a seductive voice.

He was gentle as he moved in and out, on top of her as he caressed her neck. She moaned, closing her eyes, trying to enjoy these few moments of pleasure, what she'd been missing while locked away. As he stroked her faster, her eyes popped open while she reached to grab his back, trying to hold on. He gazed into her eyes and she into his. She saw tears of passion, tears of love, as he was about to explode.

"I can't take it no more," Bengee groaned. "I'm about to bust."

"I don't want you to, baby," she said as Bengee shook his head, with sweat dripping on her as he slowed down until he couldn't hold it anymore. His eyes rolled in the back of his head as he sighed. He lay on top of her for a few minutes, then licked sweat from her dripping, wet body.

They took a shower together, and Bengee decided he needed a nap. Yarni lay down beside him. He fell off to sleep. Yarni sat in the bed, flipping channels. Bengee's eyes popped open at the *click, click* of the TV. He felt bad he left her awake. He sat on the edge of the bed, got up and stretched.

He told her to get dressed so they could go out. Yarni didn't know what to put on. So much weight had fallen off of her while she was in the clinker. She knew that the style had changed, so she didn't know what to wear. Then she realized one thing: When she shopped she bought classy attire, not faddish clothes. Fads are in today, gone tomorrow. On that note, she dressed.

Bengee took her to the mall. He wanted to take her out of town to shop, but it was too late. Drive to Georgetown, spend the night, go shopping, and come back the next day, was what he suggested. She said no, she wanted to sleep in her own bed her first night home from the clinker. They could do that the next morning. They ended up going to eat at Outback Steakhouse. Bengee watched as she ordered her food and he thought to himself how much he had truly missed the little things about Yarni while she was gone away: her charisma, her bubbly personality, as well as her classy ways.

When they arrived home, Bengee had arranged for the whole living room to be filled up with balloons along with *welcome home* streamers and banners. He had a path of rose petals leading to the bedroom. When she reached the bedroom the fireplace was going. He made passionate love to Yarni while lying in front of the fireplace. This was the best sex they'd ever had. After the love-making they laid awake in the bed whispering sweet nothings in each other's ears. He stressed to Yarni how much he loved her and how she was a soldier. On that word—*soldier*—she sat up in the bed and gazed dead into Bengee's eyes. He hit her with the pillow, to break her crazed gaze.

"What is it? Why you looking at me like that?" Bengee said.

"Please don't call me a soldier again. I'll never consider myself a soldier. Soldiers are expendable, and I've long outgrown that position. If you want to address my strengths, call me a warrior, a champion or a survivor. But never, ever refer to me as a soldier. No offense taken, just please never call me that again." Yarni laid back down, turned on her side, with her back facing Bengee, and pulled the covers over her shoulders. Bengee put his arm around her.

"Baby, I apologize. I love you so much. Good night."

The next week was almost like a fairy tale. He took her shopping, and spent every second with her. Never did he leave her sight, only to use the restroom. After being up under Yarni for a whole week nonstop, he told her he had an appointment the next morning. She didn't want to go with him. Rest was all she wanted. He told her he'd be back by 1:00 p.m., so she needed to be dressed. A long velvet Gantos box was what he placed on the bed for her before he left. "Here, put this on. We're going to lunch, and I'd like to see you in this."

He arrived back earlier than she expected. Lying across the bed watching Yarni get dressed, he fantasized as she put on her teal Christian Dior thongs with the bra to match. He fantasized about all the good times they had the past week. He loved Yarni so much he wished that he could be the man that she needed and deserved. He wondered to himself: *Damn, I'm a cruddy nigga. How in the world did God manage to bless me with such a submissive woman?* He knew in his heart he wasn't deserving of Yarni. He prayed that she'd never draw those conclusions.

Once Yarni was dressed, he told her that they were going to the Fisherman's Wharf for lunch in Virginia Beach on the water. She loved seafood. As they left the house she noticed an SUV parked across the street with a big red bow tied around it with thirty-day temporary tags on it. She glanced at the truck, and made the comment of how somebody was blessed to receive a new truck. She mentioned to Bengee, "That must be the new body-style Land Cruiser, and it is tight"

"Yeah, it's the top-of-the-line, baby. Only two other people in Richmond got one besides you," Bengee said and handed her the keys on a key chain that said *I love you.* Bracing herself, she was full of astonishment. She'd been given an array of cars, but this was top-notch. She jumped in the truck. Bengee had taken it upon himself to stop at Willie's Records and Tapes and purchase all the CD's he thought fit. They were already placed in the CD changer. She displayed her tender thanks with oodles of hugs and kisses.

"It was the least I could do. You're worthy of more than this. That's for sure, sweetness," Bengee said as he kissed her and smiled in a modest way.

When they reached the Fisherman's Wharf, she caught sight of a chartered bus. "If you want, we can go somewhere else to eat. I know how impatient you are, and it looks as if it may be a lengthy wait," Yarni said.

"Sweetness, I don't care about a delay as long as I am waiting with you," Yarni said as he kissed her on the forehead. "I love you, baby."

As they walked in, the hostess immediately took them to a back reserved section. As the door opened she heard voices in a harmony. *"Welcome home, Yarni."* People started to clap. She observed all the familiar faces, such as her mother, her aunt, and practically her whole family. Her godson's mother, Cara, was there as well as Rita, the deputy sheriff, Stephanie, and loads of friends. Gloria made it known to Yarni that Bengee had arranged everything: The chartered buses to transport everybody to Virginia Beach, the decorations, the guests, the photographer, and paid in full for everything.

"Yarni," Gloria grabbed her arm, "I'd like you to meet somebody, a dear friend of mine."

The handsome, light-complexioned, clean-cut, conservative-looking man wearing small, oval-shaped brown Fendi frames with freckles on his face interrupted with his deep voice. "Oh, I'm just your friend, huh?"

Gloria's face glowed. "Pardon me," as she held her hand over her heart. "This is my fiancé, Sam, and Sam, this is . . . my Yarni."

Yarni smiled as she watched her mother blush. She extended her hand to shake Sam's hand. He took her in his arms and hugged her. "Yarni, I'm glad to see you home." Yarni embraced him back.

"Thanks for being there for my mother, Sam, I owe you big-time," Yarni said in appreciation.

"No, you don't have to thank me. I love your mother."

"Judging by the look on her face, I would say she loves you too." Yarni moved in closer to Sam and spoke to him in a lower tone. "I can't recall when I've ever seen my mother glow over a man. To be honest, I've never ever seen my mother with a man." Sam laughed.

"Yarnise, you have a roomful of people here to see you. Don't you think you should tend to them?" Gloria interrupted with an embarrassed look on her face.

"Sam, it was very much a pleasure meeting you." Yarni looked at her mother and smiled, then looked over to Sam. "Don't worry, Sam, we'll talk soon." She winked and walked off.

After Yarni greeted all her guests, she opened her arms and embraced Bengee, to show her appreciation for everything.

For the next two weeks, everything was peaches and cream between Bengee and Yarni. She fully understood that Bengee had business to attend to in the streets and she tried not to blow up his cell phone while he was away from home. She was completely aware that in the street life, he couldn't trust a living soul, every bush shook, and it was easy for somebody to make a mistake.

As far as Yarni was concerned, there was no room for any errors regarding Bengee. Yarni felt that when Bengee was in the streets, he needed to be totally focused on what he was doing. She never distracted him unless it was an emergency. Bengee would check in on a regular basis anyway. They'd always eat dinner together. After dinner, he might go back out for a little while, but he'd always return home at a respectable hour.

However, one particular Friday night, she'd been out all day shopping with Cara. Cara and Yarni checked in with Bengee, and he mentioned that he was not feeling well, and would probably beat her home.

When she arrived home at 12:35 the house was empty. Bengee's number wasn't on the caller ID. She took a shower, jumped in the bed, and fell off to sleep. When she rolled over to hug Bengee, there was no Bengee and now it was 5:26 a.m. He wasn't in the den, and his car wasn't in the garage. What the hell?

This was so unlike Bengee, so she began to worry. She called his cell phone. He didn't answer. The voice mailbox was full and he didn't answer at the shop. She immediately began to imagine the worst. Was he locked up? Was he hurt somewhere? Had he been in an accident? Or even worse, was he dead? Oh, my God! Lord, please.

Yarni called the Richmond city jail, Henrico, Hanover, and Chesterfield county jails. She called MCV, St. Mary's, Henrico Doctors', and Chippenham Hospital. None had heard of Benjamin Whales. Yarni felt panicked. She didn't know whom else to call. All she could do was wait. After all, she was his next of kin, so if anything happened, they'd have to notify her. She began to pace the floor. She sat down on the couch, turned the TV on, and flipped through the channels. Her mind couldn't focus on anything, wondering if Bengee was dead or alive. Tears started forming in her eyes, when she pondered the fact that she'd been incarcerated for seven months, totally separated from Bengee, and now that they'd finally been reunited, she'd couldn't deal with the thought of him being removed from her life. Just then the phone rang. She hesitated. Was it a nurse from the hospital, a homeboy of Bengee's calling to present her with bad news of Bengee's whereabouts? Her heart was racing. Her palms sweaty as she grabbed the phone; she saw it was Bengee's cell-phone number. *Oh, thank God, he's alive*, she thought. *No, maybe it's someone else using his phone.*

"Hello?" she said into the receiver, holding her breath.

"Hey baby, it's me," Bengee said.

"Are you okay? I've been worried sick!"

"I am okay. now. I am on my way home. I'll explain everything when I get there." Yarni began to breathe again.

After hanging up the phone with Bengee she started to cook breakfast. When Bengee came in, Yarni ran over to him and exploded in his arms. But when she smelled the strong scent of Irish Spring soap, a soap that they didn't use, she knew there was someone else. The whole time he was out, never once was she worried about Bengee being with another girl. His well-being was her only concern. *The nerve of him, to have me up worrying myself to death. If he wanted to stay out all night, all he had to do was pick up the phone and call to let me know he was staying out.* Her body stiffened, and in response, he intuitively began to run down a well-rehearsed version of where he was.

"I stopped by Tank's house for a drink. I ended up having a few. I was drunk as hell. I laid on Tank's sofa and fell asleep, and when I woke up, it was light outside. I jumped up and came ."

She looked as the words fell clumsily out of his mouth, studied every facial expression and memorized it in her mind.

Damn, does he really think I am that dumb to believe this bull? Yeah, I might've been lovesick and stupid enough to throw my whole life away for him, but, trust and believe, brother, I am not as naive as you perceive me to be. This dude don't believe shit stinks until he's knee-deep in it. As bad as I want to jump out of this chair and throw a freaking "Yarni attack," I will not. I will keep my composure. And guess what, Mr. Bengee? I will teach you a lesson about being an inconsiderate nigga and playing on my intelligence as well. These words that Yarni wanted to say to Bengee, she kept to herself. She would bide her time.

Yarni recalled something she'd overheard Des tell Slim. "When somebody does you wrong and you feel they need to be taught a lesson, you don't always act right then. You play your position. Make them get so comfortable with you not reacting. They start slipping because they think you are weak. Then you react by doing the same thing to them. But you do it in a keener way, the way that it should have been done in the first place. Once you make your move, the cat won't know what hit him."

Yarni laughed to herself, thinking this joker was wild. She recalled the initial phone call. She realized what that was all about. It was a "vibe call". He was only calling to check the vibe, to see if she was upset at him for staying out all night, and so he wouldn't be caught off guard, and he could prepare on the ride home. She was not mad because she played cool. Now she had the upper hand. She could look in his eyes and see he felt guilty and guilt will make you *tilt!*

Bengee continued to play his hand, saying whatever he thought Yarni wanted to hear. "Baby, we're going to Regency Square Mall to Fink's Jewelry to look at a Rolex. I want to buy a new one for myself and we need his and hers Rolexs anyway."

She went along, fixed his breakfast, straightened up the house, dressed, and accompanied Bengee to the mall where he purchased the watches, plus a new Movado watch just for everyday, kick-around wear. He spent the rest of the day with her, but it was clearly timed. He informed her he had one vital run he had to make. He claimed it would only take an hour. Yarni did not object. That was perfect. It was just enough time to execute her plan.

Yarni gathered some things, threw them in an overnight bag, and left the house. She was hurt and didn't want to leave, but as she contemplated, one thing came to her mind that gave her the inspiration to walk out of that door. *A girl's gotta do what a girl's gotta do!*

On The Way Back Home:

Darchelle was very pretty. Some said she and Yarni favored each other a bit, physically. They both had the same caramel complexion and smooth skin. Darchelle had recently streaked her hair with bronze color exactly like Yarni. Their builds were the same. The only difference was that Yarni was more shapely and about two inches shorter than Darchelle.

Darchelle was an upscale freak, and boy, could she give a blow job. She had a nice set of false teeth; she would take them out when it was time to give her state-of-the-art blowjob. With her having no teeth, she could suck the chrome off of a '64 Chevy. He never took her anywhere. He only saw her at her apartment. Occasionally, he helped her out with bills, as well as gave her pocket change. One hundred dollars was her maximum. He'd never give her, or spend more on her, more than that at one time. One hundred dollars was nothing to him. He wiped his butt with that chump change. Darchelle tried her hand with Bengee every time she saw him. It was the same conversation, day in and day out.

"Bengee, can I have five hundred dollars?" Bengee would laugh hysterically and look into Darchelle's face, holding his stomach as if what she'd asked for was so funny.

"Darchelle, now be real, how am I going to get five hundred dollars' worth of pussy out of you when I'm a two-minute brother and my girl is at home straight taxing me? I gotta make sure home is taken care of, first and foremost. You can take this hundred dollars or I can keep it in my pocket."

As he continued to drive, he reflected over the stunt Darchelle had pulled last night when he told her that he couldn't be bothered with her anymore. Like a champ, she accepted the rejection, but only had one request. She wanted to freak him one last time before he walked out of the door for good. She did everything humanly possible. After she finished, she asked him did he still want to call it quits. He said, yes, although he wanted to give her a standing ovation for the encore performance she had just put on. Instead of her cussing and fussing, she freaked and sucked on him, until he fell asleep. When he looked at the clock, he dozed off to sleep. He hadn't realized that this scandalous broad had set the clock back so he wouldn't realize the real time and leave. When the sun started to beam through her window, he woke up, and looked at his cell phone for the real time. He cussed her out, smacked her around, took a shower, and raced home to Yarni. Darchelle was history, a done deal!

What else could I do to make this up to Yarni? he asked himself. *I bought her a Rolex, plus I am going to take her to a bed-and-breakfast*

*this weekend. She'll get over this. She loves me.
It ain't like she is going to leave me. Leave me?
Yeah right, where she going? Who's going to
treat her as I treat her? Who's going to provide
for her as I? Des? But where is Des? Locked up!
And he's seven hours away. Yeah, right, she
can't run to Des. She'll be okay in a few days
when this blows over,* he convinced himself. He
drove up to a street vendor selling flowers and
bought the whole bucket.

Back at the house he didn't see Yarni's truck in
the driveway. He walked in the house. No lights
or TV were on. His immediate thought was that
she ran to the store. He cut the light on in the
bedroom and saw a note in the middle of the bed.

> *Bengee,*
> *There's no need to worry. I will be back.
> Don't know a definite time. No need to go
> through the hassle I went through calling
> all the jails, and hospitals, because I am
> just fine.*
> *XOXO,*
> *Sweetness*

"That bitch," he screamed, dialing her cell
phone, but the phone started ringing in the house.
He looked on the night table and the phone was

there on the charger. He flipped through every single contact in her cell phone, and he called every number on the caller ID, looking for Yarni. He called Cara, but Cara hadn't heard from Yarni since the day before at Awful Arthur's. Suspicious of Cara, he rode past her house to see if Yarni's truck was parked anywhere in the vicinity. Yarni nor the truck was nowhere in sight. He called Gloria, and of course she was going to say she didn't see Yarni. Later he drove past Gloria's house at 4:00 a.m. to see if Yarni's truck was there. He even parked three houses down the street, walked to Gloria's house, and crept around the back to see if Yarni's TV was on in her old room. He knew Yarni couldn't sleep without the TV on, so if it was on, she would be there. There wasn't any TV playing, which meant no Yarni. Bengee returned home to lie in the bed, awake all night long. His mind started playing tricks on him as he lay there. He'd hear a noise as if someone could've been at the door. He jumped out of the bed, only to realize it wasn't anything at all. He saw a light through the bedroom window. He got up to look, wishing it was Yarni's car lights.

Eleven o'clock on Sunday morning, Bengee got dressed to go to her church. If Yarni did nothing else, every single Sunday she was at church, but this Sunday Yarni wasn't there. *Maybe something happened to her. Did the truck get a flat? Yarni doesn't know how to change a flat. Did she get car jacked?*

Yarni coasted down the street to scope out the house, after her long journey from seeing Des. She didn't see Bengee's car anywhere in sight. There was no need in calling him. She knew he would be bothered that she didn't come home the night before, especially since it was now 11:15 the next night. That's exactly what she wanted. *Now he's got a taste of his own medicine.*

She was a little frightened when she approached the house. She kept in mind that Bengee was on the psycho side. He had never pulled any crazy stunts with her, but she heard rumors of him being abusive in his other relationships. He'd even admitted some of it to her. He'd promised her that he'd never put his hands on her. So far, he had kept his word. She never gave him a reason to fly off the handle at her. She was the perfect girlfriend. At the same time, just because she was obedient and very submissive to him did not mean that she was weak. The walk up the sidewalk was a very long one. Yarni's heart was beating three times its normal rate. She was prepared for whatever was about to happen. She had already drawn the conclusion that things

were about to hit the fan. Men always try to
reverse the charges and put everything on the
woman when they are the ones who are wrong.
This was exactly what she was expecting from
Bengee. She started laughing as the thought: *He
may fight, he may fuss, but nothing he can say
or do, can take away how he felt lying in that
bed lonely by himself worried about me!*

Yarni entered the house. The kitchen light was
the only light on. She walked through the living
room. She could tell that Bengee had a tantrum.
One of her lamps was broken along with a couple
of her crystal figurines. She proceeded down the
hall and noticed a clothes hanger on the floor.
She took three more steps. There was another
clothes hanger. She walked in the bedroom.
The bed was unmade. There were hangers and
some empty shoe boxes all over the bed and the
floor near the closet. She looked in the closet. All
Bengee's clothes were gone.

She laughed to herself and came to the conclusion that if he took his things, that was something
he wanted to do anyway. *Rest assured. It's not
over yet. It's too easy.* She smirked knowingly as
she shook her head in amusement. They had too
much invested. Bengee could be unpredictable,
but one thing she knew: He'd be calling. *Maybe
not tonight, oh, but trust and believe, Bengee is*

going to call. He's going to want an explanation about where I've been. Yarni unpacked her bag, took a shower, pulled out a book, and began to read.

At 2:00 a.m., the phone rang. She looked on the caller ID and it was an unavailable number. She answered. The caller hung up. Thirty minutes later, the phone rang again. She saw Bengee's number on the caller ID. *I knew he'd be calling. I know him like a book*, she thought as she picked up the phone.

"Hello?" Yarni said.

"Oh, you'd finally remembered where you lived, huh?" Bengee said in a sarcastic tone.

"You moved out, so why do you care when I come home?"

"Yeah, I might've moved out, but the last time I checked, you had a routine, out by nine in by five, playing housewife and shit, so where were you? You got lost, took a wrong turn or what?"

"What is this, the third degree? You wanna play twenty questions? I didn't bother to question you about the other night, did I?"

"On the real, you can't question me, I'm the man. I'm the one who makes all this possible. I pay the mortgage and every other bill and tab you run up."

"Yeah, you right. But keep this in mind—what's good for the goose is good for the gander."

"Yarni, we're not going to get into a heated debate because there is just no win with you. The bottom line is, I was worried about you. I didn't know if you were dead or alive."

"It ain't so nice when the tables are turned. Reminds me of that old saying, it ain't fun when the rabbit got the gun," Yarni said.

"You always got something slick to say out of your mouth.

"Look, baby, I'm on my way home." As upset as he was and determined to leave Yarni, he just couldn't.

"Home? Look, Bengee, this house isn't a revolving door. Either you're here permanent or you can stay wherever the hell you are at."

Bengee returned home and Yarni never had another problem with him pulling an all-nighter.

9

Love Is Blind

After the all-nighter episode with Bengee, Yarni knew that he could not be trusted. Yarni ran to Ukrop's in Bengee's car, and when she opened the trunk to put her bags in it—"Oh my God!" She got the shock of her life. She stood in the parking lot in astonishment as she stood there looking at the explicit photos that she saw scattered across the trunk of the car. She guessed they were taken while she was locked up. Some of the explicit photos were of stripper broads, and some were of Darchelle.

Darchelle was planning a shock of her own. She called Yarni at the beauty parlor and told her that she was pregnant with Bengee's baby, although she really wasn't. Plus, she played the dirty-drawers trick. She went and purchased a duplicate pair of Bengee's boxers and washed them to make them look worn. And when she saw Yarni's truck parked in the mall, she hung the boxers on her side-view mirror with a note: *Are these your man's boxers?*

Yarni would not be outdone. *No, no, no, I won't get mad, I'll just get even.* She pulled out her address book, and addressed a bunch of envelopes to all the guys she knew that were in jail. She made copies of the photos she found in Bengee's trunk, extra copies of the one of Darchelle with her legs wide open, and mailed them off. She sent the extras along with a chain letter so they could pass it on to their homeboys locked up with them.

Yarni also acquired Bengee's code to his cell phone voice mail. It was easy for Yarni to figure out the code. Men would like to think they were so smart, but they really didn't apply themselves. Men codes were usually their kids' birthdays, their address, mother's address, last four digits of their Social Security—6969, 1234, 9999, or something to that effect. She'd listen to his messages secretly. Never would she speak on anything she heard, nor would she erase any of the messages. She'd leave them new and would only use the information to her advantage, like if a female left a message about a time they were supposed to meet. Yarni would simply have something planned for Bengee and herself to do around that same time.

When Yarni arrived home from her friend Cara's baby shower, Bengee was lying across the bed with a nonchalant look on his face. Immediately, she knew that there was something wrong. She drew the conclusion that Bengee was a little frustrated because the past week, she'd been taking so much time planning the shower that she hadn't spent much quality time with him. She jumped on the bed and gave him a seductive kiss. He kissed her back, but she could tell by his body language that something was wrong.

"What's wrong, baby?" Yarni asked, in a whiny tone.

"I need to tell you something, but I just can't." She could see the hurtful expression on his face, and was trying to read the look. It was a look she'd never seen before.

"Baby, all the things we've been through, it's nothing that you can't share with me. You know that." She was as comforting as she knew how to be. What could it be? Bengee just shook his head, as his eyes got tearful.

"Oooohhhh, baby, it's going to be all right. I can't help you if you don't let me know what's bothering you," Yarni said putting her arm around Bengee to console him. "Is it someone else? Did you get somebody pregnant? Is it something I did? Do you want me to move out?

Did somebody pass away and die? Do you want to break up?"

Bengee shook his head in disgust, "No, Yarni, I love you so much. Everyday I'm around you I realize just how lucky I am to have you in my corner. I never want to live life without you."

"Then, what is it?" She was anxious to know just what had him so distraught. He kept hesitating to tell her and he wouldn't speak a word. There was a lump in his throat and now he was sweating. Tears started rolling down Yarni's face as she sat on the edge of the bed beside Bengee. She had her arms around him, hugging him tight to show him security. Bengee had never been so afraid in his life. What was he to do?

Bengee took a deep breath, and pulled himself together. The look she saw on his face was enough to confirm that Bengee was carrying something heavy around.

He couldn't look Yarni in the eyes as he told her, "I can't tell you." He continued slowly. "If I tell you, you are going to leave me!"

"No, I am not. I am not going anywhere," she assured him. "But stop the act and tell me right now!" He gazed into Yarni's eyes then looked away, in shame.

"Yarni, I fucked up," he said, dropping his head and rubbing his temples. "I let this girl suck my dick and I got gonorrhea."

"What? You got what?" Yarni yelled. "Oooh, hell nah! Oooh, hell no!" She picked up her shoe and clucked him upside the head. She started picking up anything in sight to fight him, but Bengee wasn't fighting back. He tried to restrain her, grabbed her, and took her into his arms.

Yarni burst out in tears, screamed, and struggled to get away. She couldn't stand the touch of him. He only held her tighter and wouldn't let her go. "Let me go! You dirty-dick motherfucker," she screamed at the top of her lungs.

"No, I won't let you go," he tried to comfort her.

"Get off of me, I can't stand you touching me. You touching me makes me feel so filthy."

"Yarni, I love you so much. Can't we work through this?"

"Hell no!" She pushed him away. "You, you love me? Stop lying!"

"Yarni, I do love you!"

"How could you possibly love me when you broke your promise to me? You fucked somebody else, and told me a lie that it was some chick sucking your dick. You don't even have enough respect for this relationship or even love yourself enough to wear a damn rubber. You could have given me my death warrant. Is this what you do to the people you love?"

"Baby, I apologize," he said in a soft, apologetic tone. Yarni never said anything. "Baby, I promise. I'll never do anything like this again. I swear on everything I love."

Yarni finally got herself together. She wanted to get as far away from him as possible. Bengee went into the kitchen to get her a cold bottle of water. Then he went to the front door as well as the back door. He removed both of the keys from the deadbolt locks and hid them in the living room. Bengee was fully aware that if Yarni left the house that night, his chances to keep her would be about as good as a snowball in hell. By the time he returned, she was dressed and looking for her keys. He'd hid her car keys as well as the spare set.

"Where are my keys?" she growled through her pain.

"I don't know where they are," Bengee responded in an unconcerned tone.

"Bengee, give me my keys." She stood there, holding her hands out.

"I don't have your keys. I wasn't driving your truck. As a matter of fact, didn't you use your keys to open the door?" Bengee said as he sat on the couch with his arms extended out on the top of the sofa. He knew she couldn't go anywhere.

"Bengee, unlock the door so I can leave." He blocked her out as if he didn't hear her. She stood there with her arms folded. "Bengee, I am not playing. Give me my damn keys." She raised her voice as frustration set in, but he still didn't respond. "Why can't you just let me leave? I don't want to be around you. If somebody didn't want to be bothered with me, I wouldn't want that person anywhere near me. Why can't you just let me go?"

"Because this is where you live and no respect- able woman would be out in the streets this time of night," Bengee expressed this in a relaxed, calm voice.

Upset, but not surprised, she went to the bathroom window, but the bars stopped her dead in her tracks, as did the bars on the bed- room window, the kitchen, and all the rooms in the house. Bengee just had the cast-iron bars installed only a month before. Yarni realized that she was doomed. She drew the conclusion that she would try to get some rest tonight, but tomorrow morning she was outta there.

Bengee got into the bed with her. She told him in a shaky voice, "I really suggest that you carry yourself in the other room because I don't trust myself laying here beside you. I may have an instant replay of what you just dropped on me and kill you in your sleep. Now, please carry your dirty-dick ass in the other room." Though Bengee knew Yarni wouldn't dare hurt him, he slept in the other room. He was compliant because he felt at least they were still under the same roof.

The next morning Yarni awoke to Bengee sitting in the chaise chair watching her. She arose from the bed and didn't utter a word to him. To the bathroom she went to pee, washed her face, and brushed her teeth. On her way down the hall, she grabbed the cordless phone and called her doctor's office. She explained to the receptionist that she had an emergency and needed to see the doctor pronto.

They asked her what the problem was, and she simply told them her stomach was hurting. The receptionist told her to come in at noon. She jumped in the shower, got dressed, and headed out. Bengee had gotten dressed to accompany her, but she told him she didn't want him to go.

When she reached the doctor's office, she had to wait an hour and a half before they called her name. She noticed that they had hired a new receptionist. She could tell the girl was ghetto. She had super-big hair with three colors and five different hairstyles in it. Skeptical thoughts set in her mind. *I hope this ghetto chick doesn't try*

to look in my chart and find out why I'm here.
As she waited, she tried her hardest not to cry.
She kept leaving the waiting room, going into the
restroom to get herself together.

"Yarnise Pitman," the jolly nurse called. Yarni
came out of the restroom.

"How are you doing?" Yarni ignored her. She
wanted to ask, "Why?"

Once they reached the room, the nurse asked,
"Why are you here today?"

"To see the doctor," Yarni simply said.

"Yes, I am aware of that, but I need to know
what to put down on this chart." Yarni felt so embarrassed. She wasn't telling the nurse anything.
"I am here to see the doctor, not you. I will talk to
the doctor when he comes in."

The nurse frowned her face up and said, "The
doctor will be in shortly," and slammed the door
on her way out.

When the doctor walked in, he saw Yarni crying. He gave her a tissue, pulled the stool over,
and sat on it in front of her. He comforted Yarni
for a minute or so and asked her, "Why are you
crying?" She opened her mouth to tell him, but
words didn't come out. Only she sobbed more.
She finally got herself together so she could
speak.

"I am ashamed to say," and looked up at the doctor as she took a deep breath. "It hurts every time I even think about it."

The doctor looked at her in a caring way. He grabbed her hand. "Just take your time. Whatever it is, I assure you that you are not the first and you won't be the last that I've seen with the same problem. I truly can relate. It's written all over your face that you are hurt, but from my personal standpoint, broken hearts can mend with time. Now, I can't treat your medical problem unless you tell me."

She was quiet for a few seconds until she got up the nerve to speak. She closed her eyes and covered her face as she began whimpering. "My boyfriend informed me that he'd contracted gonorrhea from God-only-knows-where." She paused as she wiped her eyes. She looked up as she inhaled, then exhaled. "And, I am afraid that he might have given me AIDS or herpes, or something I cannot get rid of."

"I know you are hurt, and you have every right to be upset. Let me assure you that you are not overreacting. I diagnose people every day for this same matter. I see some of the same people four and five times a year being treated for STDs. I only wish that some of them took it as serious as you are." He gave her the examination and asked if she would like to be tested for HIV.

"Test for anything and everything you can pick up," Yarni said.

The doctor smiled at Yarni and said, "Listen, Yarnise, I am going to send you over to the lab to have blood work done."

Yarni nodded. The doctor reached into the pocket of his white lab coat to pull out his prescription pad. As he wrote on his pad he informed Yarni, "Your results won't be back for two days, and we'll call you. In the meantime, it is best to get you started on some antibiotics just in case." He tore off the prescriptions and handed them to her. As she reached to take the paper from him, he asked, "You're not allergic to penicillin, are you?" She shook her head *no*.

Bengee called her all day long. She hung up the first few times. "Baby, please don't hang up. Just give me ten seconds. I am fully aware that you are probably going to leave me. Whatever your decision is I am going to respect it, but at the same time, I need to talk to you. I am not going to try to talk you out of your mindset, but whenever you are finished running around, I am going to be at the crib waiting on you."

Yarni also had a hair appointment at 3:30. She almost cancelled the appointment, but after all the drama from the night before, her hair was in a frenzy. Maybe the change in atmosphere would make her feel a little better. As soon as she arrived, she noticed her stylist pick up the phone and call somebody. She started getting agitated. *Did she not see me walk through the door and now she gonna get on the phone? I am going to count to sixty, and if she ain't off the phone by then, I'm going to tell her to just reschedule me, because see, I am not in the mood for this. I can just keep my seventy dollars in my pocket.*

Co-Co finally called her for her wash. Being a people person, Co-Co already knew something was wrong; she had talked to Bengee a few times. Co-Co was like any other female trying to pry and be nosy on the sly, but Yarni wasn't breaking. She didn't give away that anything was going wrong for her. Co-Co looked at Yarni as she paged through the *Sister 2 Sister* magazine nonchalantly. Co-Co's look was saying: *You are so . . . fake, I know something had to happen between you and your man because he's been calling me all day, sounding desperate. You sitting here playing the role as if you are so happy. Yeah, whatever!* Yarni didn't catch the look because she was really trying to focus on the magazine and not what she was dealing with. Just then, a big Care Bear walked into the shop, asked for Yarni Pitman, and started singing a singing telegram. *"I just called to say I love*

*you/ I just called to say how much I care/ I
just called to say I love you and I mean it from
the bottom of my heart."* All the stylists and
customers thought it was so sweet what Yarni's
man had done for her. *What a good man,* they
all commented. She wanted to come back with: *If
you only knew what I had to go through. If you
could only walk in my shoes. You only see my
truck, my custom-made jewels glistening, and
my tailored designer clothes. You hear about
and see the pictures from my extravagant trips.
But what does that mean? People on the outside
never know what you have to go through to get
it. People think that everything that glitters is
gold. Whoever said that lied. And when I look at
the big picture these are just the bribes to put up
with the bullshit. So, is it even worth it?*

After Co-Co tightened her hair, she still could
not get a word out of her about what was going on, Yarni went by the pharmacy to get her
prescription filled. She arrived home. Bengee
had cooked lobster and steak, and met her at
the door with sunflowers. She dropped them
in the trash as she walked past the trash can.
She wasn't buying it: not the singing telegram,
dinner, flowers—none of it. She asked herself:
Why am I even here? Damn, is love this blind?
Although she was hurt, as well as furious with

Bengee, she still loved him. She never knew this side of love. She was confused and distraught. How could someone that you love so much, give you so much pain?

10

Breakup To Make Up

Yarni was shaken by the doorbell. She wondered who it could've been because anyone hardly ever visited them. She could hear Bengee's voice as he answered the door, but she couldn't make out the words. She tried to go back to sleep, but couldn't because of the racket Bengee was making. She decided to get up and go see what was going on.

As she was walking down the hall, Bengee called out to her, "Yarni, is that you?"

"Who else is it going to be?" she asked.

"Wait a minute before you come in here."

"Why? Do you have to hide the ho you have in there or something?"

Just then, she walked in and she saw a four-piece Louis Vuitton luggage set sitting in the living room. "Oh, my God!" she screamed, as she opened up and looked at each piece. When she got around to the duffel bag there were two plane tickets in it to St. Kitts. St. Kitts was on her must-see list. When she looked at the ticket and saw Bengee's name on it, she burst into laughter. Bengee looked at her with a puzzled look.

"Now, this is a joke!" She continued to laugh.

Bengee smiled in on the laughter too. "What's so funny, sweetness?"

"Do you really think that I would dare go with you on a vacation after you've done one of the ultimate betrayals." She looked at the pictures of the resort they were staying at. "Oh, this place is beautiful. But tell me, Mr. Dirty Dick, why would you even plan such a romantic vacation in such an exotic place when your wiener is dripping with gonorrhea? No sex is going to hop off."

He smacked his lips as he looked at her. "I know the sex is a dead issue, but I feel we need a vacation to work on the healing process of our relationship. Yarni, I am desperate right now. I know that we are on shaky grounds. I'm aware I made a stupid mistake."

"—a stupid mistake," she interrupted. "How about a mistake that could have and may still cause both of us our lives? How about I got to live in bondage for the next seven years to find out if I've got HIV or not. Yeah, so always remember, it's easy to just slide your peter up in something, but the consequences can be fatal for a few moments of pleasure." She shook her head in frustration, anger, hurt, and confusion.

"Yarni, please forgive me, baby." He stood up with arms out, trying to explain. "I am so sorry."

"You're right." She nodded. "You are sorry."

"Yarni, whatever anger you feel you need to get off of your chest, I can take you lashing out on me, but please take a look at everything we've been through. We've really had some good times. Don't just throw it all out of the window for one foul-up." Yarni stood with her hands folded as he continued. "Look, baby, I don't care about any sex on this vacation. I just want to be around you. Listen, this vacation is the least I could do for all the pain and shame I've caused you. At least take the vacation, and if after the vacation you want no parts of me, I'll just let you go your own way. I won't try to stop you or change your mind," he said humbly. "Now, the flight leaves at eight. Please, baby, please."

As bad as she wanted to decline the offer—shit, this was a free trip. When would she get another opportunity like this? She was leaving Bengee and Des wasn't coming home anytime soon. She'd have to save for a while to make a trip like this happen. She started getting prepared.

When they arrived in St. Kitts she had no idea that there was any place on earth that was as beautiful. The mannerisms of the people were flattering. She enjoyed the way the people catered to them.

They lay under a coconut tree in rented beach chairs, with pina coladas in tall glasses. Yarni was reading a *Sister 2 Sister* magazine, and he was looking at a rim book. She looked up and stared at the peaceful green water with the waves washing upon the baby-powder white sand. Bengee noticed her in a daze. He said, "What are you thinking 'bout?"

She didn't answer right away. "Bengee, do you know how humiliating I felt laying on that table getting examined because my man gave me gonorrhea?"

"I can't begin to imagine. I do know how embarrassed I felt when I went to the doctor." He got up from his chair and sat facing her with his legs straddled on the edge of her chair. "Baby, I apologize. I know nothing I can do will ever make it right again, but I hope everything I have planned will ease the pain."

He did have some phenomenal plans for her. He arranged for them both to get massages at the same time. Every night he'd outdo himself. He presented her with a ring from the David

Yurman collection. The second night, he had a picnic planned for them and presented her with some diamond earrings. The third night, he granted her a deed to a building. He told her that he'd been planning to help her open a business, so at least she could have her own income coming in until she figured out exactly what she was going to do about school. He felt that this business would be a task to keep her mind off the fact that she would never be able to practice law due to her felony conviction. Also, in Bengee's mind, this would be considered as another one of the perks for taking the gun charge for him.

The next night, he gave her a note that promised that when they returned home he'd give her twenty-thousand dollars toward her start-up fees for her business. The final night he gave her a voucher to go to New York for the next week. Along with the voucher were gift certificates for Tiffany's, Saks Fifth Avenue, Lord & Taylor, and Henri Bendel. He'd also arranged for Cara to go with her. He provided them both spa packages at the Ritz, tickets for a Broadway play, and a helicopter ride over all five boroughs.

When Yarni and Bengee returned from their trip, Yarni began to think of what she could possibly convert that building into. She considered making it into a restaurant for her mother, but her mother's catering business was going quite well with just doing the elite parties for city officials and prominent businesses in town. She weighed the options of opening a beauty salon versus a nail salon. Then she decided she didn't want the headache of dealing with all of the females, but at the same time she knew that there was money to be made in a salon. She then came up with the perfect idea, one thing; a tanning salon.

She mapped the whole thing out from start to finish. Yarni's first concern was that it had to be a tranquil environment. She had the walls painted with palm trees to give it a beach look and feel. She purchased neon color-lamp palm trees. Each room was individually painted as well. She started out with four tanning beds. She had a Jacuzzi installed in the back. She sold beach towels, tanning lotions, and supplies. She named it Sunshine's. She bought a massage table, hired a massage therapist, and turned one of the back rooms into a massage parlor. She also sold top-of-the-line massage oils and bathing suits for all size women. She recruited a Swedish woman to work there who specialized in facials and body waxing. This drew all origins of women to her salon.

Bengee was set up with a new Colombian heroin connection. He was generous with any monies she needed to enhance the salon. Bengee was impressed with what Yarni had done with the building and money that he'd given her. Gloria was proud of Yarni, but very disappointed that Yarni had not attempted to check into anything pertaining to school. The truth of the matter was that Yarni was so disillusioned about not finishing college that she blocked any thoughts about college totally out of her mind. Yarni took photos of every room in the salon and sent them to Des. Des was exhilarated about Yarni's accomplishment; at the same time, his constant pressure for Yarni to finish school never let up.

> *My Dearest Yarni,*
> *Just wanted to drop you a few lines to let you know that I love you to life. The reason why I haven't called is because we are on lockdown, Richmond and Tidewater got to fighting, so the whole joint is on lockdown.*
> *Thanks for the photos. I am very impressed with your salon. It looks to be a very classy place. However, I am still wondering what the hell is going on with your school situation. I can't understand why you won't finish. I know you are sick*

of me bitching about this. But, if you were going to drop out of college, you should have done it in the first-semester, not in your last year. Come on, baby, you've come too far to give up now. We'll talk more on this later. This topic of discussion is not closed fully, just for now. They just turned the lights off, so I'll write again tomorrow.

Unconditional Love,

Des

11

Price To Pay

With Bengee's new Colombian supplier, he was able to step it up to the next level, a level that Richmond's hustlers hadn't seen in a few years since the late eighties. He was large. He was Virginia's and North Carolina's major supplier. Riding high on his success, Bengee got very arrogant. One of his childhood friends owed him some money and when he went to pick it up, it was five-thousand dollars short. Bengee put the guy in his car, took him up on Midlothian Turnpike, right at Cloverleaf Mall's intersection, and stripped him down of everything but his tiger-striped briefs. Bengee created a sign and made him put it around his neck: *"I am a man who does not pay my debts off."* Bengee made him walk up and down the mall's intersection. The whole experience was humiliating to this guy because people were riding past, honking the horn, waving, pointing, and laughing.

Flamboyant became Bengee's first name. He now stepped out from the background and wanted to be seen. Whenever he bought a new vehicle, he rode all around town with cases of toilet paper in his car. When he pulled up on the scene and people would be in awe over the automobile, he'd just reach behind him in the backseat and throw a roll of toilet paper out of the window, so they could wipe their mouth from drooling or shitting on themselves. He'd go to the clubs and put locks on the bars, so if you didn't know him or somebody in his crew, you were not going to be served a drink. He talked down on the small-time nickel-and-dime hustlers. Big money had turned Bengee into a monster.

Yarni realized that Bengee was turning into a person that she didn't even know. He became preoccupied with a whole lot of other things. He still came home every night and they still ate dinner together, if he wasn't out of town. But it was clear to Yarni that Bengee was going to slow up or blow up, and he was 1,000 miles and running. He wasn't slowing up because he was in too deep and loving every minute of it. For the first time, Bengee didn't have anything mapped out, a goal, an aspiration, and not even a getaway plan. He was living each day as if there was no tomorrow.

Des had made Yarni fully aware a long time ago, that there was only three ways out of this drug-kingpin game. The most common two ways were death or prison, or the third way—which had only about a 2-percent survival rate—just walking away and becoming legit. Yarni knew the third way was out of the question for Bengee at this point. Yarni knew that she had to get out, or get caught up in his madness when the curtain fell on Bengee. But she had to prepare before she could close this chapter of her life.

The first step she took was she cut back on her spending habits. Every time Bengee gave her any money for herself, she would simply save half of it. She began looking for her own place. She desperately wanted a house. Because she had lived in a house with Bengee for the past two years, it would be hard for her to move into an apartment. She knew that when you buy a house, they dig into all your business and she really didn't have any credit. Cash was how she paid for everything she'd bought. She talked to Gloria about signing to get her a house and she agreed, but Yarni decided against it because she really wanted to dig herself out of this mess without her mother's help.

Then came the process of getting her criminal record expunged. She vowed to herself that she'd write the governor one letter a week until he granted the motion to reinstate her rights. She didn't care how long it took. Almost missing the cutoff date for registration, she enrolled back into school to get her undergraduate degree, which after two semesters, she acquired. She submitted her resume and interviewed with a lot of companies in the Richmond area. The whole interviewing process was very tricky because she was a convicted felon. She never let on of her criminal background due to the fact that she knew the white-collar world would have no understanding of it. Hell, they wouldn't dare give her a chance to prove herself. Thankfully, her tanning salon was profiting. That, however, wasn't enough for Yarni. She wanted a career.

After going to a midnight-madness sale at Hect's, Yarni arrived home. She noticed that all the streetlights were out in her neighborhood. She had a bad feeling. She pulled her truck in the driveway and she struggled carrying in all of her bags of groceries from Ukrop's as well as all the bags she acquired from Hecht's. When she approached the door, as soon as she put her key in and turned the knob, a man, dressed in black, jumped out of the bushes on the side of the porch. He kicked the door in and pushed her into the house. Another guy appeared and he was also dressed in all black with a ski mask on. They pinned her down on the floor with her mouth covered. They tied her hands and feet up, put masking tape on her mouth and put a bandanna over her eyes. She was scared, but she never cried. The third guy brought her bags in the house, pulled her truck into the garage while the other two began to ransack the house. Of course, Bengee didn't keep any drugs there or any real money, but they found sixty-five thousand dollars of Bengee's money as well as her stash that she'd been saving, nineteen-thousand dollars. That wasn't enough. They took Yarni out through the garage door, put her in the backseat of her truck, and one guy rode in the back with her while one guy drove. The third guy rode in another car behind them. She knew the chances of her living were slim-to-none. She remembered on an episode she'd seen on either 20/20 or Nightline, that if a kidnapper moved you to another spot, that the odds of your being killed were very high. She wouldn't even know who killed her because they had their heads covered, and now she was blindfolded.

They took her to an old, raggedy house near where Belle Meade used to be. The house had a stale smell to it. She could tell that they had been smoking weed. Though she didn't smoke weed at all, she knew the scent. Whenever somebody who smoked came around, she could always pick up the scent.

It was natural for Yarni to be very observant. Des instilled in her that you always had to put your other senses to work when one of the others was disabled. She knew that they were near a railroad track because she heard the train. Yarni timed the trains by the way the TV shows came on. She drew the conclusion that she was somewhere near a track that was used frequently. They put her in a room with a TV with cable. She was blindfolded, but she still could listen to the TV. As the dude threw her in the room, she noticed his scent of Issey Miyake cologne. She thought to herself, *This isn't a bum nigga wearing this hundred-dollar cologne.* She also could tell that the house didn't have central air. There were individual units, as well as ceiling fans in the house.

"Hellllllooo. Excuse me. Please, please allow me to use the restroom. I promise I won't try anything crazy," Yarni said in a humbling tone.

"Go take her to the bathroom, but take off that broad's shoes before you untie her," she overheard one of the kidnappers instruct another. Yarni could feel the cheap carpet on the floor. They removed the blindfold so she could use the restroom. She noticed the bathroom had a lot of mildew on the tub and around the sink.

The dude who was in constant patrol over her tried to persuade her to eat, but she wouldn't. He spoke out to Yarni: "It's nothing personal against you, and you will be outta here as soon as your man comes through with the dough."

Ransom! Ain't this some shit? These niggas done put a price over my head! She was confident that Bengee was going to come up with whatever amount they asked for. Right then another guy came into the room and hooked the speakerphone up into a plug in the room. She heard a dial tone, which was followed by a bunch of numbers. The guy was using a Wal-Mart calling card. She heard the automated operator say, "Thank you for using Wal-Mart, prepaid calling card."

After a series of numbers she observed the phone ringing. She heard Bengee's voice, "yo", and she felt a sense of security.

A flashback of when he'd given her gonorrhea came about. He'd promised never to forsake her again.

"Yo, we got your girl, man. We need $250,000 for her return," one of the captors said, Bengee hung up the phone on them, thinking about what Robert De Niro told Al Pacino in *Heat*: Never let yourself get attached to something that you are not willing to walk out on in thirty seconds flat if you feel the heat around the corner. He'd violated that rule.

He felt indebted to her. He owed Yarni his life. He felt no matter what he ever gave her, it wasn't enough to repay her for sacrificing and giving up everything she ever wanted to take the gun charge for him. She never asked him for anything, but in all actuality, he felt obligated to her. Now that he was a certified big hat, he didn't really want a relationship with Yarni anymore. He knew that at any given time she was the only person who could hurt him, so he'd never have the gall to leave Yarni. He selfishly thought to himself that if he did not pay the dudes, it would kill two birds with one stone. Maybe they would kill Yarni and he'd be free of that eternal debt he felt he owed her. See, Bengee could never walk the same streets and deal with Yarni being with the next man. Yarni was indeed the ideal woman. He could deal with her being dead better. At least no other man could experience the way she made him feel, like a king. He wouldn't have to report to anybody. He could be rid of Yarni and live his life openly as the whore that he longed to be. Plus, he'd be able to keep the $250,000 dollars for himself, which was chump change to him anyway.

On that note, his phone rang again, and he recognized it as the voice of the kidnapper that called before. He simply told them, "It's cheaper for you to keep her," and hung up the phone.

Yarni couldn't believe her ears. After all the bullshit she'd put up with from him. She realized at that moment, that everyone plays a fool some times, and there are no exceptions to the rule. Love don't love nobody!

Yarni couldn't even sob. She could only remember something her pastor said one Sunday in church. "When you are in danger, call on Psalm ninety-one." She couldn't remember the whole thing. The only parts that came to her mind was: "I will say of the Lord, He is my refuge and my fortress, my God in Him will I trust. . . . Surely He will deliver me from the snare of the fowler, and from the nuisance of pestilence. . . . Thou shalt not be afraid for the terror of night: nor for the arrow that flieth the day. . . . A thousand shall fall at thy right side and ten thousand at thy right hand, but it shall not come nigh to thee. . . . Only with thine eyes shalt thou behold and see the reward of the wicked. . . . Because thou hast made the Lord, which is my refugee, even the most high habitation."

She kept repeating it over and over again. She went into round-the-clock-prayer. She asked

God to enter into the kidnappers' heart and minister to them not to hurt or kill her. After coming out of prayer, she claimed her victory and put it in God's hands. Then she was not scared. She knew that she'd be delivered from this madness. She realized that it was only one man in her world that wasn't going to leave her or forsake her. That was God, not Bengee. She felt a sense of calmness within herself as well as in the house she was being held captive.

She overheard the kidnappers say, "Man, we gonna have to kill her." The other said, "Let me hit her first, she got a fat ass."

"Look, we ain't in this for murder or rape. We're in this for money!" the leader of the kidnappers screamed.

The kidnappers entered back into the room. They asked her if there was anybody else she could call to get the ransom from. She hesitated about calling her mother because her mother had endured so much with Yarni already. Then she didn't want to put her mother in jeopardy either. She called Uncle Stanka. He'd surely know what to do. The kidnappers allowed her to explain the situation to him, while one listened on the other phone and the other held her at gunpoint. They lowered the ransom to one hundred-thousand dollars. Her uncle agreed. He and her mother paid the ransom, and the kidnappers let her go free. The kidnappers kept her truck and took it to the chop shop in New York. She didn't care because she knew that the insurance company would cover it anyway.

Once Yarni was free, she knew from that moment on that she could never deal with Bengee again. She'd heard that while she was being held captive, Bengee was having parties, still balling out of control, along with his normal strip parties.

She called Bengee and told him, "Since you left me for dead, just pretend I am dead. I want the hundred-thousand dollars my uncle and mother put up to pay the ransom, and as far as I am concerned, never, ever bother me again or there will be consequences, and may you die a long, slow painful death, you grimy motherfucker!"

"Oh, you're threatening me?" Bengee raised his voice, but Yarni wasn't intimidated.

"Just bring my mother and uncle's fucking money or else," she firmly said and hung up on him.

He called back. His attitude reflected as if they had an argument and he could fix it.

"They will get their money. All you need is a hundred-thousand dollars? I'll bring the money when I come pick you up to come home. A'ight?"

She knew she could've gotten more money out of Bengee, but she didn't want anything else from him. She thought to herself, *It's bad when I don't even want this nigga money*.

She cried just thinking about him. Although Yarni loved Bengee, she realized two things. She loved herself more and it's a very thin line between love and hate. How you could love someone so much and as soon as they cross over that line, the same amount of love you had for them can turn to hate in an instant. She cried for six days. She remembered reading somewhere that it takes thirty days to make or break a habit. If she could make it through twenty-four more days, she'd be okay. Yarni remembered all the turmoil she'd accepted from Bengee. It was in lieu of the money. Money was an addiction in itself. She contemplated, *A girl's gotta do what a girl's gotta do*. On that note, she picked up the phone, called her girlfriend Jewel, who was a drug-abuse counselor, and asked Jewel about kicking a habit. She gathered some books on dependency habits. Her habit may not have been chemical, but she sure had two dependencies that she needed to be rid of, Bengee and the love of money.

Yarni moved in with Gloria until she could find an apartment. When she checked into renting an apartment, she realized that it was more economical to buy a house, condo or townhouse, rather than renting an apartment. The rent on apartments that she liked averaged out to be more than a mortgage payment would be. Delayed gratification were two words she hated to think 'bout. Although she wanted instant results, she realized she'd have to save and sacrifice to purchase a house. She reasoned with herself that it really didn't make sense to have a fifty-thousand dollar vehicle and no driveway of her own to sit it in. She decided that she would accept the fact that if she couldn't have instant gratification with her own place right then, she'd get a job and save toward her goal.

Yarni received a letter from Des.

Dearest Yarni,
I am going to keep this short and sweet. The streets are talking about what that bitch-ass shit Bengee did by not paying that little funky-ass $250,000 ransom. The whole six and a half years I've been down, not one time have I put locks on you or hated on any man concerning you. But straight up, a pipe can't take but so much steam and it busts. The bottom line is this, Remember back a few years ago when you

gave me the ultimatum, either hustling or you? Now it's either this joker or me. I can't sit and watch this nigga play craps with your life. I'm going to always love you regardless because I've got unconditional love and that's the love that don't wear off, but I can't allow you to be in my life if you continue to deal with this Bengee cat. So you make the decision and let me know.

Unconditional Love,
Des

She began to cry as she thought about the price she might have to pay if Des didn't want to be with her anymore. Then she thought about the cost of all the things she'd been faced with. What's the price for someone giving you gonorrhea? What's the price to fix a broken heart? What's the price doing a day in jail? How much does it cost for you to give your life? What's the price of breaking your mother's heart? How many chances do you really have at love? *I can't lose Des in spite of my stupid choices. What am I going to do?*

While she was sitting there thinking, Jay-Z's new song was playing on an underground tape she bought a while back when she in New York. There were only a few words of the song, she could make out, but those words were her inspiration, her stimulation, her encouragement, and what gave her the will to move forward . . . *"order to survive/ you gotta live with regrets."*

Yarni pulled herself together. She grabbed her cordless phone. She called Jewel and read the letter to her. "Listen, Jewel, I need you to do me a favor. Just play along, okay?" Yarni said and Jewel agreed.

Yarni had Jewel call the prison where Des was, to speak to the chaplain. She spoke in her professional, proper voice. "Hello, my name is Jewel Rogers and I am a nurse here at Charter Westbrook, and one of our patients is asking to speak to her husband. We feel that this may help her. It's an emergency."

"What's the nature of the emergency of the patient?" the chaplain asked.

"Sir, that's confidential. I can't disclose that."

"Yes, ma'am I understand," the chaplain said in a concerned tone. "Who's the inmate?"

"Ahhh" Jewel hesitated as if she was flipping through pages. "Desmond Taylor."

"Your patient is what relation to him?"

"His wife."

"Is there a number I can reach you at?" the chaplain asked.

Jewel gave him Yarni's number, and when the chaplain called back, he had Des right there. Yarni answered the phone, "nurses' station" and played the whole charade out to the fullest. When Des got on the phone, she dropped the act and told him that it was an emergency and to call when he reached his pod. When he called, she explained that Bengee was a done deal and she would never speak to him again. She kept her word, and vowed to herself to never let Bengee anywhere near her.

12

Every Dog Has Its Day

Gloria was so furious with Bengee that she wanted to kill him herself. She even talked to her brother, Stanka, about eliminating Bengee, but Yarni overheard them contemplating and interrupted the conversation. As she walked into Gloria's kitchen, looking in the refrigerator, she said to them, "Mommy and Uncle Stanka, save your energy and your money. Killing him is a waste. Eventually, he's going to commit suicide indirectly sooner or later. His lifestyle and actions are going to be the cause of his death. He's too bigheaded, selfish, and the streets are watching. He'll self-destruct one way or another. He'll crumble to the ground." Gloria and Stanka looked at Yarni, astonished, as she looked in the cabinet to grab a glass to pour her some juice. She put her hand on her hip, about to take a sip of her juice.

"And Mommy, I am surprised at you. You've always taught me vengeance isn't ours, and you reap what you sow."

She drank from her glass. She slammed the glass on the counter hard as she said casually, "After all, I had considered shooting him myself, but I realized that was just too easy of a way for him to die," Yarni said, shaking her head with a giggle. Gloria and Stanka looked at each other as she took another sip of her juice. "The real punishment was cutting all ties with him completely. I'll get the last laugh when the reality hits him in the face." She laughed as she continued. "Whether it's the feds picking him up and handing him back-to-back life sentences, once he gets behind prison walls, he'll realize how much he needs me because you see, them other chicks, they ain't going to be thinking about him. All they gonna do is run to the next dude with a dollar. So, he'll need me and want me to show him some love, write him a letter, send him a card, some pictures, accept a call. Then I'll leave him for dead, just as he left me for dead. The only difference is I'll be able to fill my life with activities and events to forget about him. He'll have a substantial amount of time to think about me and how he—excuse my language, Mommy—fucked that up. I know that none of the women he ever had or will have could measure up to me. I feel that that's the best revenge. And if it doesn't play out like that, just wait and see just how Bengee will fall victim to the streets, and the drug game will see to it that he dies a slow, painful death one way or another. So, just hold your horses and watch what I tell you. His is coming. Just watch and see. Every dog has its day!"

Gloria didn't know what to say. She was caught up in the right now. She never analyzed it as Yarni had. She wasn't sure if Yarni was only saying this to soothe her heart or if she really meant what she was saying. Gloria got up from the table and walked to her prayer room. She began to pray and ask God to make some sense of this situation.

But months passed, and Bengee still stayed on top. Yarni would sometime hear that he just purchased something new and would wonder to herself, *When is his going to come around? How come all the good guys always get caught up? The rotten cats always seem to come out on top. They never get theirs. It always seems like the innocent people die, never that nasty dude. It's always the dude that treated everybody good, the dude that bought all the kids in the neighborhood ice cream, never the dude who is*

making crazy money and don't have respect for
his own mother, won't give her a dime and will
cuss her out, call her everything, but a child of
God. Never the cruel, nasty dude who doesn't
mean anybody any good, the dudes like Bengee.
I wonder why it is like that?

People all around town started hating Bengee.
He sold his dope so cheap and it was the best
dope down south in a while. He kept it flowing,
but there were still a lot of jealous and envious folks. Plus, he'd stepped on too many toes.
Bengee had given some dope to his right-hand
man, Tank. Shortly after, Tank wasn't anywhere
to be found, leaving Bengee in debt of $325,000
dollars. Bengee could've gone into his stash and
got the money, but he refused to touch any of his
money. He felt like that was hustling backwards.
He ended up going to Baltimore, and buying
some dope so he could sell it quickly to pay off
the Colombians. The dope he brought from B-
more was straight garbage and wasn't cheap like
the drugs he was getting from the Colombians.
He knew that he was supposed to see the Colombians two weeks ago. He'd been ducking their
calls, not only was he out of the $325,000 dollars
that Tank had got him for, but the $250,000
dollars that he'd went to Baltimore and brought
the garbage with. When he finally told the Co-

lombians he had their money, they told him they were sending someone to pick up the money personally. He knew right then that they were cutting him off. It wasn't the money, and what he was getting from them was considered nothing to them. It was just the principle of how he didn't communicate with them, and that was larceny and he couldn't be a part of their organization anymore. There was only one way out . . . *death!*

Bengee knew he had to go on the low now until he figured out what to do. He wasn't giving them anything until he acquired another connection some way, somehow. He went into hiding at a house he had purchased in Caroline County that no one knew about. How could somebody with so much knowledge of the game go into hiding forty-five minutes away from Richmond? The Colombians had people everywhere. They knew somebody who worked at the electric company, and they pulled up his recently opened account. They went to his house out in Caroline County. From the woods they watched him for three days. They waited for him to come out of the house to get some wood for his fireplace. They beat him unmercifully with a baseball bat, shot him in the knees, and dragged him in the house where they tortured him with a blowtorch.

He pleaded, "Oh, please, don't kill me." He whined and begged like a little girl.

"Just please, pleeeeaaassse," he said, struggling, looking for a way out of the tub, but there wasn't any. With the gun in his mouth, they finally shot him right there in the bathtub of his own house. If that wasn't enough, they went outside and put him in his newly purchased trash barrel, buck naked, with two concrete cinder blocks at the bottom, and tossed him into Lake Anna.

It just so happened that two little girls were missing in that area and they were last seen playing near the river. Search teams were dispatched to Lake Anna, and divers found the barrel with the number 5509, Bengee's address on it. They could tell the barrel was recently dropped in the river. The color wasn't completely gone. It was extremely heavy. They called in the bulldozer to bring it up. They were expecting to find the little girls in it, but to no disappointment, it was Bengee. The little girls were found unharmed. They had wondered off in the woods.

Yarni was at Gloria's house playing spades with her mother, Sam, and Cara when there was a knock at the door. Gloria looked out of the window. It was the police. She automatically put up her guards and was in fear for her daughter. Taking precaution, she went into the kitchen and told Yarni to hide because she didn't understand why the police would be at her house. Gloria answered the door, cracking it only enough so she could peep through.

"Yes, what is it?" Gloria said with a stank attitude.

"Is Yarnise Pitman here?" the officer took his hat off and asked.

"No, but I am her mother. Is there something that I can do for you?" Gloria asked in a hostile tone.

The officer was very hesitant, "Well, we're here to inform Yarnise Pitman that Benjamin Whales is dead and we need her to come downtown to identify the body. She's listed as his next of kin," he stated.

Gloria simply said with no emotion at all, "I will let her know when I see her," and she slammed the door right in his face.

After she was sure the police were gone, Gloria went into the room that Yarni was hiding in and broke the news to her. Yarni's response was, "I knew that this day would be coming." Gloria, Cara, and Sam accompanied Yarni to identify the body. It wasn't as easy as Yarni had expected it to be. She never cried, but the remorse was all over her face. Even with all the rotten things that Bengee had done to her, she still loved him. When she saw that he'd been killed in such a brutal way, she began to have a little compassion in her heart. She felt a little guilty because she remembered the Bible said you can speak life or death into somebody's life, and she had wished death on Bengee.

She called his mother, who'd never been a mother to him. The mother's simple response was, "You've always been his family as far as I am concerned, so now the ball is in your court. Whatever arrangements you decide upon, is how he is going to be put away. If it's up to me, the state will just handle it."

Yarni thought to herself that the best way to get back at him would be to just leave him there for the state to bury, and not even be acknowledged with funeral services. That would be the best revenge ever, but Yarni's heart wasn't like that. She immediately thought about all the generous things and pleasant words he'd ever said to her and put the negative out of her mind and heart for just a minute. She simply told herself that it was nothing personal with her; it was just that Bengee got caught up and couldn't survive the game. Most can't, most won't, and most don't.

On that note, she called Scott's funeral home on Brookland Park Boulevard, and started making the funeral arrangements. The next day, she purchased him a suit from Franco's. Cara suggested that she just go to Cavalier on Broad Street and get him a suit, but Yarni refused to because Bengee went to Francos's when he was living, and this was his final appearance. At the last minute, Yarni decided to do a closed-casket funeral. She drew the conclusion that Bengee wouldn't want to be remembered with all the makeup the funeral home was forced to put on him to cover all the bruises. Yarni wasn't sure what type of turnout Bengee would have for his funeral. He'd turned into such a nasty nigga. She flooded the funeral home with flowers, as he'd done for her the two and a half years that they were together.

The turnout of the funeral was enormous. No one would ever be able to tell that he wasn't a well-liked guy. All the towns' and surrounding counties' drug dealers showed up. Although it was a funeral, it was a fashion show, a car show, and a circus. People rented stretch limousines to roll up in. Most people were there to be nosy. All the girls that he messed with were there falling over the casket, including Darchelle, who was being absolutely as dramatic as possible. Of course, the stripper broads showed up wearing as little as possible. Joyce was there to demonstrate her support and to be there for Yarni on behalf of Des. The Colombians sent flowers and a representative to show their respects. The news crews appeared there to do a story on the life and death of the city's kingpin. The feds were there as well, taking photos of everybody that showed up.

After the burial, Yarni rented the Marriott grand ballroom and had a big party for him. She had Gloria cater the party, and it was far better than any of the parties he'd ever had for himself. Throughout the whole proceedings, Yarni never shed one tear.

After Joyce witnessed exactly how nicely Yarni had put Bengee away, she developed a great deal of respect for Yarni. She admired her for the lady that she'd grown up to be. Yarni and Joyce became loyal friends from that moment on. Joyce had her heart set on Yarni becoming her daughter-in-law. If Yarni could show such compassion for Bengee after he left her for dead, Joyce was secure that her son was in good hands with Yarni.

The day after the funeral, Yarni went to check her P.O. Box. It was mostly junk mail, catalogs, and three very important letters. One was from the governor expunging her criminal record. One was her check from the insurance company for Bengee's life-insurance policy. She had a hundred-thousand dollar policy on him, but since the cause of death was murder, it was considered accidental and it paid double. The final was from a law firm offering her a job as a paralegal negotiator for personal injury cases.

She sped home and displayed the letter on the refrigerator so that Gloria could see it. Once settled at home, she called the law firm to accept the position. She also stopped off to pay the funeral home the money she owed them, as well as pay her mother the money she had loaned her to bury Bengee and the money from the kidnapping, which Bengee had never paid. He only kept leaving messages telling Yarni he was on the way to bring the money, but never did. Her mother never stressed her to repay the money, but Yarni felt obligated. She visited Bengee's mother and gave her two-thousand dollars. She really didn't deserve that, but that's what kind of heart Yarni had. She gave Cara some money to help toward the down payment of a new car because Cara drove a hooptie. She bought Zurri's kids new beds and gave her some money as well. She invested a great deal of the money, and the remainder of the money she saved, to put down on a condo for herself. There was no way that she could get either of Bengee's houses due to the fact he'd brought them under an alias. The utilities were only in his name. She didn't want the furniture. It was too much of a reminder of Bengee and that whole chapter of her life. She gave his mother some of it and sold the rest.

A week later, she found out that the police raided a house over Southside near Belle Meade for illegal cable. They found the guy Tank in the house. Tank was high as gas. He was locked up for about six months. He bragged, while in jail, on how he'd stolen so much from Bengee and how he had kidnapped Yarni. A few guys stabbed him up, but he still survived. Des heard and ordered Slim, who was on the streets by this time, to kill Tank. When Slim saw exactly how Tank was living, he felt that he wouldn't put Tank out of his misery. Tank was experiencing a part of death on earth. Tank's self-esteem had been stripped from him. He had been a big-time drug dealer, and was now a junkie, who went around begging to wash people's cars. Tank eventually overdosed anyway.

Taking everything into consideration, Gloria and Joyce gave Yarni a *Waiting To Exhale* party.

Before Yarni started her new job, she used some of the money to take a vacation. She wanted to go somewhere very different from the tropical places she'd been going to. She wanted to experience a different type of vacation. She decided to go to the Galapagos Islands. The islands put her in a totally contrasted mindset. These islands were located 600 miles from the mainland. They are volcanic islands and range from dense rain forests to stark and barren terrain.

The islands were fascinating. Yarni did a seven-day cruise visiting two islands a day. Her main purpose was to see the rare flora and fauna: tortoises weighing nearly 600 pounds, marine iguanas, frigate birds, boobies, penguins, and sea lions. She watched the sea lions swim near the divers. She adored the huge sunflowers. She wished she could've spent more time on the islands, but the time visitors could spend on the islands was regulated by the government. Yarni was truly not a nature person, but she absolutely was able to appreciate this vacation. She was ready to start a new chapter in her life.

13

The Jumpsuit

Yarni gave Cara a ride up to McGeorge Toyota to pick up her car. Whenever they were together they always laughed and joked. They were tell-it-like-it-was friends, as her and Zurri were also. There was a difference between Cara and Zurri's friendship with Yarni. Although Cara and Yarni hung out more than she and Zurri, she always felt closer to Zurri.

Yarni said, "I can't believe that Bengee's been dead for a year."

"I know time flies, right?" said Cara. "Do you remember when Bengee flew us to New York? Didn't we have the best time?"

"We sure did," Yarni responded slowly.

"Yarni, you miss Bengee, don't you?"

"Honestly?" asked Yarni.

"Nah, tell me a lie, yeah honestly!" joked Cara. When Yarni still didn't respond. Cara questioned, "Did I touch a soft spot? I am sorry if I did." Yarni didn't respond. They both were silent for a minute.

Cara asked Yarni sympathetically, "Yarni, what are you thinking about?"

"How come everybody I love has to be taken away from me under the hands of another man? I mean my father, Des, my grandmother, Castro, and now Bengee. I mean Bengee was out of my life before he died, but I am mainly speaking on Des. I love him so much, and it seems like they're never going to let him go. Am I supposed to be lonely forever? Then it seems as though when I meet somebody else, they aren't worthy, and I'm the last person to figure that shit out. Why?" Yarni continued, "Do you think somebody could've put a root on me so I won't have a companion?"

Cara responded, "Yeah, you definitely had a lot going on in your head. I don't think it's nothing against you per se, no offense—you promise?"

Yarni responded, "No offense taken, so give it to me real." Cara went on. "As far as Des, I think he was on his way to jail when you met him. The police wanted him long before you even came into the picture. The reality of it is, Des was notorious. He did a lot of blatant things, and he covered up his madness well. Des was a real gangsta. He moved in silence and violence. So, police could never catch him slipping. So, they played dirty with him, and you just happened to be the love of his life. Yarni, it's just a part of the game. As far as Bengee, he just started getting money out of control and it went to his head, and the way he was living, the streets weren't going to tolerate it much longer anyway. I'm just glad you left when you left."

"Yeah, you're right," agreed Yarni.

Cara told Yarni, "Well, at least they can't hold Des forever." Yarni pulled in the parking lot at McGeorge Toyota; Cara noticed that her car was parked out in the visitor spot.

"Yarni, by the time I pay for my car, I should be on my way; I'll call you later." She shut the door and Yarni pulled off.

Yarni was running into the Lucky's convenience store to play some numbers, when her cellphone rang. It was Cara.

"Hey girl, what's up?" Cara said.

"What ya need?" Yarni asked, as she passed the lotto card to the clerk in the store. A man spoke to Yarni; she gave him a fake smile.

"Damn baby, you walked right in front of me," the man said.

"Excuse me, I didn't notice you standing there," Yarni said, apologetic.

"That's because you're too busy on the phone." He added, "That's why you can't pay attention."

She shot him a look, then she spoke into the phone, "Now, what were you saying, Cara?"

"Who was that?" Cara inquired.

"Some rude-ass nigga," Yarni said as she walked out of the store, holding the phone to her ear. As she was pulling off, Mr. Rude came running over to her car. Yarni blew into the phone as she saw him racing to the car.

"Should I roll over this joker or what?" Cara laughed as Yarni braked and rolled down her window.

"You walked right out of the store, paid the lady and forgot your lotto tickets. I told you that phone really got your attention."

"Why, thank you, Mr. Attentive," Yarni said in a sarcastic way.

"Not a problem, Miss Preoccupied." Then Yarni noticed his Rolex President on his arm and as she eased off the brakes, she looked in her mirror to see what he was driving.

Just then, Cara asked, "What is he driving?"

"An Expedition. It's chromed out . . . I think he got TV's in it too," Yarni responded.

"VA tags or out-of-towner?" asked Cara.

"This joker is local," said Yarni as she threw in a disappointing giggle.

"Keep it moving then," responded Cara.

"Anyway, what are you into, girl?"

"Nothing much. I want to know if you want to go out tomorrow night, you know, grab a couple of drinks, mingle and maybe meet some guys. Who knows?" Cara said.

"No, I don't really feel like being bothered."

"Yarni, every since you got your job—no, way before that, when you started messing with Bengee—we hadn't been out to a club, so tomorrow we're going out, my treat."

"Nah, I'm not really feeling the club," said Yarni.

"Come on, you might meet somebody. You need to get out and meet some new people, plus you getting your hair done tomorrow anyway," said Cara.

"I'll go with you, but I am not interested in meeting any man in a club. Any man hitting on something is not going to be at the club looking for a woman."

"Okay, what are you wearing?" asked Cara. "You know you can't wear any of your business suits you wear to work."

"Yeah, I know," responded Yarni. "I guess I'm going to have to go to the mall to buy me something to wear."

"Make sure it's sophisticated as well as sexy. You've been dressing so conservative lately."

"Yeah, whatever," said Yarni as she hung up the phone.

The next morning was Yarni's day off. She got up, took a shower, dressed, and headed out.

When she got in her car she called over to Cara's mother's house. She informed her that she needed to have her godson, Li'l Ronny, ready because she was running late and was going to only blow the horn.

After dropping Li'l Ronny off, Yarni went to the beauty shop. Co-Co did her hair in spiral curls. The way each curl hung down complemented her round, fat face. Yarni went to the mall after she left the salon. She went to Up Against the Wall in Cloverleaf Mall. As soon as she walked through the door, Tonya, the saleslady, flocked to her. She knew one thing about Yarni. Yarni was going to spend her money and tip her for helping her as well.

"Hey girl," said Tonya.

"Hey!" Yarni said. "What y'all got in new?"

"We got a lot of stuff, but we haven't put it out yet." Tonya went into the back and brought out all the new things in Yarni's size that hadn't hit the floor yet.

"Yarni, you going out tonight?"

"Maybe, girl, I don't know." Yarni never told anybody her exact moves ever since the kidnapping. She knew nobody could really be trusted.

Tonya told Yarni, "Well, whatever you buy, I won't put it out on the sales floor until tomorrow or so, so you won't have to worry about nobody having the same thing on that you are wearing."

"Good looking, Tonya, but I don't want you to get into any trouble. If somebody else gets the same thing, they won't be able to freak it like me anyway."

"Yeah, you right. They'll get the four-hundred-dollar outfit and put some ten-dollar Payless shoes on with it," Tonya said and they both laughed. Yarni picked out a few things that she wanted to try on. As she breezed through the store, she noticed three dudes throwing things on the counter. She didn't make eye contact with any of them. They were all too loud for her. Plus, she knew they hustled.

As bad as I want to holler at a hustler right now to help me get into my condo, I'm trying to do the right thing. I've had enough of that lifestyle.

Yarni glanced at one through one of the store mirrors standing in the middle of the floor. He was counting a wad of cash.

That's a damn shame. Why would you even have all that money on you like that? Shoot, you at the mall buying clothes, not buying a yacht. I betcha he lives right at his mama's house, no game plan, nothing going on, just flossing until the feds come. See, he's the worst kind of hustler, all that money and don't know what to do with it. He needs a sister like me to show him what to do with that cake. Buy some property, with property comes capital, with capital comes credit, and with credit comes mo' money. Even though all that money looks good, and it damn sure would expedite my process to getting into my condo. On the other hand, easy come, easy go. On that note, I'll keep working my nine-to-five, to get mines the right way. That way, can't no brother try to come with some Indian-giving-type drama or worse, the feds come trying to confiscate what's mines. I'll pass this time. Boy, he better be glad that I'm trying to stay away from that lifestyle because he would definitely be my target. Anyways, let me go and try this stuff on.

Yarni went into the dressing room. Tonya told her to come out and show her the things she tried on. Tonya continued to look around the store to see if there was anything Yarni might've liked that they had missed.

Yarni came out of the dressing room to show Tonya everything. Tonya hyped her up about each outfit she tried on. She worked on commission and she knew how Yarni spent money when she came in there. Yarni was more likely to buy since her hair was done. That alone added a touch to any outfit she tried on. Yarni usually didn't try on clothes unless her hair was fixed. She felt she wouldn't be able to get the full effect of the outfit.

Yarni decided that she was going to buy two pair of Parasuco jeans and the little T-shirts to match for kick-around days. She also bought two other outfits. She debated back and forth on whether to purchase this Guess leather jumpsuit that she wanted.

When she came out of the dressing room from trying it on, Tonya boasted about how good it looked on her. She even called over another sales associate, and they both agreed. The loud guys were quiet and looked in astonishment. Everything paused when she looked in the three-way mirror. It was $430 dollars. It definitely looked nice on her. It fit her like a glove. Guess was something that she really didn't care for anymore, but this jumpsuit, she really wanted. She didn't care whom it was by. It wasn't something that she'd wear to Diamonds and Pearls. She dressed up when she went out. It just wasn't the effect she was trying to get tonight. She needed the other outfits for kick-around. She knew that the jumpsuit was something that would hang in her closet. But at the proper time and place, and no doubt, with the right shoes, she knew she could turn heads and have mouths dropping.

She said to herself, *This jumpsuit would really come in handy for knockout purposes only.* Then she reminded herself, *I am closing on my condo in a couple of months. I work a nine-to-five, no ballers in my life to supply my extravagant spending habit. Which was really more important? The furniture at La Difference that I am saving for or this jumpsuit?* She tried to convince herself that the jumpsuit was an investment. She reasoned with herself that she could charge the jumpsuit. Then she asked herself, *Self, what sense does that make, to wear something that I haven't even paid for and would still be making payments on it long after I've already worn it? That's only making a crazy bill for what, when I got plenty of shit in my closet now running over. With this $430 dollars, I can buy my washer for the condo. Gloria isn't going to be allowing me to be running back and forth over there using hers. I can't see the Laundromat in the vision at all.*

On that very note, Yarni laid the jumpsuit on the side of the counter. She started to tell Tonya to put it on hold just so no one else would have it. She turned to the guys, "I apologize for holding the line up." She grabbed her bags and walked out of the store.

She looked at her watch. She knew she still had to go to Regency Square to Caché; she knew for sure she'd find something in there. She started eliminating things she could wear at home so that she could go back and get that jumpsuit. She could not get her mind off of that jumpsuit.

As she walked toward the mall entrance, she heard somebody calling out her name. She turned around and it was Tonya. She was running over to Yarni with a bag. She peeped in the bag. *Lord, thank you so much.* It was the jumpsuit in the bag. She couldn't believe it. Did Tonya give it to her? She knew she didn't pay for it. Tonya saw the expression on Yarni's face.

"The dude name Rich bought it for you," Tonya explained. "He said you looked so nice in it and he wanted you to have it."

"Girl, who is, Rich?" Yarni asked with a puzzled look on her face.

"The dude walking down there, with the . . . umm . . . Tims on and the butter-soft leather coat to match," said Tonya.

"What's his story?"

"He's loaded, I mean caked up! I haven't really heard any gossip or anything about him. But I do know, he comes in the store a lot, but never with a female, no wedding ring, and never made a female purchase until now. I think he's very available, annnd . . . a potential vic for you."

A *vic* was a victim, someone a gold digger considered a sucker for her to get a substantial amount of money from.

Yarni looked sad when she told Tonya, "Thanks, sweetie, but, I've got to catch him, because I can't accept this from him."

She took off walking quickly trying to catch up with the dude and his crew. They were walking in the opposite direction than she was going. She was a few feet behind them. She called out, "Rich . . . excuse me, Rich." Just then he turned around and stopped. "Can I speak to you for a minute, please?"

Damn, he looks so familiar. I don't know where I know him from. Ooh, ummp, ummp, ummp, Lord, he smells good. I wonder if that's Joop!? He was clean-cut, fresh haircut, and his fingernails were dirt-free and manicured. Tims were smacking new. The first thing Yarni looked at was a man's shoes. She felt like if his shoes weren't right, then he'd never come correct.

When Rich gazed into her eyes, he thought to himself, *Damn, she looks good with her hair like that. Ummp, ummp ummp, she is sexier than I remembered.*

He looked at her as she spoke. "Thank you soooo much for the jumpsuit. And . . . and—" she took a deep breath then continued "as much as I would like to, I can't accept this."

He said with the most sincere look on his face, "Yes you can, and you will because I am not taking it back. I want you to have it."

"You have to take it back," she said with the most sincere look on her face. Yarni extended her hand.

"Baby, I'm no Indian-giver, and frankly, darling, you're straight insulting me." He stressed to her by shaking his head, pushing the bag back to her.

"You don't understand, I really can't accept this and—and you're making this very difficult for me." Yarni was almost unsure what she was saying herself.

"Look, there are no strings attached, so please just take it. It's my pleasure. I needed to make someone's day, and it happened to be yours today. Now why make such a big deal?" asked Rich.

Game, game, game! Would you listen to this game he's kicking to me. "I have my own personal reasons, and nothing in life is free, and if much is given, then much is required," Yarni said.

"I am insisting that you keep the jumpsuit, baby. I would feel totally disrespected if you even asked me to take it back again." He then walked away with his tons of bags in his hand, leaving Yarni standing there speechless.

He knew that he'd see Yarni again. After all, this wasn't New York. This was Richmond, a town where everyone basically knew everyone or knew someone who knew that person. Yarni tried to figure out where she knew him from, but she couldn't. She had no clue. On her way to Regency she tried to remember each and every one of Des and Bengee's friends to try to see if maybe she'd seen him through one of them. That wasn't it. She wondered, *Maybe I know him through Uncle Stank.* No, that wasn't it either.

Yarni went to Regency Square Mall, bought a pants set from Caché, and then decided against wearing it. She wore her Coogi dress with the hat to match, which she'd bought from New York when Bengee sent her. That was a year ago. A lot of styles and fads got to Richmond a little slower. She'd never worn it before. The dress and the hat were a big hit that night. No other females had on anything Coogi. Coogi had just hit Richmond. There were a few ballers in the club wearing Coogi sweaters.

14

The Big Payback

As Yarni, Cara, and Stephanie sat at the table, Cara whispered to Yarni, "Don't look now, but you ain't going to believe who's here?"

"Who, girl?" Yarni blurted out. "Girl, Rallo."

"Stop playing," Yarni said as she took a sip of her drink. "Don't look, but he's on his way over here now," Cara said.

Rallo walked up to the table bling-blinging with a nice, expensive Cuban link necklace and an iced-out cross on his chain, a big baguette pinky ring, crème linen suit, some colorful shades of brown, gator shoes, and some Cartier glasses.

"What's up, Cara? Hey, Stephanie." Both of them said "hi." "Yeah, I just want y'all to know that I'm buying everybody at this table drinks except you," he said, pointing to Yarni. Yarni laughed.

"Rallo, I don't need you to buy me a drink. I can buy my own. I am glad that you're in a situation where you can buy somebody a drink, 'cause not too long ago, I heard you couldn't even buy yourself a Snickers bar, let alone somebody a drink." On that note, Yarni got up and when she walked past Rallo, he grabbed her arm.

"Don't try to get slick out the mouth, because I made you," Rallo said.

"You made me? Yeah, right." She smacked her lips. Yarni leaned over and said, "I'm happy for you and your newfound fortune. And you would like to think you made me, but guess what, baby? I played you." She smiled and proceeded to the ladies' room. Cara came in behind her.

"I told him that if he couldn't buy all of us a drink, then I don't want any," said Cara.

"By all means, if that nigga is paying, drink him up under the table! And order some chicken baskets too." They both laughed and walked out of the bathroom.

As they walked out of the restroom, Cara said, "Let me put this bug in your ear," as she put her hand up to Yarni's ear. "Girl, Rallo looks like he back on, getting money. You should holler just to get some quick loot out of him. You know he's always peeled cash off to you. Shit, just play with him." Yarni never responded.

Yarni saw Rallo as she was on her way to check on Stephanie who was sitting at the table. Rallo looked her up and down and rolled his eyes. *The nerve of him! He acts just like a little girl rolling his eyes. Just for that watch this move I'm about to make on him. Gonna fuck his head up. Just watch and see.*

Yarni approached Rallo. *Ummp, she sho is looking good, ass is still fat as ever. Looks like she's still maintaining. Somebody gotta be taking care of her. Wonder who she messing wit now?* Rallo couldn't keep from smiling as he realized she was stopping right in front of him.

"What you coming over here for? To ask me for a drink?" Rallo said.

"Pleeasse, Rallo," Yarni said with a little giggle. "It's funny you should say that." Rallo had a grin on his face. *Oh, she see a nigga getting money again. She done caught the vapors. I'm gonna try my hand wit her. Let me see what she drinking. I'll buy her a drink just to show her I'm the bigger person.*

"Rallo, the reason why I came over here, is because I don't want war with you anymore. I want peace. I am throwing in my towel," Yarni said as apologetic as she knew how.

"Yeah, right." Smiling, but still trying to give her a hard time. "When has Yarnise Pitman ever thrown in the towel?"

"Rallo, I am dead serious." Yarni threw up her hands. "I surrender." Rallo nodded and continued to smile. "And to show you that I harbor no ill feelings, drinks are on me tonight!"

Oh hell, she really trying to get on a nigga's good side. She got mad game, but I got just as much . . . oh, I'm going to get pissy drunk at the expense of this gold-diggin' bitch, Rallo thought to himself.

"So, what you drinking, Rallo?" Yarni asked. He held up his cup and said, "Henney and Coke."

"Look, I gotta run to my car to get some more money because I know it's going to cost me. You going to straight try to drink like a fish, but by the time I get from my car, you should be finished with that one." Yarni pointed to the glass he already had in his hand. "And I'll bring over your drink, okay?" she said as humble as she knew how. Rallo shook his head.

"Don't try to leave, cuz a promise is a promise."

"Yo, I got you, Rallo. That's my word. I got you, baby," she said as she was walking away. She glanced back over. He was looking at her butt. She smiled, waved a cute, sexy wave to him, and really put the seductive walk on as she exited the club. She hesitated for a minute. *Should I?* Then she thought again: A girl's gotta do what a girl's gotta do, and she ran as fast as she could in her Charles Jourdan stiletto ankle boots across the street to the Racetrack service station. She hurried back to the club and rushed over to the bar. She ordered Rallo's Hennessy and Coke, and a plain Coke for herself. She had decided not to drink tonight. She had to be sober to execute her plan that she expected to go down in about an hour and a half or so.

On the way over to Rallo, she dropped two Ex-lax tablets in his drink. She was almost sure that the breakdown of the alcohol would dissolve the ex-lax. She read the ingredients on the back of the box while standing in line at Racetrack. She had also remembered this from one of her chemistry classes. She handed him the drink. He drank the drink straight while she stood there. He handed her the glass back and said, "Next, please." Smiling. *This was easier than I thought. Better believe I am glad I paid attention in chemistry.*

Yarni walked away, back over to the bar. She returned with two Hennessy and Cokes this time, which each contained two more ex-lax tablets.

"Rallo, I'll be back in a few with your next round, so hold tight. I need to go check on my girls, and then I'm going to hit the bar for you again."

"No problem, baby, just keep 'em coming." He raised his glass up and drank the first one straight down. Yarni walked away.

As Yarni made her way back through the smoke-filled club, someone grabbed her hand, squeezed it tight, and pulled her over to them. When she looked, it was Rich with the same print and color Coogi sweater as her dress. His friend joked, "Ooh, they got his and her matching outfits." They both laughed. Just as they laughed, the picture man approached them as he was walking around the club snapping pictures. He totally caught Yarni off guard. Yarni secretly was glad to see Rich, but the timing was wrong, due to the fact she was on a mission and couldn't be sidetracked. This was the revenge she had been waiting on for years.

"Let me get another one," Rich said to the picture man. They both smiled. Rich gave that photo to Yarni.

"Look, I don't usually pick up women at the club, but I want to take you and your girls to breakfast after this is over."

"No, I don't want to break your clubbing habits. If you haven't been picking up women at the club, please don't start now on my account." Yarni walked away, and made her way through the crowd back to the bar, getting Rallo two more Hennessy and Cokes mixed with ex-lax, and headed back to her table.

"Where have you been?" asked Stephanie

"Oh, I forgot to tell you, I decided to sponsor Rallo's drinks tonight. So, I had to go get him a round." Yarni smiled.

"What?" Stephanie said, "Have you lost your damn mind?"

"It's not what you think, Steph," she whispered. "Don't you know the one who laughs last, laughs the longest?"

Yarni got up and walked away as she smiled at Stephanie.

"I know she is not thinking about backtracking to Rallo." Steph shook her head in disgust.

"She just probably going to juice him for some quick cash. You know he's always been a sucker for Yarni," Cara said with her arms folded.

"Yeah, I know that's right," Steph said, as they laughed.

Yarni took Rallo two more drinks. She could tell he was feeling the alcohol. She walked back over to her table. She looked at her watch and laughed to herself. She knew the show was about to begin. "Y'all, let's stand over there."

"Why? So, we can get a good view of Rallo?" Cara asked while winking and smiling as if Yarni really wanted to watch Rallo.

They slid their way through the musty crowd. She looked at Rallo talking to a girl, whom looked like she was wearing a 34DD with a flat butt. They made eye contact as he lifted his drink up and smiled. He was sure Yarni wanted him. He was only talking to the various girls to make her jealous.

Yarni smiled back at him, and right then, she saw the look on his face. A sharp cramp hit him and he grabbed his stomach. He walked off quickly, leaving Ms. 34DD standing right there. He was holding his stomach while trying to squeeze his butt tight, while walking with his legs tight, putting one leg in front of the other. He approached the long restroom line. He couldn't hold it any longer. He screamed out as he rushed to the front of the line. "It's an emergency!" He was as wild as a bull in a china shop. He barged into a stall, pulling out some Steve Urkel-looking guy with his pants down. He threw two one hundred, dollar bills at him. He dropped his pants only to realize he had already gone on himself. He plopped on the toilet as the watery waste gushed out of his rectum. He made loud noises of relief. A few guys knocked on the door of the stall.

"Everything all right in there man?" someone called.

Rallo couldn't even answer. He didn't have the will to respond. The foul stench filled the

bathroom, which chased every man out of there.
The bathroom was vacant besides Rallo. He shit-
ted so much that when he got up, his knees were
weak. He reached for some tissue to wipe the
sweat from dripping from his face only to realize
there was no toilet paper on the roll. He realized
that he had shit running down the insides of
his legs and all over his brand-new gator shoes.
When he walked out of the stall, he immediately
headed right back in. "Oh God, God, Lord have
mercy!" he shouted out.

He was very confused. He walked to the mirror and threw water on his face. He had beads
of uncontrollable perspiration on his face. He
looked like he'd been in a fight. He walked out
of the bathroom lump-sided, barely standing up
straight. His shirt was out of his pants with shit
stains on the back. His linen suit was ruined. The
first person he saw when he came outside of the
bathroom was Yarni holding another drink in
her hand.

"Want a drink?" she said, as serious as a heart
attack.

He was dehydrated and thirsty. He grabbed
the drink out of her hand, drank it in one gulp,
and handed her the glass back.

"What happened to you? Were you in a scuffle?" Yarni asked with a sincere voice and look.

"Naw, sick as hell," he said, walking off. She walked beside him, trying to show him her concern.

"Ohhh, my God," she said while holding her nose, "You stiiiink! Where are you going to be? I'll run and get you another drink."

"Naw, I'm fucked up, Yarni, I had too much to drink and I didn't have nothing on my stomach. I'll catch up with you another time."

Rallo staggered off. She watched him bypass people as they laughed and fanned him off as he finally exited the club.

What better way to get revenge on a fly guy than humiliate him in the club? She knew the right opportunity would come one day.

She looked out of the window and watched Rallo try to make it to his car, when she focused on the fact that he had white or crème-leather piked-out seats in his car. A childhood song popped in her head, "Diarrhea, diarrhea, some people think it's funny, but it's really wet and runny . . . diarrhea, diarrhea." Then she laughed hysterically, almost peeing on herself.

That was the best laugh Yarni ever had in her life.

15

Your Worry, Not Mine

Stephanie suggested that they go to the Waffle House when they got out of the club. Yarni hadn't been out in God knows when, so there was no need to rush home. There wasn't anybody waiting for her there anyway. Everybody went to the Waffle House or Aunt Sarah's after the club. When they walked inside the Waffle House, there was a wait. They decided that they'd go to Aunt Sarah's instead. Aunt Sarah's wasn't as packed, but there was a time lag. Cara walked through Aunt Sarah's to go to the restroom, Rich noticed her. He and his homeboys already had a table.

"Excuse me, shorty girl, weren't you with the girl with the Coogi dress on?"

"Yeah," Cara responded.

"Tell her Rich is over here and y'all can come sit with us. It's three of y'all, right? We can make room," Rich said as the guys with him slid over and around in the large booth. Cara told Yarni what Rich said.

"I feel straight uncomfortable going over there to sit with them. He da one that I was telling you about from the mall today and the jumpsuit," Yarni said with a serious look on her face.

"He seems like good people, he got a nice Rolex President on," Cara said.

"Cara, you make me sick with that always measuring a brother by what he drives or what he got."

Cara ignored Yarni and asked the hostess, "What's the wait on the Pitman party?" The hostess answered, forty-five minutes. Cara and Stephanie looked at Yarni. Yarni smacked her lips and said, "Oookay."

They headed over to the back of the dining room. Rich and his boys had a table and a booth. Yarni, Cara, and Rich sat at the same table. Stephanie sat at the other table with the other two guys. Yarni watched Rich, still trying to figure out where she knew him from.

Rich asked, "Why you looking at me like that? You see something you like over here?" He caught Yarni off guard.

"No, I was actually wondering where I know you from. You look so familiar to me."

"I do, do I?" Rich said.

"Yeah, you do," said Yarni.

"Oh, nigga, that's the oldest line in the book," Rich said to Yarni as he took a sip of his water. Rich and Yarni joked all night. Cara got a kick out of seeing Yarni laughing and actually interacting with a man. Yarni had been through so much with Bengee that Cara was just ecstatic that her friend had a smile on her face.

When they all finished eating, of course, Rich picked up the tab. Yarni said, "Oh I'll leave the tip."

Rich shot her a look and said, "Your money is bogus when you're with me."

He asked Yarni, "When can I see you again?"

"Chances are, you'll see me around town," said Yarni.

"Look, straight up, I don't want to play your little cat and mouse game anymore. Since I first seen you yesterday, I thought you were beautiful. Then, I ran into you earlier at the mall. I couldn't read the strong look you had on your face when I had to beg you to accept the jumpsuit, and as persistent as you were about leaving the tip, I don't understand why you wouldn't allow a brother to be a man, to treat you like the lady you are."

"All right now, I like you already," Cara said jokingly.

"Long story," Yarni simply responded, as she rolled her eyes.

"Well, I've got time. I don't have to go to work tomorrow," Rich said as he went in his pocket to leave the tip.

"Well, I don't discuss my life story with strangers. Now, let's leave it at that." Yarni got up to go to the bathroom.

Cara asked Rich, "What's your motive with my friend?"

"My intentions are all good," said Rich while looking into Cara's eyes. He added, "I am feeling your friend."

"Let me tell you this, my friend has been through a lot, and the drama she doesn't need or deserve. If I find out at any given time, your motives aren't good, I will personally fuck you up myself," Cara stressed as Rich chuckled. He wrote his numbers down on a piece of paper.

"Make sure your friend gives me a call," said Rich.

"I'll see what I can do," Cara said as she rose up from the table.

Yarni asked, "Are y'all ready?"

The girls replied "Yeah."

"Thanks for everything," Yarni said to Rich and passed him a rose. She'd seen the man selling them outside when she went to the restroom.

"I definitely want to see you again. Let's do lunch tomorrow," said Rich. "Your friend has my number. Excuse me," he shouted as he put his jacket on, "Ms. Preoccupied, I don't even know your name," he called from a distance.

"It's Yarni," she shouted back at him.

The whole way home, Cara went on and on about Rich, how he was a perfect gentleman and how he seemed so patient with a genuine kind spirit.

"They all seem that way when you first meet them. They put on their best faces," Yarni interrupted.

Cara was impressed with him. He had pretty white teeth. His attitude and disposition rated well above normal. Cara had gotten the scoop on him while Yarni went in the restroom. He had his own pick-up and drop-off business. He had purchased old houses over in the historic Church Hill area, renovated them, and then sold them at market price. Cara was convinced that this was definitely what her friend needed in her life. She knew deep in Yarni's heart that Yarni desired companionship. Could this be? Cara wondered. Cara reasoned with herself, even if this wasn't permanent for Yarni, this would be a temporary relief for her.

Cara hated the fact that Yarni was so devoted to Des. For what? Cara felt like it was a waste of time, gas, energy, and putting all that wear and tear on her car. Who was to say he was even going to be with Yarni when he came home? Who was to say that he could look past the relationships Yarni had been in since he'd been gone? Who was to say he was not just stringing Yarni along because friends got fewer and fewer the longer one is incarcerated? Who was to say that he was not using Yarni? It didn't have to be for money that he was using her for. It could be her time; he might use her for a visit or just as a connection to the outside world. Who was to say that they were going to have anything in common when he came home? What could he do for Yarni while in jail?

Cara could never understand why Yarni felt so obligated to Des after all these years had gone by and no matter whom Yarni met and was in a relationship with, Des was always her first concern. The love that Yarni had from when she was seventeen for Des has never died or lost any sparks. Cara used to voice her opinion on the Des situation, but she respected Yarni's feelings, so she no longer brought it up. She would elaborate on it if Yarni brought up the topic. Whenever Cara would meet any suitable candidate that she thought might be any good for Yarni, Cara would always push him at her.

They dropped Stephanie off at home and Cara decided that she'd stay over Yarni's house, so Yarni wouldn't have to drive her all the way home. Besides, Cara's son was over his father's house.

The next morning, Cara was standing over Yarni with the phone. "Yarni, wake up. The phone's for you," Cara said.

"Is it Des?" Yarni asked, partially asleep.

"No," Cara said, covering up the phone.

"Take a message then," she said slowly.

"No, get up and get the phone. Wake up!" Cara said while pulling the crème-and-gold comforter back off of Yarni, who was curled up in a fetal position.

"Tell them to hold on," Yarni said. Yarni got up, brushed her teeth, and washed her face. When she was finished, she jumped right back under the covers and took the phone from Cara.

"Good morning," Yarni said.

"Good afternoon, Ms. Preoccupied. How are you feeling today?" said Rich.

"What time is it?" asked Yarni while yawning in Rich's ear. "Excuse me," she said in a sleepy tone.

"It's one-twenty-three p.m.," responded Rich. "I wanted to know what time you'd be up for lunch?"

"Uuummm, I'm not going to be able to go because my friend Cara is here with me."

"Baby, that excuse is not going to work because Cara can come right along with us. Now, what time should I pick you up?" Yarni hesitated before answering him.

"We will meet you there. Where do you want us to meet you?

"You can pick the place," he told her.

"No, this was your idea so you pick the place." She wanted to see what his taste was like.

"How about Byram's on West Broad Street? Is three-fifteen okay?

"Yes, that'll be fine."

"The address is three-two-one-five, so don't be late!" Yarni hung up the phone.

Cara was dancing around Yarni, "Go Yarni. It's your birthday. You going to Byram's, on your first date!" Most men would only take their wife to Byram's for a special occasion or something of that nature. Byram's Lobster House was one of her favorite places in the city to eat. It was a real classy place. She liked everything about Byram's. Byram's offered the best of everything. Their customer service was beyond reproach. They

pampered one as if they were a king or queen.
The food at Byram's was scrumptious and they
employed world-renowned chefs.

Yarni jumped off the bed. "What am I going
to wear?"

Cara added, "Definitely put on something re-
fined. You know the type of place Byram's is. We
may run into someone famous there." Yarni and
Cara got dressed. As they pulled up to Byram's,
the valet driver welcomed them both with a rose,
courtesy of the guy waiting at the bar.

Rich greeted them both with a kiss on the
hand. Cara admired the exotic fish in the aquar-
ium. He pulled both of their chairs out. They
both were moved by his manners. He ordered
the best champagne in the house for them. "I'd
like to make a toast," he said. "To everlasting
friendships." Yarni could feel the chemistry
between them. She liked the way he seemed to
have his act together. It was so hard to find a
brother who had it going on for himself. The
odds were very slim to find a brother who wasn't
living with his mama, leeching off some woman,
who wasn't getting high, sold drugs or had some
type of illegal hustle. To come across a man who
didn't have any of those things, with a little class,
and didn't have his head stuck up his own butt;
that was very rare.

It was something about his eyes Yarni couldn't pinpoint. She would always look at people in their eyes when she addressed them. She felt as though the eyes told it all. There was something peculiar about the way he looked. She couldn't figure it out.

The food was extraordinary. When the bill came, she offered to leave the tip, but he wouldn't allow it. He explained to her that whenever they were together, she never had to go in her pocketbook for anything. She explained to him, "I really appreciate the gesture, but at the same time, for my own personal reasons, I would like to contribute. Please understand and accept this."

"Okay, I will compromise with you. For every three times I take you out to eat, the fourth time you'll cook me a hot meal. Since I am a bachelor, a brother never gets a home-cooked meal. Is it a deal?" Rich asked.

Yarni, agreed. "There's only one problem. I live with my mother and I am real protective of my mother and selective of who I bring around her."

"Well, you could always come over to my place to cook. I'll buy the groceries and all you have to do is show up and cook," he said in a soft, subtle tone.

"Well, I guess you've got this all figured out, huh?" said Yarni.

"There's one more thing," Rich said hesitantly.

"What is it now?" Yarni asked sarcastically.

"How about we go to the park and talk a little more extensively?"

Cara interrupted, "Drop me off at my car. I have to go get Li'l Ronny. I am already late, but it's all good."

Rich said, "Well, we can drop you to your car, Cara. Yarni, you and I can go to the park, and I will drop you back at you car later."

"No, I don't ride with arbitrary men," Yarni said rudely.

Cara cut in, "Don't worry, Yarni, I got his license-tag number." Yarni didn't really feel comfortable riding with him. Cara pulled her to the side and told her to loosen up.

"Rich seems to be a good guy and if he tries something crazy, just Mace him." As Cara exited the car, she turned to Yarni, "Don't forget you have to take me to the train station in the morning, so don't hang out too late. I need you to be at my house at four-thirty a.m. You know I have to be there by five a.m."

"I won't, just don't forget to call me in the morning to wake me up."

"Make sure you call me tonight as soon as you get in the house," Cara said while bending down, holding the car door open.

Once they dropped Cara off, the conversation seemed so natural. Yarni relaxed more. Rich made her laugh. Since the whole ordeal with Bengee, Yarni was very skeptical about men. She knew how hard it had been for her to get over Bengee, and she never wanted to subject herself to such pain again. When they reached the park, they got out and walked around the big man-made lake and watched the water and light show on the lake. Rich asked Yarni, "Can I ask you a personal question?"

"How personal?"

Rich stopped walking, turned, and looked Yarni in the eyes.

She could smell his Joop! cologne. *He smells so good,* Yarni said to herself.

He shyly asked Yarni, "Did you have a horrible experience of some sort? I notice you're so defensive and cynical when it comes to men. May I ask how come?"

That threw Yarni for a loop, of course. She wasn't expecting him to ask that question.

Yarni responded, "I've been hurt tremendously."

"We all have, baby. It's a part of life. But does that mean that you won't ever love again?" Rich asked.

"I don't know. It would be very hard for me to love," Yarni said.

"Damn, what could cause you to be so uncertain if you'd ever love again?" Rich said.

"I loved somebody with all my heart, and it was terribly too late when I found out that his love wasn't genuine. It almost cost me my life. I guess you could say I was blinded by all the material things."

"Well, that can happen to the best of us, Yarni," Rich said as he sat on a bench.

"You really think so?" was Yarni's response.

"May I ask, how come you didn't want to accept the jumpsuit in the mall?" Rich said, with an earnest look. "I am curious to know."

"Because I didn't want to feel like I owe you anything," Yarni replied.

"No, you don't owe me anything," Rich said in a compassionate tone.

"Well, honestly, Rich, my last couple of relationships, the guys provided a lot of lavish things for me. The relationships became based on material things. It's almost like if a man gives you something, he feels he has the upper hand. He acts as though you need him!"

"That's those insecure clown-dudes, they feel that's the only thing they can bring to the table. Don't judge me, please. Give me a chance to change your disposition concerning men," he said.

Yarni just looked at Rich. She thought to herself, *What could you bring to the table? What makes you different?* She couldn't put her finger on it, but it was something about Rich's voice and his eyes that puzzled her.

Yarni looked at her watch. "I need to get home because I've got to get up bright and early and take Cara to the train station. Plus, I need to get prepared for work tomorrow," Yarni said.

The park experience was good for Yarni. She couldn't believe that she had actually enjoyed herself. It was almost like therapy for her.

The next morning at 4:00 Yarni's phone rung. She was so sick of these early wake-up calls. She was sure it was Cara waking her up. However, it was Rich.

"Good morning, I'm calling because I need the address where to pick you up so we can take Cara to the train station. I'm not comfortable with you being out at four a.m. by yourself."

Oh how thoughtful, and this is surely a convenience, because I can take a nap in the car.

When Rich arrived to pick Yarni up, he handed her a little teddy bear. The card attached said, *I never believed in love at first sight until I met you.* When they reached Cara's house, she was surprised that Rich had gotten up so early. Cara thought selfishly to herself, *How come Yarni always gets the dudes that bend over backwards for her?*

Yarni and Rich became companions. They enjoyed long, intimate talks. He'd shower her with sentimental things, and sometimes would send them through the mail. He once gave her a picnic inside on a rainy day. He'd write her unexpected letters. They liked the same movies. He always committed a public display of his affection for her. He showed interest in her work. She would stay over his house. It would get late and they'd just fall asleep.

Rich also made it a point to celebrate everything so he could surprise her with generous gifts. He was very selective as well as careful of the gifts he gave her. He always made sure that the presents had some type of sentimental value to them so she would be comfortable accepting the gifts. He presented her with some aquamarine earrings, the matching ring and pendant, along with a note attached: *Found in a range of blue shades from pale to dark, this gem embodies the beauty of the seas. It was thought to give its wearer knowledge and foresight and assist in an individual's inspiration.*

Any time he would send her flowers, the card would give the origin of the flower, what it meant, and where it came from. He gave her a gift certificate to Custom Cruisin' to have TV's installed in her truck, so she wouldn't have to listen to the soaps on the radio.

She also would do thoughtful things for Rich as well. He was very appreciative of the least little thing she did.

They finally took their relationship to the next level. He begged her to move into his place with him, but she refused. She was focusing on her goal to buy her own condo. She'd never lived solely on her own. She promised herself that she'd never live with another man until she was married. However, Rich was very persistent, so she spent a lot of time over his house. She usually spent the night regularly, and when she didn't spend the night, they'd stay on the phone until the wee hours in the morning.

One day, she'd just finished having lunch with Rich and she bumped into Amy. Amy, who knew everybody's business in Richmond, of course. Amy was going to throw some salt Yarni's way. Yarni prepared herself for Amy's negative input. She thought to herself, *I swear I don't even feel like speaking to this bone-carrying broad.*

"Heeey, Yarni," Amy said.

"Heeeey Amy, how are you doing?" Yarni said while thinking, *I wonder what dirt is this toxic chick kicking today?* The truth of the matter was there was nothing Yarni could do to prepare herself for the news that was about to be dropped on her.

"Girl, everything's fine with me," Amy said, looking Yarni up and down on the sly.

"It's been a while since I've seen you. I'm glad to know everything's going well for you. Tell your mother I said hi," Yarni said.

Amy told Yarni, "Girl, I heard your mother is big-time catering all of those high-society parties. Tell her I said hi."

"I will, and you take care," added Yarni. *Woo, that was short and sweet. Let me keep it moving.* As Yarni was walking off, Amy called out to her.

"Oh, Yarni, I thought I seen you a couple of times with the guy Rich. Yarni thought to herself, *Here we go. I knew that was just too easy, being around Amy and she didn't kick any dirt my way!* Amy continued. "I know my eyes didn't deceive me. Y'all were surely looking like lovebirds to me."

"And your point?" Yarni said.

"Yarni, I've known you a long time and I know enough about you that I feel obligated to tell you this.

"Rich messes with Darchelle, the one that used to creep with Bengee?"

"For real?" Yarni said.

"Yes, and he has been for a while, since Bengee cut her off."

"Thanks for telling me."

"No problem. You know I puts you down with latest, breaking news, right?" Amy said to Yarni with a smile.

Yarni kept her composure until Amy walked away. She wanted to cry but she just couldn't. *I can't believe out of all the chicks in the town he has to be messing with that tramp. Damn, the world is small! I've gotta cut him off. It could have been anybody but her.*

She simply called Rich and left him a message.

"I know you mess with that dirty trick Darchelle, so you be with her."

Rich called Yarni for weeks trying to reconcile, but she wasn't having him back.

Yarni received the news that Des had been transferred from Red Onion Correctional Facility, which was a seven-hour drive, to Haynesville Correctional Center, which was only an hour away from her. She was happy and relieved by the transfer.

After the good news, she wasn't thinking of Rich because her real man was closer to her.

She went to see Des faithfully. Their relationship grew stronger and stronger. His calls were
cheaper, and Des called each day. She never got
tired of talking to him. He was her best friend.
He always made her day. It really bothered
Yarni that jail was wearing on Des. He was
aging, getting a few gray strands of hair. His eyes
were filled with a multitude of feelings within,
some good and some melancholy. Love, hate,
confidence, fear, optimism, depression, comfort,
and pain all struggled for dominance for him to
prevail.

16

With Friends Like These You Don't Need Enemies

Cara and Yarni decided to go out. Cara was avoiding her live-in boyfriend, Mike. Mike was very jealous and abusive to Cara. Yarni could not stand Mike. Cara told Yarni to meet her over a male friend of Cara's house. Yarni questioned Cara about the meeting place. The club they were going to was in Shockoe Bottom. Cara lived in the historic Church Hill area, which was five minutes away from the club. Yarni lived on the other side of town in Western Henrico County, which was twenty-five minutes away from town. Cara told Yarni to meet her at her friend's house, who lived in Newtown. Yarni wanted to meet over Cara's house, so when the club was over she could just hop in her car and go home from there, versus Cara having to come back over her friend's house to drop Yarni at her car. Cara insisted that Yarni meet her at her friend's house. Yarni had a gut feeling that she should've just driven to the club. Cara informed Yarni that she wanted her car to be parked at the club so if Mike drove past, he would see it out there and would assume that she was in the club. She added that she didn't want Mike to see Yarni's car outside because if she decided to stay with her guy friend then she would use the excuse that she had to take Yarni to the far West End and just spent the night over there.

Yarni agreed. When Yarni arrived to the guy friend's house, Cara introduced her to his friends. Yarni wasn't interested in any of them. They were all loud and out of order. She could tell that they had been drinking long before she'd gotten there. Once Yarni was introduced to the fellas, Cara and Yarni hopped in Cara's car and went to the club.

They arrived at the club. Cara sat at the bar the whole time with her guy friend. Yarni mingled throughout the club with different sets of people. She kept going back to the bar, checking on Cara.

Gloria paged Yarni while she was at the club. She went into the restroom, pulled out her cell phone and called her mother right back. Gloria answered in a groggy voice.

"Mommy, what's wrong? What are you doing up this time of night?" Yarni asked.

"I have indigestion," Gloria explained. "Sam and I went to that new Greek restaurant, and something I ate didn't agree with my stomach. Please stop and get me some Tums on the way home."

"I'll be there soon. I am riding with Cara and this club is wack, so we should be leaving in the next few minutes."

Yarni went back over to the bar where Cara was sitting. Yarni said to Cara, "On the way back to my car, I'm going to need you to drop me at the store, I need to get my mom some Tums. She isn't feeling well." Cara never looked up while she was sipping on her drink.

"Oh, I'm not going to drop you at your car. I am going to let you ride back with my guy friend and his friends."

"What?" Yarni said.

Cara said, "Oh, it doesn't make sense for me to go back to Newtown when I live five minutes from here, and they're going back up there anyway."

Yarni was angry. "Cara, I told you this from the beginning, I wanted to park my car at your house or drive myself. You insisted that I ride with you."

"Yarni, I'm not going up there and Mike is blowing up my pager and cell phone calling from my house. I need to get home ASAP."

Yarni responded, "Look, Cara, I don't feel comfortable about riding with three dudes who I don't even know who have been drinking, and who probably got bitter feelings toward me anyway because I haven't given any of them the time of day. Please, Cara, drop me at my car."

Cara said hastily, while never looking at Yarni in the eyes, "I know them and I wouldn't send you with anyone who I thought would hurt you."

"Cara, I feel uneasy about riding with them," Yarni desperately pleaded.

"Well, I'm not going all the way back to Newtown," and Cara meant what she said.

Yarni offered to pay Cara. Cara refused and didn't give Yarni a ride to her vehicle.

Yarni's feelings were hurt completely. She couldn't believe that Cara would just leave her. She thought about just walking up to Cara and just smacking the spit out of her mouth, but she didn't. She could only think about the kidnapping. She wanted to cry because she felt stranded and betrayed by one of her dearest friends.

She pulled out her cell phone and called Manhattan Cab. They said it would be an hour before they could pick her up. She agreed, although, she knew plenty of people in the club, she didn't want to ask anyone to take her anywhere. As she waited outside the club for her cab to arrive,

Stephanie called her. She asked Stephanie to give her a ride. Stephanie was there in fifteen minutes.

After she evaluated the situation and talked to her mother, she reflected on the fact that those guys could've possibly raped and killed her. They probably wouldn't have, but three strange dudes that had been drinkin—who's to say? A real friend would have never left another friend in that kind of bind.

Her mother said, "Yarni, I know you are hurt, but let this be a learning experience. From now on, drive your own car so you are in control. You'll never have to worry about being in this kind of predicament again."

Yarni never spoke to Cara again about this ordeal. She later forgave Cara in her heart, but Cara and her would never be friends again.

Two days passed. Yarni just got the good news that she'd be closing on her condo in thirty days. She was ecstatic to have been blessed to be able to buy her own condo without the help of a man. This was a triumph that she'd accomplished on her own.

Yarni was lying across her bed making a list of the things she had already purchased and wanted to purchase for her townhouse. She was distracted when her phone rang loudly. She checked the caller ID. It was a bizarre number, a 329 number. She automatically knew it was a North Side number but she didn't recognize it.

"Hello?" she answered.

"Hello? Can I speak to Yarni," the harsh voice said. Yarni was puzzled because she didn't recognize the voice.

"Who's calling please?" Yarni asked. It couldn't be a bill collector, because they'd be asking for Yarnise, she thought.

The caller said, "Darchelle"

Yarni hesitantly said, "This is Yarni speaking."

"Yarni, this Darchelle, Rich's girlfriend, Bengee's ex." Yarni was silent for a brief second. Yarni then asked, "And why would you be calling my house? We have nothing to discuss."

Darchelle said—wanting to snap back at Yarni, but didn't. "I am calling for Rich. He asked me to call you."

"Oh, he did?" Yarni chuckled.

"Yeah, he's locked up down in the city jail, and I need somebody to cosign to get him out because my job isn't enough. His mother is out of town in Atlantic City. He told me to call you."

"He told you to call me?" Yarni asked.

"Yeah, so where can I meet you at, or if you can't cosign how much can you contribute to his bail?" *The nerve of this chick. Shit, the gall of* him.

Yarni stood her ground. "Darchelle, you are his girl, not me. So, that's your worry, not mine. Now, please don't call here again, thank you in advance and good luck on your mission to get your man out of jail." Yarni hung up the phone. "The *nerve*" she screamed.

Yarni called Stephanie, and Steph called Zurri, to link them all together so she could tell them all about Darchelle and Rich. They were all on the three-way going on and on and making jokes on the whole ordeal. When Yarni's phone beeped, it was someone calling on her other line. She clicked over to the other line.

"Hello?" she said.

"Yarni, this is Rich. Please don't hang up." She thought he must be on a three-way himself, because it wasn't a collect call.

"Yes, Rich," she said in a joking way.

"I really need to talk to you," he replied.

"I'm listening, Rich, and I hope it's not about me cosigning to get you out."

"Look, Yarni, they got me down in the city jail now. I already got a warrant out in Chesterfield. The computers are down now, and I need to get up out of here before the computers come back up 'cuz I know for a fact, they ain't going to let me go nowhere when them computers come back up," he said in an over-worried, urgent tone.

"Well, this matter sounds real urgent to me. You better stop wasting your time on the phone with me and call somebody who can and will actually help you," Yarni responded. Rich screamed into the phone.

"The least you can do is come through for me. You owe me that."

Yarni raised her voice, "Lower your voice before I hang up. I owe you?"

"That's right, I spared your life!" Rich said.

"You spared my life?

"Yes, when Tank kept saying he wanted to kill you, I was the one who told him *no!*" Tears started to fill her eyes.

"What exactly do you mean?" Yarni said in an unsure voice. Rich said, "Yeah, I actually felt sorry for your stuck-up pitiful ass when your sorry-ass nigga left you for dead! I wondered how could a man leave his woman as he left you." Yarni begin to cry and Rich continued with no remorse. "Remember you kept saying it was something about my eyes? All you ever saw was my eyes when I was holding you at gunpoint. Remember that day when I borrowed two hundred and fifty dollars from you and later that day I gave a thousand dollars? That's because I had done a kidnapping. Her man paid. I been doing this shit for years! You never believed me when I told you, I didn't sell drugs. My hustle is kidnapping. You were the only woman I ever got personal with. I never lied to you about anything, except I didn't tell you I was married. Now, please Yarni, I saved your life. Please come through for me," Rich pleaded in a humble voice. "As I said Yarni, you owe me, big-time."

Yarni was quiet for a while. She was speechless. "Hello?" Rich said. "Yarni, are you there?"

"You know Rich, I don't owe your ass shit!" she screamed into the phone. "I paid you a hundred-thousand dollars for my return. Had you just let me go free, I might feel some type of pity for you! Why don't you send your boys to pull off a quick heist real fast to get your bail money?"

Yarni slammed the phone down. She sobbed. *Am I that naive that I would be involved with my kidnapper?* she wondered. *I need to step back and reevaluate myself.* She began to cry hysterically.

She called Stephanie and Zurri and explained the whole conversation with Rich to them. They comforted her. "How would you have known? Don't blame yourself. He's the sicko, not you. He treated you like a lady and conducted himself as a perfect gentleman. There were no signs. So, it's not your fault."

Gloria began to worry about Yarni. She was concerned that Yarni might snap at any moment. Gloria secretly called to Richmond's city jail to alert them of Rich's warrants in Chesterfield. Rita was more so worried that since Yarni didn't help him get out of jail, he might come after Yarni. Gloria, on the other hand, was worried that if he was released, Yarni was going to hurt Rich. Yarni had been through enough. Gloria wasn't sure of Yarni's breaking point.

Rich never made bail. Once he was finger-printed, he was charged for warrants he had in North Carolina and Georgia, along with the warrants in Chesterfield and Richmond. Rich was going to be in jail for a long time.

Yarni was relieved that Rich was going to be locked up for a long time. Her only concern was that she hoped that Rich wouldn't be housed in any of the state prisons Des had been or was currently at. Des still had people all across the Virginia state prison system who'd kill under his command. As much as she hated Rich, she didn't want his death to be on her conscience. She also didn't want Des to have any parts of hurting Rich. She wanted Des to come home and not put himself in any kind of situation to jeopardize his being released.

17

Champagne Taste, Beer Budget

Yarni finally closed on her condo. She felt blessed and relieved. This was hers. No one could kick her out. She could do whatever she wanted. If she wanted to walk around butt-naked, she could.

The first thing she did prior to moving any of her furniture in was an initial cleansing of her townhouse. She burned frankincense and myrrh to purify the house. She lit a house-blessing candle. Her Aunt Andrea came over to pray.

Stephanie, Rita, and Zurri tried to convince Yarni to allow them to give her a housewarming party. She declined the offer because she didn't want anyone knowing exactly where she lived. She didn't want to seem as if she was begging for the things she needed for her condo. They completely understood, taking in consideration everything she'd been through. Stephanie, Rita,

Andrea, Zurri, and Joyce all gave her gift certificates. She was appreciative. Gloria had some
saving bonds that she'd gotten when Yarni was a
baby. She cashed them so Yarni could purchase
some furniture. With Yarni's expensive taste, the
money from the saving bonds didn't go very far.

She went to La Difference Furniture and purchased an exquisite imported sofa. She went to
Circuit City and purchased a big-screen TV. The
salesman talked her into buying surround sound.
She didn't know anyone personally who'd had
surround sound. She'd only read about it in the
magazines. Stanka bought her a state-of-the-art
stereo, hot off the streets from a crackhead. She
couldn't afford the dining-room set she wanted,
so she bought two bar stools for her bar. Her co-
workers at the law firm got her a gift certificate to
Linens 'n Things. Right after Bengee died, when
she received the insurance check from his death,
she purchased herself a new bedroom set because
the bed her mother had purchased years ago was
so juvenile. So that bedroom suite was still pretty
new. While she was still living at her mother's
house, she'd been picking up odds and ends that
she knew for sure she'd need. Yarni was glad that
she was finally in her own place. But now, how
was she going to finance the rest of her furniture?

When her mother saw what little Yarni had done with the money, she lectured her, "Sweetie, you've got to buckle down. I can't believe this is all you got with the money. I saved those bonds for you over a course of twenty-odd years? The bottom line is: Yarni, you can't have champagne taste with a beer budget."

Yarni had only been living in her condo for three months. When she arrived home from visiting Des, she couldn't believe her eyes. Her condo door was cracked open. Yarni walked through the door and stood in disbelief. She couldn't make sense of the whole situation because the person didn't take anything. They only broke in and trashed her condo. They used a knife to cut up her sofa. Her big-screen TV was turned over and broken. All her minks and most expensive clothes were tossed in her marble bathtubs in both her bathrooms and bleach was splattered all over her garments. They even spray-painted *BITCH* all over the walls. They snatched her comforter set off of her bed and cut it and put cigarette burns all over it. They went through the house and poured bleach all over the carpet.

Yarni was devastated. She was already so frustrated that she couldn't afford all the things she wanted for her townhouse as it was—and now this. It really hurt her heart because these were all the things that she acquired on her own; no hustler or fast cash got her any of these things. She had worked an honest job for these things. Her home-owner's insurance conducted a full investigation because there was no sign of forced entry. After they finally decided to pay her, it didn't cover everything that was destroyed. She decided that she'd purchase the large things that were trashed with the money the insurance company gave her. She could pick up the little things and the clothes, here and there. So, she was back at square one. What was she to do now? She couldn't go running to her mother because she was a grown woman, not a little girl anymore. She tried to look at the bright side of it.

At least this happened before I actually got my place the way I wanted it. I'm grateful that the insurance company did give me some money, and now I have ADT coming out to install a security system, and I guess some type of break will come so that I can get this place like I want it.

18

Yea, Though I Walk Through TheShadow Of Death . . .

Yarni's phone was ringing as she walked in the house from working out at the gym. She sprinted over to the phone to answer it. It was Castro calling Yarni collect. This was the first time in all his years of being locked up that he ever called her from prison. Her heart started pounding. She was nervous. Was something wrong? Was it Des? What could it be? What happened to Castro? What? She kept trying to push zero to accept the call while the automated voice was still talking, but she had to wait until it prompted her to press zero. She did. Once they connected the call, she said, "Hello?" holding her breath.

"Hey, Yarni," Just then the automated voice interrupted. "This call is from a correctional center and this call is subject to recording."

"Damn, it's bad enough they charge us all this money for these calls and then they want to talk more than we do," Yarni laughed. She was relieved when she heard Castro's voice fussing about the phone situation. She knew that it wasn't anything bad.

"What's the dealeyo, Ms. Yarnise?"

"Nothing much, what's up wit you?"

"Nothing much. Where you been? I've been calling you all day."

"You've been calling me all day? What's up with that? What do I owe this pleasurable once-in-a-decade moment? Please explain?"

"Remember, I am the big brother, and no matter how grown you get, you will always be my little sister. You got dat? Now where ya been?"

"Oh, go to hell, Castro. No, all jokes aside, I've been at work and—" Castro interrupted.

"Work? What the hell is going on? I can't believe you've been at that job this long. Des told me you had a job. So, it's official, huh? You finally decided to hang your shovel up and pass your gold-digging crown on, huh?" Yarni burst into laughter.

"You crazy, Castro, I miss you, sooo much. I am so glad you called."

"Don't go and get all teary-eyed on me," he said in a modest tone.

"I do miss you," she said to her friend and fake brother. "Well, come pick me up tomorrow at eight a.m," Castro said, cutting to the chase.

"No problem! Why you didn't tell me before now?" Yarni inquired.

"Because when you get to talking about these type of things, people try to throw a monkey wrench at a brother 'cause he short. So, I didn't tell nobody."

Yarni picked him up from the Deep Meadow Correctional Facility. She took him to the mall and bought him a couple of outfits, some Timberland boots and a cell phone after she got Des's approval.

Castro called Yarni at work, and asked if he could take her to lunch. He explained that he had something to talk to her about. Yarni met with Castro that afternoon.

"Listen, I need you to get me this apartment in your name. I want only a six-month lease. I have a bag of money in the car. I will give you six months of rent when we go outside along with the security deposit. I'm going to look out for you too." Yarni didn't have to think twice about it.

"Cas, I don't have any problem with getting you an apartment in my name, but first I have to okay it with Des."

"I spoke to Des this morning. Out of respect, I ran it past him first. He is gonna call you, but he said it was up to you," Castro said.

"Now, why are you riding around with a bag of money in the trunk of your car? That's just careless and ghetto." Yarni reached over and playfully hit him. He looked at her again.

"What is it now?" she asked while rolling her eyes, "I know that look," Castro spoke slowly and unsure. He twisted his words.

"Need, I Ya—" Castro mumbled. Yarni laughed.

"Come on now. Get your words together!" she demanded as they laughed.

"Yarni, I can't shit where I eat," he said, very serious.

"Oh, you've had to give them people a decade of your life to realize that," Yarni said sarcastically.

"Basically," Castro said to Yarni in a sarcastic way, and nodded his head and then they both burst into laughter.

"Yarni, I have somewhere to stash my drugs, but nowhere that I feel comfortable leaving my money unattended. I mean, I know I could probably hide it somewhere in my mother's house, but you and I know how nosy she is. The only other place I can think of is with you."

"Look, there's rules to this. Don't keep running back and forth to my house every single day for your money, making my spot hot. Don't bring anybody along with you when you come through with money. I never want to find out you're stashing drugs where I lay my head at," Yarni stated.

Castro paid Yarni five-hundred dollars a week for allowing him to keep his money in her house. Anything hot, stolen that came across his path, he bought it for Yarni.

Castro filled Yarni's Louis Vuitton duffel bag with money. She noticed that he purchased a safe and placed it in one of the closets. When she noticed the safe, she automatically knew that Castro was doing major things.

One day Yarni met a man at a Caribbean restaurant. He had been watching Yarni, who was having lunch with Castro. When she got up to go to the restroom, the man followed her. He wore light blue jeans, a white and yellow polo shirt with some brown leather sandals that strapped around his big toe. His perfect pearly white teeth, yellow 18-karat gold chain and pendant he wore, brought out his tar-black complexion. His short, nappy hair was all over his head. He was medium build, standing at five feet six, with huge ears.

"Excuse me, miss, you are so bootiful," the man said to her, speaking slowly, trying to camouflage his accent.

Yarni could smell money, but she knew under any circumstances she could not exchange numbers with this fellow, not while Castro was with her anyway.

Forget about this small conversation, just give me your damn number.

"You live here, in Richmond?" the man asked.

"Yes," Yarni said, as she looked timidly around the corner, not wanting Castro to get suspicious of her.

"Do you live here?" She knew he didn't but wanted to pretend she didn't know for general conversation.

"I am Levi, and I would love to get to know you better. No, I am not from here, but you are very, very bootiful," he said, while looking into Yarni's eyes and grinning.

Levi, who was from Nigeria, lived and owned a castle on St. Thomas. He also shared with Yarni that he owned a house in L.A. He asked about Castro. She explained that Castro was her brother. He asked Yarni, Did Castro hustle? Yarni simply said, "I don't know what you're speaking on?" She knew that Levi might be "the connect" that Castro had been longing to stumble upon ever since Des went to prison. Levi flocked to Yarni while she ate. Castro just sat back and got a kick out of the way Levi catered to Yarni, something he could not have.

On that note, they kept in touch. Castro went to St. Thomas to visit with Levi, and Levi gave him a price that would change his whole lifestyle.

Castro returned and began slanging more heroin than a little bit. He and Levi worked well together. He was fond of Levi because he wasn't one of those guys who constantly called the next day after he departed with the dope for his money. Levi played fair with Castro; in return Castro never shorted him his money.

Yarni walked into her condo from work and she overheard Castro in her living room talking on his cell phone. She knew he was speaking to Levi by the depth of the conversation.

"Man, I can't send her. The broad is seven months pregnant. I can't risk her going into labor with the pack on her. The doctor has put her on bed rest, man." He was silent for a minute, listening. Castro spoke out again. "There's no one else I feel safe sending, and know for sure they're kosher. I'm looking out for everyone's best interest." He never heard Yarni enter the house. The moment he saw her, he brought the conversation to an end.

With a very agitated look on his face, he plopped down on the bar stool.

"What's wrong?" She walked over and rubbed his back.

"Talk to your little sister." Castro looked at Yarni and rubbed his forehead as if he had a headache.

"The girl that I normally send to the West Coast to get the pack is seven months pregnant. The doctor put her on bed rest. Levi is paranoid as hell of anybody else I send and is demanding that I send the pregnant girl. I'm afraid if I don't send her, he'll cut me off. And Yarni, this is the cheapest dope I ever got or could get my hands on," Castro said.

Yarni thought long and hard. She tried to think of something for him as well.

"I am going to just try my hand with the pregnant girl one last time." He called her on his cell phone. As the phone rang, he stated, "Shit, instead of paying her the eight Gs she usually get paid, I'm gonna pay her ten."

Yarni looked in amazement at Castro, and the only thing that flashed in her head was the ten-thousand and the dining-room set at La Difference she'd special ordered and the baby grand piano she'd been wanting every since she'd closed on her condo. She blurted out, "Ten Gs—shit, I'll go!"

Castro was relieved when Yarni said she'd go, but at the same time he knew it wasn't right sending her. How would he explain this to Des if something was to happen? He felt guilty, but at the same time he didn't want to lose his connection with Levi. He tried to ease his guilt by telling himself that this was only temporarily and he'd hurry and find someone else to replace her.

He explained to her that usually he flew the pregnant girl out there to L.A. and she rode back either in a limo or a hearse. The police rarely bothered with those two automobiles.

Yarni objected and spoke, "In this lifetime I'm not riding in any hearse until I'm dead and gone."

Castro laughed until tears came to his eyes. "Come on, Yarni," he said.

Yarni put her hand up, blocking Castro's words. "And don't even suggest Greyhound," said Yarni.

"Come on, sissy, now you know good and well I wouldn't put you on no damn Greyhound."

"Well, big money grip, you getting the cheapest dope ever so it's nothing for you to fly me both ways," she said.

"Keep in mind, I do have a nine-to-five. Plus, flying is more convenient and quicker, not a lot of anticipation going on. It's over and done with in a matter of hours versus a matter of days."

Castro nodded. "You're right."

Yarni added, "Even if somebody was to drop a dime on me, how much time would the police have to set up a roadblock? Not much if I flew." It was settled, Yarni flew.

When she arrived in L.A., Levi was overjoyed to see her. They went sightseeing all over L.A., and he took her shopping. He even drove her to Hollywood where they went to watch the *Family Feud* game show. He took her to the ghetto part of L.A. to a raggedy house with chipped paint. This is when she really learned the true concept of never judge a book by its cover. She was skeptical.

She didn't want to seem nosy or make him paranoid, but she couldn't keep from asking, "Does someone actually live here? Why are we going here?" As she stepped onto the dry-rotted step on the porch of the house, she walked as light as she could on her tiptoes, afraid that the step might cave in at any time.

"This is for your safety," Levi said to her in a casual tone and patted her on her back.

Yarni asked herself, *Is he taking me here to shake me up to secure that if something goes down, I won't tell?*

Yarni and Levi entered the house. The house was a full-running ghetto imitation of the CIA!

They were printing Social Security cards, birth certificates, and state-issued ID's. Computers were everywhere. The documentation looked authentic. They also had the capabilities of clearing negative ratings on credit reports. Yarni looked in amazement. *Damn, people are bootleg as I don't know what. Always finding a way to skin the cat.*

Levi purchased two different identities for Yarni. He paid $3,500 dollars per identity. He explained to Yarni that they usually sold for at least five-thousand dollars for all three pieces, but she could take the Social Security card and birth certificate to the local DMV and get a real photo ID. Yarni said she wasn't going to try DMV like that. She took the paperwork. He made her mail whatever ID she wasn't using express mail to her house in case her bags were searched. She wouldn't carry all multiple ID's on her.

Yarni's flight left in a few hours. She was curious as to how she was going to transport the dope back. Levi took her to the mall one last time, and asked her to pick out something to go with some yellow shoes, something comfortable, nothing too flashy. She did. She picked out a cut multicolored sundress. Levi picked out a big, yellow straw hat and a straw pocketbook. They returned to his house. He instructed her to change into the outfit.

She did. He went into a bag and pulled out some big, bulky, Spice Girls platform bright-yellow high heels. He told her to put them on. He informed her that the dope was concealed in the heels of the shoes. She couldn't believe the fact that she had 300 grams of uncut heroin in each of her platform shoes. It was easy as pie going back to Richmond.

Yarni began to make this trip twice a month. She was able to furnish her house off completely. She only bought the best of everything, including the baby grand piano she wanted. She never told anyone, including Des, what she was doing. She was living a double life.

Yarni and Levi became more than just business partners, but they never had a sexual relationship. Yarni looked to Levi as a brother. Levi always made it his business to show Yarni a good time whenever she was in Cali, and whenever it was time for her to execute the plan, he made her feel safe and secure. On one occasion, Levi asked Yarni if he could give her half of her money right then and he'd wire her the rest in two days. At limited times he requested the favor. She agreed because he always sent the money as promised. One time, he didn't send the money. He cussed her out when she called to ask him very innocently about the money that he'd promised to send her two weeks ago. "Shit, I don't have no fucking money right now. Everybody fucking calling me begging for money like I am some kinda fucking bank, ATM or something . . . shit, you act like a nigga ain't never tipped you or look out for yo' ass. Shit, I'll call you later when I get yo' money 'cause yo' ass ain't no different, you just like the other motherfuckers!!"

He slammed the phone down in her ear. At this point, it wasn't about the money. She was more so hurt that he would even take her kindness for weakness.

Andrea had been asking Yarni for months to come to her church. Yarni really had a bad taste in her mouth about churches every since she'd been kidnapped. God had always been a major part of Yarni's life from the time she breathed air in this world. Gloria instilled God into Yarni's life. Yarni went to her preacher when she was returned from the kidnapping. She sought out some spiritual leadership. She explained to the pastor what she'd been through and she proclaimed it was a wake-up call from God. The pastor simply said, "It wasn't a wake-up call from God. God would never allow you to experience any bad, if you're his child." Yarni began to cry and she described to the pastor how she had prayed while being held captive and how God answered her prayer. The pastor said, "Maybe somebody else was praying for you at the same time. God didn't even hear your prayers because you're a sinner. He doesn't acknowledge a sinner's prayers," said the minister.

Yarni was agitated with the pastor. She thought to herself: *And you're supposed to be saving souls from going to hell.* She simply spoke out to him in a firm tone, "Matthew 7:1 says 'Judge not, that you be judged.'" She stormed out of the church. She stopped paying her tithes at that church. She tithed faithfully to TV-broadcast ministries, but never stepped another foot into that church again.

One Sunday, Yarni and Andrea had dinner. Andrea greeted Yarni with a gold gift bag. Enclosed in the gift bag was a tape *No More Sheets* by Juanita Bynum. Andrea and Yarni had a nice dinner. Andrea asked Yarni, "Why don't you come to church next Sunday with me? After church, we're having dinner. Don't answer now. Just don't rule it out. Promise me you will watch the tape."

"I promise," Yarni said.

Andrea whispered in Yarni's ear as she embraced her with a hug, "Promises aren't meant to be broken."

Yarni sat on her sofa. She flipped through all the channels and nothing was on cable. She contemplated slipping on some clothes and going to the video store, then she remembered the video Andrea had given her. She popped the tape into the VCR. She listened and watched in disbelief. She pressed *stop* and *rewind* so many times. The uncontrollable tears would not stop rolling down her face. This woman, Juanita Bynum, was so raw and to the point that, the realness of the message on the tape, just about broke Yarni down. Yarni watched the tape two times. She called Aunt Andrea and graciously thanked her for the enlightenment and informed her that she would be visiting her church the coming Sunday.

The next morning Yarni pulled up in the parking lot of the church. She thought, *Should I leave and return in a few minutes so I won't have to deal with all the church people looking at me all crazy because they don't know me. Or should I just turn around and go home?* She backed out of the parking space and went to the stoplight. *This is nothing but the devil. It must be something in that church he doesn't want me to hear.* On that note, she made a U-turn. She reasoned with herself. *Forget these people; I am not going to think about them. I am not here for them anyway. They can look at me all they want to. I am just going to look right back at them and eat up their food and leave. Simple as that!*

Boy, was Yarni wrong. As she exited her car, a cheerful lady, who looked like Diana Ross, walked up and hugged her. "Thank you, sister for stopping by. Ooh, it's so good to be in the house of the Lord. God wants you to know that He loves and I do too," said the lady.

As Yarni approached the church, another jolly lady gave her a hug.

"Sister, has anybody told you they loved you today?" Yarni was stunned. She couldn't even answer. The lady continued, "I love you and God loves you too." Yarni begin to feel relaxed and at peace. She proceeded to the door and the usher greeted her with a bulletin and a hug as well.

"It's so nice to see you, sister." She was no longer nervous about entering into the new church.

Everybody was hugging each other as if they were on a church-member recruitment commercial. Yarni felt they were sincere, that no one was pretending. They all seemed so excited and exalted to be in the house of the Lord. They all hugged her and made her feel that she wasn't a stranger at all. She spotted her Aunt Andrea and joined her. Nothing could prepare Yarni for what she was about to witness.

Church started, and Yarni watched in disbelief. It was like these people were having a *big* party for God. She'd really partied the night before, but these folks were shouting, jumping around, dancing, (not the hoochie-coochie dances), and swinging their hands from side to side. They had the tambourines shaking and drums playing. Yarni thought she knew how to party and attended all the finest, top-notch social gatherings, but Andrea reminded her that she'd never been present at a "Holy Ghost" party.

Yarni wanted to join in, but she couldn't, she thought. She had been out partying the night before. Was God going to approve of her? She listened to the music and observed the people. She couldn't stop the tears from rolling down her eyes. She asked God for forgiveness for all her sins. She listened attentively to every word that the minister spoke. She realized at that moment, that whatever church she went to, it would have to definitely be a teaching church. It felt as though the pastor was talking directly to her. Everything he said pertained to Yarni. When church was over, the members embraced her with hugs and love. She could feel the anointing over her.

Yarni attended church every Sunday. She would run into the people from her old church.

They would make comments, as if her previous church was the only church in Richmond. They would make the assumption that she was off in the world, simply because they didn't see her at their church. She would make it clear, "Oh, I go to the Holy Ghost Deliverance Church,"

"Oh, well it's okay to visit, but it's nothing like your home church," they would say in doubt. *Why couldn't people be content for me that I was attending church somewhere?*

One Sunday after Yarni got in from church, she received a call from Levi. Months had passed since she last spoke to him. He apologized and asked for forgiveness. He informed Yarni that he had her money. He was going to send it the next day. Yarni thought that was her blessing. What Yarni didn't realize was sometimes the devil could disguise things as blessings.

Levi called every day until Thursday. He simply said to her: "Yarni, I need you to do me that favor." Yarni thought about how Levi had done her wrong before. She reflected on what Gloria used to say to her in reference to Yarni's girlfriends.

"If the snake bites you one time, it's the snake's fault. But if you allow that snake to come in and bite you the second time, it's your fault!"

She fully took Gloria's quote into consideration, but she also thought about the stuff that she had put down payments on that she needed to pay off. She ended up going anyway under the conditions of, Levi would send her the money he owed her, as well as half the money up front he was going to pay her. Levi followed instructions as she explained to him. The next day she received the money. She contemplated back and forth if she should just buck on the money he sent and not go. But, she reminded herself that her word was her bond. She'd given him her word, and she couldn't go back on it.

Yarni took a red-eye flight to L.A She usually would sleep on the flight over. This particular night, she couldn't sleep. She listened to her Sanyo CD Walkman. She listened to the newly released Mobb Deep CD, *Murda Muzik* track number 2—"Streets Raised Me." It was one of her favorite songs on the CD. As she listened to the words of the song—*street life/ why you have to raise me this way/ I'm surprised we're alive today . . . but who am I to say . . . forever you're a part of me . . . street life*—Tears filled her eyes. They began to roll down the side of her face. She felt doomed. She was at the point of no return. This was the first time that it had actually registered in Yarni's head how enormous the risk was she was taking. Yarni realized that she could lose everything for ten-thousand dollars.

Her freedom, her life, her job, everything she'd fought so hard to have and establish. She knew that there was no turning back. There wasn't a way she could get out of this.

She only called upon God. She started with Psalm 23:4: *Yea, though I walk through the valley of the shadow of death, I will fear no evil: for thou art with me; thy rod and thy staff, they will comfort me.* She began to pray; she promised God, "Lord, if you spare me this one time, I promise you, I will never attempt to do this again."

Yarni made the trip back from L.A. safely. Levi pulled the same stunt. He told her he'd send her the balance of the money. She knew in her heart, he wouldn't until the next time he needed her. She was certain that there would be no next time for her. See, not only did she promise herself; she made an oath to God, and she knew the repercussions. The five-thousand dollars that Levi owed her, she never called him to ask him about it. She counted the money as a loss.

She knew that no matter how bad things got for her, she could never go back to trafficking drugs anywhere. Every time she reflected over the ordeal, she thanked God for keeping her in His care because had she ever gotten caught,

Yarni would be under the jail. Some people would say she was lucky. But Yarni would simply say she was blessed.

19

Faithful Mommy Dearest

Yarni continued to go to church every Sunday. She thought, *If I can give this job five days a week, the least I can do is give God one day a week.* She began to look at church the same way she looked at her job. She was on time to work, so therefore, she never stepped into church a second late. When she was at work, she participated in work to the fullest. At church, she just didn't sit in her seat. She involved herself in the ministry. She also included herself in church functions. She dressed herself neatly for church as she did work.

Yarni continued to visit Des faithfully every week. Des could see a change in Yarni. Des saw a sense of maturity within her. He wasn't into religion. He had studied different religions and didn't agree with all the facts of each religion. Whenever Yarni spoke on her religion, he listened to her attentively, simply because he was interested in anything she had to say. Yarni sent Des tapes from Sunday's services. She would also send verses and any kind of propaganda she came across.

Yarni was very proud that Des had taken a bad situation and made the best of it. He used it as a growing experience. He read and studied everything. He taught himself different languages, took college courses, and acquired two different degrees and was pursuing his master's, when in 1994 the governor of the state of Virginia cut out college courses in the prison systems.

Yarni expressed to Des that the only kind of man she knew she could be happy with, was a man of God. She came to grips that a man who is of God was going to live upright. He was not going to intentionally do anything to disappoint God. So, if this man of God thought so highly of God, she knew he would treat her as she needed and longed to be treated. She then told Des that she wanted him to go to his Bible and look up Proverbs 31:10–31. She informed him of the fact that she felt she was growing into a virtuous woman. That was one of her strong qualities she brought to the table. She told him she wasn't going to settle for a man who wasn't equally yoked.

Des thought long and hard about what Yarni said. She also told him that she wasn't going to pressure him to commit his life to God. She never did. She always spoke the word to Des and continued to give him scriptures to encourage him to want to develop a personal relationship with God. Before she knew it, Des was quoting her scriptures and speaking the word to her. He graciously thanked Yarni for introducing him to God.

Yarni also began getting in touch with her inner spirit. She read and studied inspirational books by Iyanla Vanzant, along with other daily devotionals and prayers. She learned to meditate. She participated in yoga. She kept a gratitude journal, in which each day she diligently wrote in it three things that she was grateful for that day. She fasted for spiritual breakthroughs.

Yarni and Castro grew distant because Yarni had explained to Castro that she wanted no parts of that lifestyle any more. He said he respected her wishes. Castro and Yarni spoke on occasion. He felt that Yarni didn't care about him any more.

Yarni called Castro's cell phone one day to check on him because she hadn't heard from him, but his mother told her he was in the States. She also wanted to invite him to "church in the park" that her church was sponsoring. She wasn't going to write Castro off as a lost cause, because Andrea never gave up on her. As the phone rang, she got a knot in her stomach. "Hello," said a woman.

"I must have the wrong number," Yarni said, hanging up. She called right back. The woman answered again.

"Hello?" Yarni said. "Is this 777-9111?"

"Yes," said the woman.

"Who is this?" Yarni asked.

"This is the FBI. if you're calling for Castro, Castro's handcuffed. Don't call him. He'll call you—collect that is!" the lady said in a joking way.

Yarni called Gloria.

"Mommy, Castro's been arrested, I just called his house and the feds picked him up." Gloria never heard this type of terror in Yarni's voice. Gloria knew something was wrong and it wasn't the fact that Castro was in jail either. Gloria knew they were close friends, but not that tight that she would get so terrified over Castro getting locked up. Yarni was uncertain that she too wouldn't be arrested. Automatically, she thought the worse.

Gloria told Yarni a few days later, "Castro called and told me to distinctly to tell you that everything is okay." Gloria never asked Yarni where she'd gotten the money to buy all that exquisite furniture on a $35,000-dollar-a year salary. The tanning salon was breaking even and profiting a very minimum. Her mother was well aware of the fact that Yarni had been doing something she had no business.

Yarni loved her job at the law firm. She worked for a lawyer named Jack Do Right. This was his given name. His name alone was a wonderful asset for any attorney. His name alone brought in a great deal of business. Jack was a very prominent attorney. He had practiced criminal law for ten years.

He dressed sharp and he always smelled good. He was especially crazy about Yarni. He liked the way Yarni could be as soft-spoken and look like a rose, but could sting like a thorn. He liked Yarni's eagerness and her drive. She was very intelligent and dedicated to her job and the clients, as well. She was more assertive than the average attorneys he knew. He could never figure out why Yarni never entered law school. Jack knew the very minimum of Yarni's personal life. He just assumed she had no personal life, because she worked such long hours, throwing herself into her work at the firm.

Yarni thought highly of Jack. Jack acted as though he had Yarni's best interest at heart. She was his paralegal, and they worked as a team. She developed the utmost respect for him. Jack never took Yarni for granted and Yarni never took Jack for granted.

Jack was a permanent reminder to Yarni of the attorney she could have become. Yarni was out to lunch one afternoon when a call came in for her supervisor. It was Cara. Cara informed one of the other partners of the firm of Yarni's background and personal life. She mentioned to the partner that Yarni had been convicted of a felony, and how she should be fired. She also expressed that Yarni was in a relationship with a convicted murderer who was in prison on death row. She added lies and exaggerated the truth.

When Yarni returned from lunch, Jack asked to speak to her in his office. He presented Yarni with the information he'd received. Yarni wanted to cry. This was definitely a part of her checkered past catching up with her. She reflected on what a quote her mother used to warn her about, "What you do in the dark will always come to light." Then she took a deep breath, and for the first time in her life, she explained everything to Jack. She knew she was fired. She left out the trafficking, but she explained the whole scenario with Bengee and the gun charge. She also told him about the expungement of her record. She explained that was the reason why she never entered law school. Jack sat looking at Yarni in amazement. He couldn't believe Yarni had such a strong drive.

He was speechless for a few seconds and then he plainly said, "There comes a time when a girl's gotta do what a girl's gotta do. And it looks to me like, it's just remarkable how you managed to pick up the pieces under the unbalanced conditions. That alone, says a lot about you, Yarnise. It would have been so easy for you to just say, 'Oh, forget about this and have a pity party for yourself,' but you didn't." Jack didn't fire her under the provisions that she'd enroll into law school.

Yarni's feelings were extremely hurt when she thought of Cara. She began to hear a lot of hurtful things that Cara had been saying about her. She never understood why Cara would go around talking about her. Yarni thought of all the ways she could hurt Cara. For every one thing Cara knew on Yarni, Yarni knew ten things on her.

When people asked Yarni, had she seen Cara, she would simply say no. Why couldn't Cara do the same thing? Why couldn't Cara just be mature about the whole situation? After Cara's latest stunt, Yarni began to think of all the ways she could get in touch with Cara's man, who she'd heard was locked up, and tell him some trifling things about her. But she simply told herself, she'd never tell him any of those things when her and Cara were friends, and she wasn't going to stoop to Cara's level. While preying on Yarni's downfall, Cara had done Yarni a favor because Yarni had lost sight of her dream of becoming a lawyer.

Yarni recollected on the service the pastor taught on Sunday morning. How you reap what you sow. It's like a farmer. He sows into good ground so he can reap a plentiful harvest. The more you give the more you get in return. She met a single mom, Sister Kenya, at her church who was struggling to make ends met. Kenya was a faithful mother and a person with good character. She approached Yarni and asked her if she needed help in her tanning salon. She explained to Yarni that she could only work between eleven until two. Her youngest child was in kindergarten and went to school only a half day. She stressed that she would have to leave work no later than two o'clock because she had no one who could get her children off of the bus.

Yarni didn't need any extra help around the tanning salon but she told Kenya that she would help her out. The woman showed up at Yarni's tanning salon with a good attitude. She took pride in all her work and she had plenty of initiative. She got a lot accomplished in the three hours she was there. She was a blessing to Yarni. She swept the floors, and at times ran errands for Yarni. She did whatever needed to be done.

Kenya expressed to Yarni that she was going to have to be off the following Friday because she had to go to court for child support. Later that Friday night, Yarni called Sister Kenya.

"Hey, Sister Kenya," she said, "How did court go?"

"Sister Yarnise, girl, I tell you. I am so at the end of my rope with my children's father and the court systems. He isn't going to pay me child support. He can spend money for a lawyer, but is so much in debt to me for child support. As bad as I need the money I want to withdraw the claim. I am sick of it. Why should the white man have to make a grown man take care of his child?"

Yarni sympathized with her. "I feel exactly what you are saying. You know I seen this number on TV that I'm going to definitely get it for you. It's a number for deadbeat dads. I am praying for you also. I know it's so easy for people to tell you, just pray on it. Kenya, I am praying for you and have faith that it's going to be okay," Yarni comforted her.

Kenya responded, "I know it's going to be okay. I believe that God is going to supply all my needs and riches beyond my wildest dreams." Yarni's line beeped.

"Kenya, I hate to interrupt, but I got a call coming in. I'll see you at church Sunday."

"Yarnise, thanks for calling. I really needed to vent."

"Not a problem" said Yarni. They both said, "Be blessed" to each other and hung up.

Kenya came over to Yarni after church to give her a hug. She also told Yarni, "Sister Yarni, ooh, I like those shoes."

"Thank you," said Yarni as Kenya's children all came over to give her hugs too. Yarni was collecting money from the singles of the church. They were going to a gospel play at the Landmark Theater.

Yarni told Kenya, "Wait a minute, I need to speak to you." Kenya waited patiently until Yarni was finished.

Yarni asked Kenya, "Sister Kenya, do you have ten dollars?" Kenya went in her pocketbook with no complaints, questions or comments, and pulled out a ten-dollar bill and gave it to Yarni. Yarni said thanks to Kenya. Kenya said, "Not a problem. I'm just glad that God blessed me so I could be a blessing to you."

Yarni went in her pocketbook and passed Kenya the deed and keys to her building. "I'm glad that God has blessed me to be a blessing to you." Kenya was confused.

"What's this?"

"I don't have the time to focus on the tanning salon any more since I've enrolled into law school now. You are dedicated to the shop more than I ever was. I know for a fact that you will be able to generate a steady income for you and your children."

"Oh, Yarnise," she said with her eyes filled with tears. "I can't accept this."

"Yes, you can."

Kenya said to Yarni, "We're going to have to work out some kind of payment plan."

"You've paid me for it, ten dollars," Yarni said as she brushed the lint off the sleeve of her coat.

"Thank you, Yarnise. I am eternally grateful to you."

Yarni knew in her heart that God had a bigger plan for her. She knew that she would be blessed astronomically.

Jack's wife left a note on the refrigerator that said she was leaving him to be with her tennis instructor. Jack was heartbroken. He began to look fatigued. Jack turned to alcohol. He drank heavily. People at the firm were whispering

behind Jack's back about how he was losing control. Yarni expressed to Jack how she could smell
the liquor on him coming out of his pores, and
the fact that he *was* falling apart. Jack confessed
to Yarni that he had been drinking heavily and
had even experimented with LSD.

During the conversation, one of the partners
barged in and informed Jack that his reputation
was at stake, and the other partners suspected
that he was on drugs judging by his appearance. He denied the accusations. The partners
demanded a drug test from Jack. Jack was at his
lowest point. He was certain that his career was
out of the window. Jack contemplated suicide.
Yarni listened as the partners spoke harshly to
him. The partners instructed Jack to report for
the drug test within the next two hours. On that
note, Yarni interrupted, "Jack I will drive you
because I've got to go over that way to drop some
paperwork off anyway. You look like you could
use the company and support."

Yarni spoke out, grabbed three folders off
of the desk, and as she walked off said, "I'm
ready now. I just have to grab my purse." Yarni
grabbed her Gucci pocketbook that matched her
Gucci pumps, and they exited the building.

As soon as they were in Yarni's spanking new
black convertible Jaguar, Jack let his guard down.
"What the hell am I going to do?" he screamed.

Yarni calmly said, as she looked in her rear-view mirror as she backed out of the parking space, "You are going to calm down and pull yourself together."

Jack looked at Yarni and said, "Has it sunk in that there's no way that I am going to pass a drug test." He slowly stressed to Yarni, "I *used LSD* last night," as if she didn't understand what he was trying to spell out to her. Yarni unpretentiously stated, "Has it sunk in that I do have street sense, and in the streets, there's always two ways to skin a cat." Jack didn't understand how to possibly get around this situation. He gazed at Yarni.

"Please explain how I am going to skin this cat alive?"

"Just trust me, okay?" Yarni said as she glanced over at Jack, while still trying to keep her eyes on the road.

Yarni pulled in the drugstore's parking lot. She looked Jack straight in the eyes.

"I am going to get you out of this bind this one time. However, you will get help. You've got to accept the fact that your wife is gone and that it's her loss. Your pity party is over *today*!" Yarni said.

Jack's eyes were glassy-looking, filled with tears as he agreed, shaking his head. Yarni told him to wait while she ran into the drugstore.

Yarni returned from the drugstore with a pill bottle and a Styrofoam cup. She pulled into the gas station across the street from the drug-test center. She entered the restroom, removed the pill bottle and cup from her purse. She emptied the pills out in the trash, preceded to wash the bottle out thoroughly with hot, scorching water, and dried the bottle with a paper towel. She urinated in the cup, then poured the pee in the bottle. She wiped the bottle off and wrapped it in a paper towel. She carefully placed the bottle in her purse. As she exited the store, she stopped by the counter to purchase a pack of gum.

She returned to the car and opened her pocketbook. She reached in and pulled the paper towel and bottle out. She handed him the bottle. She instructed him, "Put this against your skin to keep it warm. You've got to keep this body temperature." He examined the bottle and then quickly inserted it in his pants. She instructed him, "As soon as you walk through the door, act as if you've got to pee, as if you cannot hold it. *Do not* leave the bottle in the bathroom." She dropped Jack in front of the building and waited patiently.

Jack came back to the car with a large smile on his face. He informed Yarni that they had tested the urine while he waited.

"Thanks so much, Yarnise!" he said graciously. "Take me to the bank. I could never repay you, but I've got to give you a monetary token of my appreciation."

Yarni straightforwardly said, "I won't take you to the bank, nor will I accept your money."

"You have to, Yarnise."

"Jack, I didn't do anything helluva. I simply had your back. That's what friends do. They have each other's back unconditionally, right?" Yarni said.

Jack said to Yarni, nodding, "You're absolutely right."

Yarni sat at her desk as she looked over the letter she had gotten the day before from Des. Enclosed with the letter was his answer from his parole hearing, another turndown. She began to weep, when the energetic secretary buzzed in her line, "Yarnise, it's your mother on line four." Yarni weakly said, "All right, put her through."

She picked up the phone. "Yeah, Mommy."

Gloria could immediately hear in Yarni's tone that something was majorly wrong. She could feel the pain and hurt in Yarni's voice. "Baby, what's wrong?"

Yarni cried to her mother, "Everything!"

"Yarni, if you don't tell me I can't help you, advise you or sympathize with you," Gloria said.

"Mommy, I am lonely. The man I love is in prison for a crime he didn't commit. They're never going to grant him parole. I'm tired of going through all the unnecessary drama with the penal system every time I go to visit him, getting searched; they implement a new rule every week. I am at the breaking point. Mommy, I understand God don't put more on you than you can bear, but at the same time, I'm only human. God must feel that I am awfully strong. Mommy, I'm going to always have Des's back as long as they keep him. I am going to be there for him, but when is justice going to prevail?"

Gloria got emotional as well. She knew Yarni's plight. She'd been down that same road with Yarni's father.

Gloria listened. This is the one time that she couldn't argue Yarni's point because her daughter was absolutely right. There was no bright side to this situation.

Gloria replied, "Yarni, God has a way of working out every situation, believe that. Where is your faith, my child? There's nothing God can't do."

"Yeah, I know, Mommy," she said slowly and still in a crying mode.

"I'm not going to preach to you, but remember this: No great victories were ever won without great trials! Also, I'm making baked ziti tonight. I need you to come over. I have something extremely important to talk to you about."

Yarni cut her mother off, even though ziti was her favorite. "I just feel so overwhelmed right now. I feel like this system is so jacked up. Mommy, I'll talk to you tonight. What time is dinner going to be ready?"

"Sevenish." Gloria said.

"See you then," Yarni said.

Jack knocked on Yarni's office door. She tried to pull herself together before she allowed him to enter. He noticed her eyes were puffy. He placed the file folder on her desk aside. "Care to share?" he asked, as he took a bite of his apple and sat on the edge of her desk.

"No, I don't", Yarni said.

"Yarnise, listen, you've been nothing but a friend to me. You saved me from the bottle, and losing my whole career that I busted my butt to achieve. You got me into a twelve-step program. You even brought me balloons and a cake and attended my graduation. Not to mention the countless times you had to cover for me while I was attending sobriety meetings. How come I'm always on a need-to-know basis with you?"

"Maybe the things I'm going through are too heavy for you to even understand," Yarni said while tapping her felt-tip pen on the desk.

"Well, why don't you try me and see." She explained to him about the situation with Des. She gave him the lawyer's name who she had working on his appeal. Jack instructed Yarni to bring in all Des's transcripts and any paperwork she had on his trial. He told her that he was very interested in the case and that he had a friend, Larry, who was a federal attorney whose son was executed by electric chair and treated unjustly because of the bad relationship his friend and the governor had. Jack promised her that he would go through Des's transcripts with a fine-toothed comb. Yarni felt relieved.

Jack said, "That's what friends do. They have each other's back unconditionally."

Yarni drove to her mother's house. She listened to "Dear Mama" by 2Pac. She listened to the words of the song, which made her think of her very own mother. Tears formed in her eyes, thinking of the countless times her mother had come through for her. When there was no one else, there was always her mother, through the bad, good, happy, and sad; countless times her mother was always the last one standing when the dust settled.

When Yarni arrived at Gloria's house, she could smell the baked ziti cooking as she approached the door. Her mother asked if she felt better since she'd spoken to her earlier. Yarni told to her mother what Jack said to her earlier that day.

After they were finished with dinner, Yarni did the dishes as she always had, from the time she was twelve years old.

"Mommy, you're so old-school. Why do you have a dishwasher and still require me to do the dishes by hand? Why do you have a dryer and yet you still hang your clothes on the clothesline?"

Gloria just laughed and said, "Your generation is too spoiled, so when you come over here, I have to enforce my old-school ways to keep you from getting caught up in this new-generation lifestyle, sweetie." She pinched Yarni's cheeks, then filled the teakettle with water.

Gloria made them some hot tea. She carried the tray with the teacups on it out into the dining room and placed it on the table. She had a serious look on her face. Yarni noticed earlier that Gloria had appeared uptight since she had arrived at her mother's house. Yarni asked, "Mommy, what's wrong?"

She told Yarni, "I told you over the phone, I've got something extremely serious to speak

to you about." Shivers went up Yarni's spine.
She was afraid. Was her mother sick? Did she
have cancer? Was it her father? Yarni couldn't
imagine what could've been so serious.

Gloria looked at Yarni and took a deep breath.
She got up from the table and began to pace the
floor. Yarni got up and hugged her mother. She
asked her, "Mommy, what is it?" Gloria began
to look out the window as if she was paranoid.
Yarni became very scared.

"Mommy, you are scaring me," Yarni said.

Gloria looked at Yarni and simply said, "I
hope that I am making the right decision."

"Right decision about what, Mommy?" Yarni
said as she began to cry herself. Gloria noticed
that Yarni was crying. She took Yarni into her
arms and she wiped her tears away.

"Sweetie, stop it, don't you start crying. It's
nothing bad. I need to get myself together, because it's so much to tell you, and I don't know
exactly where to begin."

Yarni looked at Gloria with a puzzled look on
her face, and said, "Mommy, just start from the
beginning."

Gloria sighed. "Well, it all started right after
you returned from the kidnapping. I had no type
of understanding of your forgiveness in your
heart for Bengee." Gloria pointed to her chest.

"I wanted him dead myself. I couldn't grasp the notion that you had let it all go." She began to pace the floor as she continued to explain. "Your feelings were impassive toward Bengee. I automatically drew the conclusion that you were only experiencing post-traumatic shock. I was convinced as soon as the shock wore off, you were going to snap and . . ." She paused as she stopped in her tracks and looked at Yarni. Gloria breathed as she continued, "and . . . and kill Bengee. Once that would've happened, the justice system wouldn't have any sympathy or pity on you, and your struggle. I felt the need to gather collateral myself in case I needed to step in to look after you. I needed a shield of protection." Yarni listened attentively.

Gloria continued, Yarni could sense the seriousness in her mother's voice, as she sat down on the edge of the chair. She made direct eye contact with Yarni. "I went out and spent close to fifteen-thousand dollars in high-tech video equipment. I begin to make movies and audiotapes of the corruption that I silently watched go on at these parties that I cater for the entire city and state officials." She shook her head. "Yarni, the contents of these tapes are so explicit. It is unreal. I have congressmen on tape giving each other blow jobs. It is so sick. I even planted a camera in the paroles chairman's car. He arrived to a party and expected *me* to park his car because the valet parkers were all tied up. At the time, I didn't know who he was, but I figured he had some skeletons in his closet as they all do. I planted a micro-sized camera, the size of a dime, behind the BMW emblem on the dash of his car. I removed the emblem, put a pinhole in it, placed the camera under it. The camera revealed him having sex with fifteen-year-old girls and boys. The eye in the sky also exposed him sniffing cocaine. I also have evidence of judges accepting bribes."

Yarni listened in astonishment. She asked, "Mommy, when did you get to be so gangsta?"

Gloria said, "I had to take precautions when you started getting exposed to this mean world. I wasn't going to let the system take you away from me as they had your father. You're all I have. I figured that you were doing something you had no business doing with you going back and forth to L.A., especially when I seen all that elegant furniture and that piano. I knew the money didn't drop out of the sky." Yarni didn't comment.

Gloria looked at Yarni and told her, "Yarni, I waited so long to tell you this, because I didn't know if you were going to get indicted. Now, since I feel secure, I am going to give you the evidence, and I want you to use it to get Des out of prison." Yarni begin to cry. She got so emotional. She couldn't believe what she was hearing. Yarni was so happy.

Gloria pointed to a box. "There is all you need to negotiate Des's release. Yarni, remember what I told when you were a little girl. 'Nothing in life is free!' That goes for the contents in that box." Gloria stopped Yarni in her tracks as she sprinted to the box in the corner. This was the first time her mother had ever asked her for money. She was surprised, but she didn't care if she had to work the rest of her life to pay off her mother.

"Mommy, how much?" Yarni said, hesitating.

Gloria said, "You finish law school, take the bar exam, and give me at least two grandchildren." Yarni smiled at Gloria.

Yarni opened the box. She was in total shock at the pictures. Gloria had tons of audiotapes and videotapes. She even had CD's that contained info. Yarni looked at her mother in disbelief. "Mommy, what about you? What about your business?"

"First of all, there is no way they can trace any of the tapes back to me. If they do, then what? I've got two sets of mastered copies. If anything ever happens to you or me, I've got people who have special instructions on what to do. Don't worry. I've got that part taken care of. Yarni, see, I'm from the old school and my friends live by a set of principles and morals that your generation really doesn't understand or can't relate to.

"As far as my business, remember the canal that they're going to be opening up on the James River in Shockoe Bottom? I've just closed on a building that overlooks the canal as well as the James River. It's going to be upscale dining. It's going to be reservation required, after-five attire, the whole shebang. So, Yarni I'll be just fine.

"Now you take the box and get out of here. You got some negotiating to do."

She hugged her mother.

"Mommy, I love you so much. Thank you for being my mother as well as being a *faithful mother*!"

Gloria simply responded, "Well, sometimes a mother has to do what a mother has to do." She hugged and kissed Yarni on the forehead.

The next morning, Jack called Yarni before she left for work. "Yarnise, I am just calling to remind you to bring Des's transcripts and paperwork," he said.

Yarni replied, "Oh, it's sitting at my front door. I should be there in about forty-five minutes."

"See you then," said Jack. Yarni hung up the phone.

She took the transcripts to work with her. For the next two weeks, she thoroughly reviewed the information that her mother had given her. She would go into work two hours earlier, to use the law-reference books at the office. When she would arrive, she would observe Jack working so diligently on Des's case. Jack stayed past 9:00 every night going over the technicalities in Des's trial. This was the first time Yarni had ever seen Jack actually enthused about something.

Jack called Yarni at 8:37 one Saturday night. He had come in to specifically work on Des's case. "Yarnise, it's Jack from the office. Are you busy?"

"No, is something wrong?" Yarni asked.

"If you're not busy, I need you to come by the office. I've got to talk to you."

"Jack, I'm on the way." She threw on some jeans and a T-shirt with her Air Max sneakers. She forwarded her calls to her cell phone. She knew Des was calling at ten. She knew she wasn't going to be back for his call. It wasn't a workday and she was going to talk to him even if Jack prolonged their talk. She would excuse herself for the twenty minutes of the call. Yarni drove over to the firm. Every stoplight caught her, simply because she was in a hurry.

Yarni finally arrived. Jack was waiting in his office. He removed his reading glasses. He said to Yarni, "Yarnise, I have to be straight-up with you. I need to speak to Desmond. He's been sold out!

"What? Sold out?" Yarni frantically asked. Then she laughed. "Tell me something that I don't already know."

"His lawyer sold him out. His lawyer may not have wanted to do it, but I guess it was greed. See, the police along with the Commonwealth attorney composed a list called the 'blackball list.' This list consists of individuals, usually mastermind criminals, who the city, county or state have spent so much money investigating and have came up with nothing. These individuals are clever. They almost never slip up. They humiliate the police department as well as the courts because they're never in a vulnerable situation whereas the police can blackball them. So, whenever they may slip up the least little bit, they set them up. The crime is usually a setup. The jury is usually rigged, typically with undercover cops posing as citizens. The lawyers they hire are a setup as well. The lawyers are paid a large bonus to keep their mouths shut along with whatever money the clients pay them. It's all premeditated down to the judge presiding over the case. See, they spend so much money in surveillance and never can get a conviction. They look like imbeciles. So, that's where the blackball list comes into play." Yarni could not believe what Jack was saying to her.

Jack continued, "It's not all the lawyers. I'm almost positive that when you were shopping for lawyers for Des, maybe one or two said their caseload was too heavy to take on the case." Yarni reflected and shook her head in agreement. Jack added, "I've already called my friend, Larry Fair, the friend I mentioned earlier whose son was killed by electric chair many years ago. He's already on a flight from Canada on his way here. He plays dirty with these folks. He's what I call — " Jack put his fingers up to make quotation marks as he said, "a gangster attorney". He's no joke when it comes to throwing salt." Jack looked at his watch. "We have about an hour and half before we have to pick him up at the airport," he said.

"Yarnise, I need you to let Des know that we are taking over his case and he can fire that other poor excuse for an esquire." Jack added, "Maybe we should allow Larry to fire him. Larry gets a real kick out of these type of predicaments."

In less than twenty seconds, Yarni's cell phone rang. She looked at her caller ID, and it was Des.

She hurried to press zero to accept the call. She explained to Des that she didn't want to talk over the phone, but she would be with Jack and Larry to see him in the next day or so. She said she'd explain everything when they arrived. They were one step closer to him coming home. Yarni left the room to have some privacy while speaking to Des. She never revealed any of the new evidence to Des.

She stood at Jack's door. Jack asked, "Why that look?"

"Jack" she said, "I think I may have something, but I would feel more comfortable sharing it with you before Larry arrives." Jack looked puzzled, but he slowly said, "okay."

"But we've got to leave now." Yarni drove them to a storage she'd rented under an assumed name. They hopped out of the car, and Yarni opened the lock on the storage. She presented the box to Jack. He looked at Yarni before he took the lid off, and she shook her head at him to persuade him. He opened it and he too was bewildered. He had a cunning expression on his face. He simply said, "This is beautiful! Yarnise, you are amazing. Where did you get these?"

"I can't expose that. I'd die first."

Jack stressed, "I totally understand. At this point of it, it doesn't even matter where you got it from with these indecent actions going on. Yarnise, we're going to definitely let Larry do the negotiating on this one."

Yarni said, "There's one more thing. I don't want Des to know anything about this evidence until he's released. I don't want him to get his hopes up too high for a letdown." Jack agreed.

Jack and Yarni arrived at the airport. Larry's flight arrived right on time. Yarni didn't know quite what Jack meant when he said Larry was a gangster attorney until she met him. She then understood fully. As wealthy, energetic, and intelligent as he was, she could detect a bit of ghettoism in him. He had a fire within his soul. She could see he was a warrior. He would die for his cause. Larry was so excited that he had these political criminals backed up against the wall. When he studied the evidence, a few times, Yarni thought he was going to do cartwheels around the office. The more evidence he saw, he jumped up and did the Carlton from *Fresh Prince of Bel-Air* dance. Yarni tried to determine if this guy was working with a full deck or not. She knew when he started to speak. He looked at Jack and asked, "Where can we go to get a blowout cell phone?"

"What's a blowout cell phone?" Jack asked with a confused look on his face.

Yarni interrupted. "It's a cell phone where you might pay seventy-five, but the phone has no limitations. You can't receive any incoming calls. It is activated usually for a month or so. I may know someone who may know where to get one from." Yarni arranged to get the phone. Larry made the necessary calls, and the next day, Des was granted an unconditional pardon. The paperwork had to be signed the next day.

Yarni was so excited. She stopped by Gloria's house to give her the update on Des. Yarni asked, "How do you prepare for your man who's been imprisoned for the past ten years?"

Gloria hugged her and said, "We're going to plan a celebration."

"Mommy, don't go all out. Something small."

Gloria looked at her. "Don't tell me how to plan my son-in-law's release party." She was ecstatic.

Yarni called Joyce. "Hello, my dear daughter-in-law," Joyce said.

Yarni said, "Who would've thought that we'd end up so close."

Joyce laughed and said, "I'm telling you. I truly gave you a hard time."

Yarni interrupted before Joyce got carried away with that whole episode. "Listen Joyce, I need you tomorrow. I know you're working but I absolutely need you to take off."

Joyce humbly said, "Say no more, I will take an emergency personal day. What's wrong, baby?"

"I can't and won't explain to you on the phone. Please just meet my mother at her house. She will explain everything in the morning."

Joyce said, "No problem, baby. I'll call your mother when I'm on the way."

The very next day, Yarni was on her way to the Haynesville Correctional Center to pick Des up. While she was on the way, she had butterflies in her stomach. She began to think, *What if Des comes home and acts a fool. What if he comes home and tries to play catch-up? What if he is released and doesn't love me anymore, because I've matured so much? I hope he don't just continue the relationship if his heart really isn't here, but he feels obligated because I've been there for him. I'm going to make that clear off the top, that he doesn't owe me anything. What if he comes home and goes* back to that same lifestyle all over again? *If he does, I will surely be gone.* Those were all the things that Yarni thought about the whole way. She was so overjoyed and scared at the same time. She shouted out, "Des, you better do right!"

20

Good Girl Gone Bad

As Yarni approached the stoplight, upon noticing a woman about to cross the street, she snapped out of her thoughts. On the median strip of Jefferson Davis Highway stood a young woman wearing an old 1992 multicolored suede jacket that was three sizes too big. It was practically hanging open off of her shoulders and she had on nothing under it but her panties, bra, and some fluorescent orange socks. Yarni felt sorry for her as she watched the girl look both ways and then drop her head before putting both her feet on the pavement to cross the street.

Damn, I hate to see a sister out here like that. It's almost 100 degrees and she hasn't got a clue. I would call the fire department because she's about to burn up. I remember I used to have a coat like that. Cara and I drove to Potomac Mills and got coats just a like. She and I used to be sho-nuff road dogs, now we don't even speak. Funny how you can be somebody's best friend one day, and one incident can show you their true colors. I wonder why she hung around me so long if she really didn't care for me.

The light changed before the girl was finished crossing the street. Yarni waited for the girl to get to the other side and she pulled off. As soon as she pulled off, she looked in the rearview mirror and then looked again. I know that walk from somewhere. She made a U-turn. When she got back down to the stoplight, the girl was lying on the ground. She pulled her car in a Chinese restaurant parking lot. She opened the door and hopped out of the car, as tears formed in her eyes. "Cara, oh my God?" She put her arms around Cara. Cara couldn't look at Yarni. She jerked away.

"Cara, I am not going to hurt you. Just please let me help you." Cara only sobbed.

"Yarni, I am soo sorry, for everything," Cara cried.

"I know, Cara," Yarni said to Cara in an understanding tone. "Now, please just get in my car."

Cara shook her head. "How can you honestly help me after all I've done to hurt you?"

Yarni was squatting in front of her. She ignored Cara's question. "Cara, please just get in my car. I don't want anybody to see you out here like this. Now, please!" Yarni said as she cried herself.

"Yarni, you don't understand. I think you're blind to the fact of everything I've done to you. I'm sorry, Yarni. I'm sorry." No matter how much Yarni insisted for Cara to get in the car, Cara repeatedly told Yarni, she was sorry.

Yarni tried to be strong for Cara, "Cara Ann Bloomfeild, I am demanding that you get off these streets half naked." At that moment, Cara realized just exactly what she was wearing. "Oh, my God, where are my clothes? All I remember is I was getting high with two white guys, and the next thing I know I woke up lying on top of my coat."

Cara said to Yarni as she wiped her tears, "Yarni, I have to tell you because I know it's probably killing you, but I was the one who trashed your condo."

Yarni covered her mouth and just cried. She got up and walked off. She couldn't believe her once best friend in the whole world had actually hated her so much. They both cried. Cara got up and zipped up her coat and walked over to where Yarni was standing.

"I am sorry, Yarni, I swear I am so sorry. I'll do what I have to do to repay you," Cara cried.

"You mean that?" She raised her voice at Cara. "Do you really mean that?" Under any other circumstances, Yarni would have probably hit anybody else upside the head, but she just couldn't lash out on Cara.

Cara nodded her head timidly and said, "Yes, anything, Yarni."

Yarni grabbed Cara's arm and pulled her over to the car's side-view mirror. "Look at yourself. You look a shitty mess! Now what you're going to do is get your frail hind parts in the doggone car," Yarni said, pointing to the car. "Right now!" She opened up the car door and pushed Cara in the car. Yarni ran around the other side, got into the car, and drove off. Yarni pulled down the mirror in the roof of the car because Cara was afraid to look at herself in the side-view mirror. "Look at yourself."

Cara had no choice but to look. She slowly glanced at herself in the mirror and screamed, "Oh, my God." They were both quiet. Yarni pulled up into the gas-station parking lot on the corner of Maury and Jefferson Davis. "Stay here." Cara shook her head and watched as Yarni went to get the key for the bathroom from the gas attendant. Yarni popped the trunk, grabbed her gym bag, and instructed Cara to go into the bathroom and put the shorts, T-shirt, and sneakers on. Cara did as she was told. While Cara was in the bathroom, she went back into the store. She knocked on the door. "Here, Cara, open up—here is a toothbrush, toothpaste, soap, and deodorant."

Cara finally was dressed. Yarni was waiting in the car. "I am glad it fits," Yarni said.

"Yarni, it's a shame. You know I was always a size fifteen/sixteen and I looked inside the label of these shorts and they are a five/six. I stared in the mirror and what used to be my voluminous butt is gone. I've even lost weight in my face. How did you even recognize me? I know I look a mess. If the tables were turned, I wouldn't even allow me to be in this car. I was really smelling, and for you to allow me to even sit on your leather seats as dirty and stinky as I was . . . I thank you so much, Yarni."

Yarni didn't respond as she pulled in the McDonald's parking lot. She ordered Cara something to eat and herself a drink.

"Thank you for allowing me to see what I was letting drugs do to me."

"Yeah, well, what are you going to do to stop it?"

"I don't know, I hadn't realized it had gotten this out of control. I thought I was handling it. I don't know what to do, or who to go to because my family has totally disowned me." She shook her head in disgust as she dropped her head. "I even lost custody of Li'l Ronny, I lost my house. I lost everything."

Yarni reached her hand out of the window to grab Cara's food and their drinks and as she passed Cara the food, she asked her, "Cara, you never even smoked cigarettes, better yet, used any drugs when we were friends, so how did it get to this?"

"Girl, I just got caught up. Right after we fell out, Mike got locked up and he started snitching on everybody in sight. He told on everybody he dealt with around Richmond, about thirty dudes, and they only took like ten years off of his twenty-seven-year sentence, and you have to do day for day. If you're sentenced to three years, you have to do every day. So, he continued to rat on people, anybody and everybody he knew or heard of. They reduced his time again, taking three more years off. See, that's the part I don't understand, how they make you tell on all of them people and yet, still make you do years. After he got another reduction, that still wasn't good enough, so he was putting pressure on me to go around to clubs in D.C. and North Carolina meeting dudes who look like they getting any type of money to get their numbers, talk to them, and find out details—where they be, what they drive, what they do or just whatever information I can get and turn it over to the proper authorities."

"And these dudes were telling you all their business?" Yarni asked in a surprised tone.

"Yarni, you know what a dude would do for a big butt and a smile! They pour out their whole game plan, trying to impress me, plus I wasn't from there, which meant, new coochie! Chile, please! And, Yarni, I put my work in faithfully for him, but it was never enough. I wasn't cut out for that doing-time-with-a-nigga-type shit. And, you know this from when I used to tell you, but I tried being there for him, but when I wasn't at home to take his calls or on time when visiting hours started, because maybe I was putting in work the night before for him, I was cussed out, called everything, but a child of God. The whole scenario just began to frustrate me, because it was *never* enough to get him released. I started feeling useless, pathetic, and hopeless. So, I started smoking weed, staying high all day, everyday. Then lacing the weed with coke, and shortly after just leaving the weed out and doing coke, twenty-four-seven, I just got tricked up in the game. And whenever I wasn't high, I would think about you, and resentment would really set in when I thought how you held it together running up and down the road to see Des for all those years and just being a devoted friend to him along with everything you was faced with in your own life. Taking all your strengths into consideration, I began to hate you. When I heard that you'd finally gotten your townhouse, I couldn't stand the thought that you were faced with almost the same struggle as I was, if not even worse, and you prevailed, and I was just smoked out!" Cara covered her face as the tears rolled down her eyes uncontrollably. "And to top it off, Mike met some girl through the prison's pen-pal program and married her right before he came home. When he was released, we saw each other. He rolled up on me in his brand-new Lexus, which he got from hustling. Can you believe he's right in this same town where he told on a rack of people not even three years ago? And these same local cats is still buying and selling drugs to his police ass. He said, he'd lost all respect for me because I'd looked so bad and had let drugs get the best of me. Well, I told him that I'd lost respect for him too because he wasn't a man, he couldn't do his time without bringing other people who had nothing to do with his case down. He beat me like he was fighting a man, and called me a crackhead, trick bitch. I told him, with what little energy I had, that he was a coward and a snitch, and that he can beat me, but while he's beating me he better be looking over his shoulder because somebody may be coming to kill him. He only got madder and stomped me with his Tims."

"Damn, Cara. I feel so bad for you. I had no idea that things had gotten so rough for you. But, Cara, you got to bind out that evil spirit, that curse, that addiction in the name of Jesus, girl. You've got to stay in the word." She reached into the backseat of her car and grabbed her Bible and gave it to Cara. "And on your knees in prayer and believe in your heart that it can be done. Take my word, Cara, that all things are possible through Christ who will strengthen you." Just then, they pulled up at the Good Samaritan Inn on Hull Street, which was a place that rehabilitated people, provided them with a structured environment, meetings, shelter, and helped them find employment.

"Cara, I was en route to do something very important when I saw you. These people here will be able to help you get yourself back on track. My boss is a personal friend with the coordinator, so they will call me if you get out of line. Don't disappoint me. I called while you were in the restroom, so they are expecting you."

"I won't disappoint you because after everything shiesty that I have done to you, you've found it in your heart to get me out the gutter and back onto the right road. Thank you so much, Yarni."

Yarni didn't want to get emotional, so she never elaborated on what Cara had just said to her. She told Cara, "I won't be able to bring you any of the things you need in here because I will be preoccupied for the next few days, but I am going to get Steph to bring you some personal items and a couple of outfits. They're not going to allow you to go out for the next thirty days."

Cara shook her head. "I understand Yarni, I owe you my life. Thank you."

Yarni drove off. She had no idea exactly how much she loved Cara in spite of everything Cara had done to her. Yarni had always said to herself that if she ever saw Cara, after everything she did—from throwing dirt on her name to sending Des letters revealing every foul thing Yarni had ever done, to calling her job trying to get her fired—if she were to see her lying on the side of the road dying and needed one drop of water, she wouldn't even spit on her. That's how much animosity she had toward her. Now, after seeing Cara, she'd realized exactly how much God had ministered her heart. Yarni knew that it wasn't her who had the will and the power to put her own feelings aside to assist Cara. It was God. This was another confirmation of God's miracle working powers.

Meanwhile . . . at the Haynesville Correctional Center on June 30, 1999:

"Desmond Taylor, B and B," said a fat, black correctional officer with sweat rolling down his face.

Des heard the announcement while he was playing chess. "What is going on?" He said.

The correctional officer arrogantly said, " B and B, bed and baggage."

"Where am I going? They don't usually transfer in broad daylight," Des asked suspiciously.

"Are you going home or not?" the correctional officer asked. Des grabbed his state-issued property: mattress, blanket, and sheets. He didn't know what type of stunt was being pulled. He gave all his items he'd just bought from the canteen two days before away. The only thing he kept was his sweat suit that he purchased from the J.C. Penney catalog. The clothes he wore in were too small. He'd gained forty pounds, all muscles from working out over the decade he'd been there.

He walked through the gates. He saw Yarni leaning on her black convertible Jaguar waiting for him. The gates shut behind him. He dropped to the ground and started thanking God. He stayed on his knees for ten minutes. Once he finished praising God, he gazed up and Yarni was standing right there. He hugged and kissed her. They hopped in her car and drove off.

21

The Best Things Come To Those Who Wait

Yarni and Des ended up in D.C. where she was taking him shopping. They enjoyed a quiet lunch together also. Yarni explained to Des the information that Gloria had produced.

"Didn't I tell you that I was going to get you out? It may have taken me a decade, but I came through," Yarni said.

"Just like you always have. Thanks for being there so faithfully for so many years," Des said, kissing Yarni with a long, passionate kiss.

Yarni felt so complete. She had never felt so comfortable around any man as she had Des. She loved him wholeheartedly. He loved her completely as well and had the utmost respect for her. As they ate lunch, they fed each other. Des gazed into Yarni's eyes. He thought to himself how he wanted to marry her right then and there. He wasn't in the appropriate position that he felt he needed to be in to marry her. The reality of it was that Yarni didn't care what Des's financial situation was. She wanted to be his wife. She wanted nothing but to marry this man, to take on his name, to bear his children, and to be with him until death do they part. They were destined. He was her soul mate.

"Yarni, I am going to marry you in the next few months, but I have one order of unfinished business I have to take care of," Des explained to Yarni.

Yarni was shocked that Des had spoken about marriage after he had only been home for a few hours. She was also alarmed that he said he had some unfinished business to take care of. She was heated.

"What do you mean, you have some unfinished business to take care of?" Yarni said.

"It doesn't involve any drugs or anything that will risk me being removed from your life again. Yarni, I'm never leaving you ever. I've just got to put some things into effect so we can live comfortably," said Des.

Yarni was still worried. She had made up in her mind that she wasn't expecting to get married any time soon. She was fully aware that the reality of the situation was that Des was raised in the streets. He went to college and was the valedictorian of his high school senior class, but he'd been married to the street life for so many years. She had promised herself that she'd never accept a hustler into her life again. A hustler had a lot of excess baggage that came with him: the women, the perks that the hustlers got for having the drugs, the late-night hours, the jealous people and the haters that could result in kidnappings, robberies and murder. She couldn't accept any of those things into her life anymore, not even for Des. She loved Des but she loved herself more.

They arrived at Gloria's house. Gloria and Joyce had planned a nice get-together for Des. Des was overjoyed that Joyce and Gloria had gone through so much for him, especially Gloria. Gloria was a remarkable woman. He could understand entirely why he loved Yarni so much. Look at the woman who raised her. He knew Yarni had doubts of him cheating due to the fact he had been locked up for so long. But the truth was, Des had done everything that the streets had to offer before he went in. Yarni proved to be everything he needed, wanted, and desired in a woman. Yarni was truly his very best friend. All he wanted to do was be her knight in shining armor.

As Des made his rounds around the party, he met the friends who Yarni had acquired over the years while he was in prison. He also was formally introduced to Larry and Jack. He gave them his eternal thanks for the work they had done on his case.

Gloria presented Yarni and Des with the picture she had taken of them on their first date. She had it painted and framed for them to hang over their fireplace once they were married.

Gloria's restaurant became one of the classiest restaurants in Richmond. She later married Sam and they purchased a summer house in the Florida Keys.

Des and Yarni went to Las Vegas, it was their first vacation away from Richmond since he had been home from prison. Des had arranged everything. On New Year's eve, early during the day, they were at the Venetian Hotel riding on the gondolas and the man rowing the boat started singing, *"When we get married we'll have a big celebration. There will be dancing and all when we get married."*

Des looked into Yarni's eyes and said to her, "Yarni, I love you so much. What do you think about us just getting married while we're out here?"

Yarni was speechless as tears of happiness filled her eyes. Des wiped her eyes and said, "Listen baby, I need you to look at me. Look into my eyes."

Yarni looked up at Des. He was holding an exquisite platinum solitaire marquise ring with baguettes on each side of the band. The sight of the ring left Yarni breathless.

Later that night on December 31, 1999 at 11:00, Yarni and Des were married at the Paris Hotel in Las Vegas on the Eiffel Tower. The ceremony was simply beautiful.

Des had surprised Yarni by flying in the guests in hopes of her accepting his proposal. Gloria gave Yarni away. The wedding was very intimate. Only twenty guests were allowed to attend the wedding. Among Yarni's ten guests were Rita, Zurri, and Stephanie. There was one of Des's guests that Yarni didn't recognize, or had never even seen before, for that matter. The ceremony was over right when the New Year, the new millennium, came in. The fireworks began right after Des kissed the bride. The timing was perfect. After the ceremony Des introduced the arbitrary guest as Rico, an old and devoted friend.

The next day Yarni and Des got tattoos on their left finger, the wedding bands. Des explained to Yarni that the ring finger had the main artery that ran straight to the heart, that was why it was so important for them to get the tattoos there and always wear their wedding rings. Des even surprised Yarni with a tattoo on his arm with a heart with Yarni's name, their wedding date, and a message reading *Death Before Dishonor*.

Later that evening, while still in Vegas, Des met up with Rico while Yarni was in the Christian Dior store. Rico handed Des a huge Bellagio shopping bag full of money.

"Congrats on your wedding are in order," said Rico. "Yeah, thanks, man," Des said, while smiling. "You've got a good wife, papi. She really loves you!"

"Yeah, I know, man! Look, thanks for everything!" said Des.

"Thanks for giving ten years. You could have so easily told, but you didn't," Rico said.

"Thanks for the ultimate get-back taking that cat Bengee out for all the pain he caused my wife."

"No problem at all, papi," Rico added. "Just for the record, I didn't attend the funeral, but I sent flowers and a representative."

"This is it for me. I'm through with the drug game and the street lifestyle. I've got my freedom, my wife, and I know God. I can't straddle the fence. I'm outta this," Des said.

"I respect you, papi, and can only pray that I retire out of this game, before I am killed. I love you, pa, and I hope to be the godfather of your children." They hugged, patted each other on the back, and went their separate ways.

THE END